THE BIRD OF DAWNING

The Bird of Dawning

or

The Fortune of the Sea

By

John Masefield

NEW YORK

THE MACMILLAN COMPANY

1934

THE BIRD OF DAWNING

THE BIRD OF DAWNING

NEARLY seventy years ago, Cruiser Trewsbury, the second mate of the homeward-bound China clipper, *Blackgauntlet*, was keeping the first watch in a September evening in the extremest Northern verge of the North East Trades. His Christian name was Cyril, but he had been nicknamed 'Cruiser' while on the *Conway*, and the name had followed him about the seas. He was a compact, forceful young man of nearly twenty-two, in his seventh year at sea. He stood about five feet eight and weighed twelve stone seven. He had a frank, friendly, good-humoured face, broad and smiling, with very quick brown eyes. The face was somewhat pale, under its wind-tan, and kept clean-shaven: his hair was brown. He was an excellent sailor and shipmate; he had a fairly good tenor voice; he had made it a rule to learn a new language on each round voyage; and had written but had not published a little manual on Compass Deviation. But his great delight and interest was the painting of sailing ships in all possible positions and situations. His ambition was to "pass for Master" on his return to England, give up the sea, go to an art-school in Paris and become a painter.

Though he was the second mate of one of the first flight of the China clippers, a ship of exceeding speed and beauty, within a few weeks of home and with a fair chance of being first in the Season's Race, the winner of the London Prize, he was by no means at his ease there.

They had sailed from Foochow on the same tide with four other of the racing tea ships, and had seen one of the most dreaded of them, the *Natuna*, bring up in the River and lose her tide. In the China Sea they had held their own against the other three, sometimes gaining, sometimes losing a little, as the luck of the current or some happy turn of judgment served. The *Caer Ocvran* had led through Sunda Straits by perhaps three miles: the *Black-gauntlet* being then, certainly, second; the *Min and Win* third, and the *Bird of Dawning* fourth. After that, they had parted company in the darkness of a gathering gale, and had gone their hurrying ways alone, seeing no more of each other, except one glimpse at dusk of what seemed to be the *Min and Win*.

All through the Roaring Forties and the South East Trades their luck had held: they had gone their best, with a never-failing power of wind behind them. Well into the North East Trades, they had felt that they were breaking all records ever known in the passage, and that the miracle of their luck might well be theirs only. Then, unaccountably, and in a way not known before by any man on board, the North East Trades had failed them. They had died away into nothing, and had left them for a miserable week, expecting but not finding the Westerlies that should have been bowling them home into the Channel. It had been like a week in the Doldrums, with hot weather, light airs, and occasional violent squalls. Day after day, watch after watch, they had felt their chance of a record passage and of the London Prize die away. The men had begun to growl at the continual heaving at the braces, to catch the chance slants of wind that fell. The work of the ship at that time had been the painting and cleaning her for her entrance to the London River. Ten times in a watch, the pots and brushes had been left at a call to the braces: the paint had been all smeared, the work interrupted and delayed, and tempers ruffled: all things had been thwarted and nothing done.

Cruiser, being of a singular good nature, had taken the weather as a part of the luck of the sea, quite as likely to affect their rivals as themselves. But his Captain was of a different temper. Young Captain Duntisbourne, of the *Blackgauntlet*, longed above all things for the glory of being the winner of the Season's Race. He had not long been in the China trade. He had served his time in a famous Australian passenger service, had been promoted early, both for a very real ability and by the influence of his uncle, who was a Director on the board. He had commanded in the Australian service before he was twenty-five: and at the age of twenty-seven had been tempted to the command of the *Blackgauntlet*.

In his first year's race, he had been fifth with her: and this with the very bad luck of losing his rudder, and having to come home with a jury rudder contrived by himself. To be fifth, under such conditions, had been rightly counted an honour to him: and the honour (very generously given) confirmed him further in his belief in his skill and in the capacity of the ship.

In his second year's race, he had been second, a very close second, so close a second, that he had felt the race in his grasp. Then his pilot had miscalculated: there had been a dispute: a precious moment had been lost: and he had had the bitter mortification of seeing the *Caer Ocvran* pick up the tug that should have been his, and precede him into the London Dock by five minutes. His feelings on this occasion had led him to accuse the pilot of deliberately letting the *Caer Ocvran* win, in order to win a private bet. However, the *Caer Ocvran* had received the prize and Captain Duntisbourne yet another incentive to make a desperate effort next time.

Now, in this third year's race, after all had gone so well, these days of squalls and calms had fallen, till heart had lost hope and mind was sick. For nearly seven weeks on end Captain Duntisbourne had driven the ship as few ships have been driven. In all that time, he had never once undressed for bed, and had seldom slept below. Most of such sleep as he had known, had been taken on deck on the poop in a long chair lashed to the rail, under a weathercloth in foul weather and screened by a canvas tilt from the rain. No man during the passage had seen him take more than one hour of sleep at a time. Usually, he would doze for half an hour, then leap up, look at the trim of the yards, look at the course, ask what she was doing, go to the weather rail and con her, then stand for perhaps half an hour watching her, before lying down again. Since the Trades had failed into this misery of squall and calm, he had hardly rested at all, but had been leaping up, pacing the deck, swearing at the men and interfering with the officers, till all hands were irritable and overstrained.

Only three hours before, in the first dogwatch, the Captain had fallen foul of Cruiser for not having finished the starboard life-boat on the skids.

"Why is not the boat painted and the gear back in her, Mr. Trewsbury?" he had asked.

"Sir," Trewsbury had answered, "we've been called to the braces so many times, with little slants of wind, that we haven't been able to get ahead at all."

"You could have scraped and painted twenty boats if you'd given your heart to it in the time you've been at her. God in Heaven, Mr. Trewsbury, look at all this boat's gear on the main deck here, as though the deck were a pigsty. Why isn't the gear in the boat?"

"If you please, Captain Duntisbourne, the paint in the boat is still wet. I've chocked the gear into the booms till the paint in the boat is dry. I thought I could get it back into her at dawn."

"You thought. You're not paid to think."

"Yes, Captain Duntisbourne, I am."

"Then if you are, sir, think to purpose, instead of making a crack ship's deck like an Irish fair, with three old crocks and a paint wipe. I never saw such a filthy mess in all my days."

Cruiser had not answered this, but had called to two men to put the gear into the boat.

"Leave it where it is, you," the Captain had called. "Let the port watch see the mess you make and clear it up for you."

"Sir," Cruiser had answered, "the port watch made the mess. They started painting this boat this afternoon. My watch has been so busy at the braces that we have not been able to clear it up."

Unfortunately, two of the men had tittered at this, just behind the Captain. They were working there at a coach work-mat on the rail of the poop ladder; and Captain Duntisbourne, whirling round upon them, had told them that if they tried any insolence with him they should ride the spanker gaff till they got to Hell or Hackney, with a bucket of sand on each ankle, what was more.

After this, things had cooled off a little, but Cruiser knew that the matter had not ended. The dogwatch had closed with that tenseness upon all hands that foretold further trouble. He knew that his watch thought that he had scored off the Old Man, and that they supported him against the Old Man, and that this was an impossible situation.

He had never liked Captain Duntisbourne. He respected him as a sailor, and was grateful to him for taking him as second mate: otherwise he thought him cold and eaten up with the sense of himself. Now that he was all frayed nerves and anger, he was anything but a pleasant commander. In appearance he was a spare slim man of about five feet ten, "all wire and whipcord," lithe, active beyond the ordinary, and ever restless, eyes, head and hands; still under thirty, excellent in his profession, continually surprising even old seamen by his practical knowledge, and an acknowledged leader in its theory. His *Theory of the Wind-Shifts in Typhoons* had won him the gold medal of the International Bureau.

In port, he went clean-shaven; here at sea he

wore a short beard. His face was ever somewhat pale and tight, with a twitchy, quick, restless look; the eyes ever querulous and hard, of a cold gray colour. The impression he conveyed to most was of restless insatiate ambition, to be Master, to be Ruler, to be Omnipotent, and that to this, all things and all people were either steps or stops. He had a way that filled many with blind rage. It seemed to ask "Can you in any way minister to my obvious superiority? No? Then, naturally, I consider that you do not exist."

Had the *Blackgauntlet's* mate, Mr. Stratton, been alive, Cruiser's lot would have been a great deal happier, but Mr. Stratton had died a week after Sunda Straits, from the effect of a broken tack block coming on to his head from a main topmast studding sail. Most Captains would have promoted the second mate, and chosen a new second mate from among the apprentices or the crew; this was not Captain Duntisbourne's way. Instead of doing this, he gave the mate's watch to the First Boatswain (the *Blackgauntlet* carried two). This Boatswain, Frampton, now kept the Mate's watch under the Captain's supervision. The eldest apprentice, Abbott, a big lad, out of his time, and a competent navigator, acted as third mate with him.

Neither the Boatswain Frampton nor Abbott was permitted to live aft; each messed and slept with his old associates, the one in the round house with carpenter and sailmakers, the other in the half deck with the reefers. The Captain used them, and gave them, perhaps, some little consideration when he met them on deck, in the course of duty, at the taking of sights, etc., but he let them both feel that they were not going to mess with Captain Icelin Duntisbourne, who was presently to be supreme in all that pertained to the sea.

As a consequence, Cruiser alone shared the cabin-life with the Captain, and sometimes sat at meals with him; unpleasant meals, for the Captain had an icy politeness just covering, sometimes not quite covering, the contempt that he felt for an officer who was not extraordinary. Latterly, on a plea, a reasonable plea, that it would help matters if only one of the two certificated officers should be below at one time, the two had had their meals apart: it was a pleasanter arrangement, yet Cruiser, who was used to getting on well with his fellows, found it lonely and galling.

'Still,' he thought, 'it will only be for one other month: then I shall be out of her. I can stick it for a month. If I pass for Master, then this will be my last voyage as a sailor. I must try to make it a good one. It is better than my voyage out, at any rate.' His voyage out had been anything but pleasant; he had had a rough time before he had fallen in with Captain Duntisbourne.

He looked down from the poop rail into the
starboard boat about which there had been the dispute. She smelt of wet paint, and gleamed out
white from it. He could see the paint-pots in the
stern-sheets where the men had left them. Below
her, somewhere among the booms under the skids,
lay all her gear: and somebody there, probably
one of the apprentices, or perhaps one of the
watch, was splashing something; or perhaps a flying fish had flown on board there.

He would perhaps have enquired into it, but for
the fact that he noticed the lower stars to be dim-
ming. It was a hot, still, tropical night: the ship
was not under way. She plowtered about, flinging
a little water through the freeing ports, and jangling her gear: the mainsail tugged like a horse at
a tethering pin. Away to the south and west there
was a blackness in heaven, that looked like a big
squall. 'Please heaven, it may be the westerlies,'
Cruiser thought.

As he looked at the blackness, something told
him that what impended was more than the prevalent westerly. Something ugly was coming on from
the south and west. Its advance guards, of a swell
upon the sea, a closeness upon the air, and a madness upon the human nerve, were already upon
them. Gradually, the air, so hot and damp, became denser, till it was liker steam than air. The
noises of the water in the freeing-ports, the gear

jangling, the kick of the wheel, and the swirl about the rudder, even the low voices of men in the waist talking about times ashore, became more and more audible, till they were nearly unendurable. The horizon dimmed itself out; the sky that had been starry, and then pallid, became obscured. Cruiser felt suddenly that it was "coming on thick."

It came very quickly and very gently, in little drifts of grayness like wool, each not much bigger, as it seemed, than the mottling in cirro-cumulus. They came in about the ship seemingly from the south and west, but upon an unfelt breath. At one minute they were not there, and he could see the sea, dark, oily, and gleaming from the side lights: in the next minute they were the world.

"Stroud and Chalford, there," he called, "Boatswain, there."

"Sir."

"Rig the foghorn."

"Rig the foghorn, sir; ay, ay, sir."

He was about to turn to windward, to tell the Captain in his chair that it had come on thick, when he found himself prevented: the Captain had stolen to his side.

"It has just come on thick, sir," he said.

"So I perceive," the Captain said. "Keep all fast with the foghorn, Mr. Trewsbury: we're far from being in the Channel yet."

"Very good, Captain Duntisbourne. Boatswain, there. Keep all fast with the foghorn."

"Keep all fast with the foghorn, sir; ay, ay, sir."

Cruiser felt that he had been snubbed: still, to snub is a Captain's perquisite: and certainly one could well spare the noise of the doleful horn.

"Perhaps, sir," he said, "this is the first sign of the Westerlies: it was growing very black in the west, and the glass is falling nicely."

"So you think that, do you, Mr. Trewsbury?" the Captain asked, in his gentle, icy voice.

"Yes, sir."

"You think much, for so young an officer, Mr. Trewsbury."

This also came in a gentle icy voice. He could not see the Captain's eyes: no one could tell from the voice whether he meant to be cutting or complimentary. He resented being called "so young an officer" by a man himself less than thirty. He knew, too, that most of the watch, under the break of the poop below him, would have heard the remark, and taken it in its most evil sense. He gave the Captain the benefit of the doubt, but did not answer, save by "Yes, sir."

The Captain seemed to doubt whether this had been meant for rudeness. Cruiser felt the restless eyes upon him with some malignancy.

"I daresay you are right about the wind, Mr. Trewsbury," the Captain said, "I hope that when the wind comes we may make good some of what we have lost. But it is the record that I regret: we cannot now make a record passage."

"We may still make a winning passage, sir."

"You think that, Mr. Trewsbury?"

"Yes, sir."

"I believe, you have not before been in one of these races with the tea?"

"No, sir."

"They break a great many stunsail booms, perhaps."

"Yes, sir."

The Captain twitched his hands suddenly and sheered away to the binnacle, then walked quickly up and down the weather side of the poop. Presently he came silently back to Cruiser, who felt the restless spirit watching him with intent eyes.

"Mr. Trewsbury," he said very gently, "I believe that I have never talked with you as perhaps all Captains should with a young officer; and Mr. Stratton's loss has made the passage difficult. He was a fine seaman, Mr. Stratton, but given to periodic intemperance when in port. However, that is all over, and forgotten. About yourself, Mr. Trewsbury, I believe that I have never rightly heard what brought you out to the East. Were you not in the *Bird of Dawning?*"

"No, sir."

"Strange," the Captain said. "But before you

joined us I could have sworn that I passed you on the poop of the *Bird of Dawning:* and I thought that you belonged to her."

"No, sir. But I think I did pass you on the poop there, while we were in Pagoda Anchorage. I went on board the *Bird of Dawning* one morning, to see Captain Miserden."

"A fine seaman, Captain Miserden: and a very beautiful ship, the *Bird;* did you not think so, Mr. Trewsbury?"

"She's got rather a loutish look aft, sir, compared with the *Blackgauntlet:* that heavy stern, and long poop, take away from her."

"Shall we walk a little, Mr. Trewsbury?" the Captain asked. "Athwartships, though, if you please, even if it be 'three steps and overboard.' An old seaman once warned me never to walk up and down a poop, fore and aft, always athwartships. 'It will be less easy for them to knock you on the head, so, from behind.' He had been mate in a Western Ocean packet, where an officer had to look out for these things. However, after a week of calm, such as we've been having, a sudden death might seem a pleasure."

Cruiser wondered at the Captain's sudden gentleness; however, it was a pleasant change: he had had no conversation since leaving the Min except an occasional chat with one of the boys at night. He turned to walk with him in the mist, in the few

feet of space between the break of the poop and
the mizen mast.

"So you were not in the China tea race before,
Mr. Trewsbury," the Captain said. "Were you in
the Navy, by any chance?"

"No, sir, never. I was in Gloucester Brothers';
the Blue and White Line they call them, big, full-
rigged ships of over 2,000 tons, the *Talavera*, the
Vittoria, the *Bidassoa*: they were all named after
the battles in the Peninsula."

"What were they? Colliers?"

"We took general cargoes to Australia or San
Francisco, and came back with grain, or hides, or
hides and tallow. I served my time in them, and
went one voyage in the *Bidassoa* as second mate."

"A South Shields firm, you say?"

"No, sir, a Liverpool firm: Gloucester Brothers,
with a house-flag of blue and white stripes. The
Fuentes d'Onoro holds the record to San Francisco."

"Did you say that you took convicts to Australia?"

"No, sir, general cargoes."

"Ah, yes. And you were never in the Navy?"

"Never, sir."

"Strange," the Captain said. There was a pause
after this, till the Captain suddenly asked:

"May I ask how you came to the East, if you

were never in this tea race before, and not in the Navy?"

"Certainly, sir. When I had passed for mate, I passed in steam, and tried to get a berth in a steamer."

"I should have thought that little effort would be needed," the Captain interposed. "There is surely little competition for a place in the Black Guard."

"Young men are taking to steam, sir," Cruiser said. "Steam is the new thing, and the new men turn to it."

"I will admit that they may be new, Mr. Trewsbury, but let us not agree to call them men. Men master the elements; in that there is beauty and fitness. The new scheme is that men should become the slaves of machines: and in that there is neither. But I interrupt, I fear. May I ask, if you were unsuccessful in your attempt?"

"No, sir, I was successful. I was given a second mate's berth in a steamer bound to Sydney: a ship called the *Thunderbird*."

"I am sorry that you should call a tank moved by a machine a ship. May I ask if you felt a little ashamed, when you stood upon the coal or oil platform to empty the cinders?"

"I was very proud, sir, to be helping to master the elements."

"Proud, did you say? But Life is continually

astounding one, with the conditions which cause pride in others. However, in this case, I ought not to feel surprise. And your pride, as you call it, maintained itself, perhaps; you grew to love your oil-rag and what do they call it, your coal-sluice?"

"Sir, she was a ship twice the size of this: and the last word in man's advance in mastery. But I had a bad time in her, for other reasons."

"Very often, a berth is not what one thought it would be," the Captain said. "So this blackened strumpet of your love was not all that she should have been as a wife?"

"The ship was all that one could ask, sir. She was as steady as a rock: and logged her seven knots day in, day out. No one could have complained of the ship."

"Yet you left her?"

"Yes, sir, I left her in Sydney."

"So the collier's joy was widowed. Perhaps you repented of the intercourse. I think you did not come all black from a bunker into this beautiful ship."

"I wished to get sea-time, sir, so as to be able to pass for Master. I shipped as third mate, without pay, in the *Natuna*, and was in her, for the passage only, to Pagoda Anchorage. Captain Elkstone told me that he would take me home as third mate if I could get nothing better."

"Captain Elkstone, of the *Natuna*; Mr. Stratton's boon companion in the frolic bursts which I remember."

"I believe that they were first cousins, sir."

"They were brothers, and more, when in their cups together, Mr. Trewsbury. So, when you reached the Min River and were paid off you were what they call 'on the beach'?"

"I was living ashore and looking for a berth, sir."

"Precisely. You were 'on the beach', offering your wares on the tray, like Spanker-Gaff-Tom, who lost the *Syringa* and Honest-Dick-Tip who put the *Redrocket* ashore. A choice marine assortment, the Pagoda Beach."

"I was not quite of that assortment, Captain Duntisbourne."

"Obviously not," the Captain answered, "for you say that you are hoping to pass for Master, and these men are or have been Masters. How well I know the faces at the Steps: the pale faces, sagging at the jowl, and the broken hat brims, and the trowsers going ragged at the heel. So you were pushing your wares with Captain Miserden, when I passed you in the *Bird of Dawning*?"

"Yes, sir, I went to ask him for a berth."

"May I ask how Captain Miserden received you?"

"Sir, he received me kindly, very kindly, but he asked me some questions about religion, especially about prophecy, and said he would think over my answers."

"Which did not suit?"

"He wrote to say that the result was against my coming in his ship."

"So that I have the honour of sailing with one paid off by Captain Elkstone and refused by Captain Miserden? I have of course long known that I was exceptionally favoured. But of course you came to me very specially recommended by Mr. Sladd, of the Firm, to whom all berths are open. May I be forgiven, Mr. Trewsbury, if I wonder at the change from your being on the beach, rejected by even Miserden, then, within a week, being favoured by Mr. Sladd, with 'special letter, tantamount to an order'? You could not have known Mr. Sladd when you begged of Miserden. Yet, within a few days you were his chosen."

Cruiser was hot at the Captain's tone. He said nothing.

"Perhaps, Mr. Trewsbury, you will explain how it was that the change occurred?"

"Sir," Trewsbury answered, "Mr. Sladd wrote to you on my behalf. No doubt he explained his reasons."

"He did not, Mr. Trewsbury."

"Did you not ask him to explain them, sir?"

Cruiser had once heard a whaler's harpooner make use of the phrase "That touched him where he lives." He repeated the phrase to himself now, having so touched the Captain. He felt the Captain draw back, on being so touched, like a snake about to strike: he felt the bitter mind flicker over him like a snake's tongue.

"But of course," the Captain said presently. "Of course the great Mr. Sladd had excellent reasons, some of which I can surmise, and others concerning which I can speculate. It is a very lonely life for these merchants, do you not think; these master brains; directing great interests at the ends of the earth, as at Foochow?"

"Sir," Cruiser said, "they lead less lonely lives than the captains in their ships. Mr. Sladd's life is a whirl of society compared with yours."

"Perhaps there is not much society in the *Blackgauntlet*," the Captain answered, "now that the sometimes drunken Mr. Stratton has gone from us. We may be poor, but we try to be select; and hitherto have succeeded, fairly; enough, well, at least to keep a beautiful ship out of the hands of coal-trimmers and beach-combers, and others, the flotsam of the Eastern ports. But about this tank or coal-engine in which you came to Sydney, Mr. Trewsbury, tell me now, honestly, were you not sickened to the soul by her, after being in these other ships of which you speak?"

"No, sir," Trewsbury said, "I found her very interesting. I am interested in engines."

"I do not wish to force your confidence, Mr. Trewsbury, in any way, but will you tell me if you left her because she was not sea-worthy?"

"She was sea-worthy, sir: tight as a nut and went along as easy as an old shoe, in any sort of a sea: and took very little water on board. For comfort, all agreed, sir, nothing could touch her, that we had known."

"That 'we' had known. Who were 'we'?"

"The mate and myself, sir."

"You speak as though 'we' were in some way in a league about her: did this mate leave her in Sydney with you?"

"Yes, sir, he did. He went up-country to the gold-fields, and did well there."

"You did not like your commander, I presume?"

"We did not, sir."

"It is very galling to be cooped in a ship with an officer of whom one disapproves. You have my sympathy, Mr. Trewsbury. But to return to Mr. Sladd, of the Firm, almost omnipotent in the East, directing thousands, yet plainly going mad from loneliness. In the solitude of that great place of his, up on the hill, he must suffer from a terrible temptation, to burn it all up and so go out in a blaze. Don't you think that the longing to shriek must be unendurable?"

"Sir," Cruiser answered, "I'm like the Irishman. An American said to him, 'I am getting too rich.' The Irishman answered, 'I wish I had more of your complaint.' Mr. Sladd seemed to me to be enjoying his life very much."

"And at what a cost of promiscuity, Mr. Trewsbury: having to snatch at every chance comer that Fortune flings upon the beach. And young women out from England. But no doubt you will say that they are his nieces."

"One of them is his niece, sir: the other is her friend."

"You will pardon me, Mr. Trewsbury, but I do not think that you can be in a position to speak with authority on this point."

"As it happens, Captain Duntisbourne, I have met the ladies in England and know them both."

"Ah, indeed; in that case, certainly, I have nothing more to say."

"No, sir," Cruiser said.

Again he was conscious of the Captain's malignant thought playing all over him as though it were a serpent's tongue. He wished that a squall might come down, or some spirit of sleep drive the Captain to his rest. There was a pause: then the Captain began again.

"With so much genius, Mr. Sladd might well have made a name in the nation, had he known ships as well as how to make money by them."

"Does he not know ships, sir?"

"But you know him, Mr. Trewsbury; you are his familiar friend and the associate of his familiar friends. Surely you know that he does not."

"Sir," Cruiser answered, "Mr. Sladd has great power of mind, and gives much of it to all that affects his interests. He seemed to me (and of course, sir, I only know him slightly) to have a thorough knowledge of ships as far as they concern him."

"You mean, as wagons in which tea can be carried from the plantation to the London market."

"No, sir, far more than that. These wagons are of a special build and rig: and demand a special life, which he thoroughly understands."

"It is impossible, Mr. Trewsbury, that he should think that they demand a special life when he sends me a chance comer to be a responsible officer on board one."

"Captain Duntisbourne, he sent you a competent officer when he sent me. I know my profession."

"Doubtless," the Captain said. "But of course some doubt exists as to what your profession is. From your own showing it might be collier or it might be pimp." At this, the Captain sheered away and walked hurriedly aft to the binnacle, looked at the card, glanced aloft, and then went fore and aft on the weather poop, snapping his fingers and crying aloud "Is this western wind ever going to blast this calm, my holy topsail?"

Presently he edged back to Cruiser, who still stood at the poop-rail, thinking that if a tack block could descend on the Captain's head it would be a weight well displaced. This time the Captain was all gentle suavity.

"And yet she is a beautiful ship, Mr. Trewsbury," he said. "You will admit that no ship more beautiful exists. You have only seen her, when she was nearly to her marks in the water. But I know her as she is in dry dock. She is the only ship that I have ever seen that will stand that test. She is beautiful even in dry dock. She is so fine in her entrance, and so clean and perfect in her run: no dolphin that ever leaped is lovelier. And above the water, she is faultless. Men tell me that some women are lovely: I suppose sex will make men say anything.

"I have her trimmed an inch or two by the stern: and if only the wind would blow, we might see, and the world might see."

"I think, sir," Cruiser said, "that this mist is a shade thinner, there is a sort of movement in it. Did you not feel that sudden breath, sir?"

"Not enough for steerage way," the Captain said. "The calm has strangled her: choked her dead. And what does your Mr. Sladd care for the thought that I have given to the making of this stagnant lump a triumph?"

"Sir," Cruiser answered, "he said that the

Blackgauntlet is the best kept ship in the seven seas."

"*Is?*" the Captain repeated. "No, Mr. Trewsbury, I know nothing about '*Is*'. That she was not altogether ill-kept at one time I had reason to believe and pride in believing. But since you came aboard, from your coal tank, all Liverpool pennants from your beach, she's looked like the parish knacker. Look at your paints in the starboard boat on the skids there: and the boat's gear strewn on deck like a derelict workhouse ward. God in Heaven, Mr. Trewsbury, she's nothing but a scavenger's tip, and the fish puke as she passes.

"This thing that's as foul as Paddy's Milestone was once a flash ship; but with a second mate kicked out of a collier . . ."

"I was nothing of the kind, sir. I was never in a collier, as you know perfectly well."

"A thing that lives by coal is a collier, sir. You were a collier's second mate: and kicked out of her, my God in Heaven, as too dirty even for her."

Cruiser during this was very keenly aware that the watch was alert, at the break of the poop, listening intently to the row. How far the row might have gone from this point he never knew, for as the Captain ceased, the last of the mist sped away with a pattering of rain, and instinct told him that a squall was on them.

It came on the instant, with a rush out of the west.

"Let go your skysail halliards," he shouted, "stand by your royal braces." He leaped to the pin, as he shouted, and let the mizen skysail go. A brief confusion of wind and rain followed, gear flogged and dripped, and men cried out at the gear: then it was all over, save for the scuppers running. The skysails were rehoisted to a stagnant air, and the gear coiled up again. The Captain had left the poop during the first striking of the squall: Cruiser had the deck to himself.

In a few minutes, after the passing of the squall, the mist gathered again about the ship, so that even the lower topsails were dim to him. It was hot and oppressive again, with the annoyance of gear jangling and drops splashing. Cruiser was filled with fury at the Captain's insolence. What on earth possessed the man to speak like that? However, he knew in his heart the cause of all the trouble. The Captain had had no fit rest for two months, and was like a madman, from the strain, from the days of continual calm and the oppression of the night. Still, it is no consolation to an injured man to be told that his injurer is mad. There would be at least another month with the madman: and the madness would grow worse if the winds still failed, or drew ahead.

'Of all the foul years a man could have at sea,'

he thought, 'I think my last year has been the foulest. First in the *Thunderbird*, with a Captain who had plainly been paid to put the ship ashore; then as third mate in the *Natuna*, without pay, with a Captain who was indeed a jovial soul, but usually drunk; and now here with a nervy lunatic whose nerves are all snapping. However, if I can pass for Master at the end of it, I'll be out of it.'

His thoughts went back to the golden time in London more than a year before: a golden time indeed.

Would such a time ever recur, ever be bettered? It did not seem likely. The helmsman behind him struck One Bell, loud voices roused the watch, and presently Frampton and Abbott were beside him, mustering their men.

"It's pretty thick, Mr. Trewsbury," Abbott said. "Do you think I ought to rig the foghorn?"

"The Old Man told me to hold on with the foghorn. But the mist is weeping out, it will be blowing in an hour, and blowing hard: something dirty is coming."

He leaned over the rail, called "Relieve the wheel and look-out," and went below to his cabin. The Captain was not in his chair, nor on deck at all, when he left the poop. 'And a very good thing,' he told himself, 'for perhaps he has turned-in at last, to get a real sleep in a bed."

He himself determined to sleep.

His cabin was on the starboard side of a little alleyway, which ran from the saloon to the break of the poop. His cabin ports opened on to the main deck, and light of a sort entered by bullseyes in the ship's side. On the other side of the alleyway just opposite to his door, was the cabin of the late Mr. Stratton, now not in use. Further aft, to starboard, was the Captain's cabin, and to port, the steward's pantry and cabin, the Captain's bathroom, and a small space known as the Slop-Room. The clipper carried big crews, renewed every three months or so from the destitute of English, Australian and Chinese sea-ports: many slops were needed.

Cruiser on his way to his cabin entered up the rough log, had a look at the glass, which had fallen during the watch, and set it against the next observation. As he passed the Captain's cabin he saw that the door was hooked back wide open. A light burned there in a safety sconce on gimbals: he saw the Captain in his bunk, fully-dressed, ready for a call, with his face to the ship's side, seemingly asleep. "Well, let him sleep," he thought. "If he could sleep for a week, he might be less of an ass with a fellow."

He was quite sure that wind was coming very soon: a storm was coming up quickly: the warning closeness and thickness was "weeping itself out," and the blast would follow during his watch below. He judged that the first blast would be from some point to the east of south; which would be fair enough. 'There'll be some desperate driving when it does come,' he thought.

As he expected to be called on deck before his watch was out, he took off his shoes, and put them ready to hand inside his bunk. He had rigged a safety candle-sconce inside his bunk, with a little metal tray for matches. He saw that the matches lay to hand there. He hung his coat on a hook; hooked the door wide open, so that all might be clear for a rush on deck; and then turned-in, like the trooper's horse. As always, he thought fervently for two minutes of that lovely girl whose beauty had so moved him: then, wondering what sort of a watch below he would get before the call, he dropped into the sleep of the sailor, which is something unknown ashore.

Deep though his sleep was, he was aware of certain things: he felt a greater uneasiness in the ship's motion, and then the greater steadiness that followed her getting steerage way. He felt the ship beginning to move, and the watch hopping to the braces and singing out. Presently the watch was just over his head, and he knew, though still asleep, that the crojick was being stowed and that the ship was running. "It's come southerly, as I thought," he muttered. "It will shift through south into west."

He knew, in his sleep, that the Captain had gone on deck the instant the wind had filled a sail. Now and then, still in his sleep, he heard the Captain's light nervy tread, which reminded him of a cat's or boxer's. The mizen skysail and royal came in, the main skysail came in and then the wind seemed to increase from the roaring of these flapping kites and the ship's gathering of speed. Then there came the Captain's call, "Get the foretopmast stunsail on her, Mr. Frampton," and the Bosun's answer "Foretopmast stunsail, ay, ay, sir." There was no doubt about the wind now; the storm was coming on fast and they were going like a leaf before it. He wondered how much more of the after sail would be taken off her. The distant cries of the men forward came to him, and the noise of the great sail going up. She felt the new sail and so did he, but the lower stunsail followed to shake her further. The ship was now alive again: she was a racer of the seas again. He heard the Captain (standing, seemingly, right over his head) stamp with his slippered foot, in a way peculiar to him, at something that vexed him (possibly, the gear of the starboard boat). Then he heard the cry of 'Heave the Log', and from the time the lads took to drag the log in, after heaving, he knew, in his sleep, that the ship was doing well. And at this point he heard seven bells and knew that he had only a quarter of an hour more of rest. Still, a quarter of an hour is well worth having, he thought. One can go very deeply into sleep in a quarter of an hour.

He lapsed into the depths and eternities of sleep, glad that the ship was alive and going like a bird again. She was going like a bird of the sea, and the music of her going was a gurgle of water and the tinkling rush of the scuppers running rain. Then all the depths, eternities, noises and tumults of ship, storm, wind and water gathered together and struck in an appalling CRASH, which lifted him in his bunk and flung him to its side.

"Holy sailor," he cried, rousing on the instant. "He's taken the masts out of her."

He knew, as he groped for his shoes and slid them on, that that was not so: from the first crash, which had flung the ship over, there had come partial recovery, followed by an immediate second crash with a rain of gear down from aloft, the thunder of sail slatting loose, cries of men, yells and curses. "She's gone into a derelict," he muttered; "something's hit her."

He slung his coat on and was out of the alleyway and on deck within twenty-five seconds of the blow.

It was, as he noted, eighteen minutes to four.

On deck it was thick wild weather, with a blinding rain; dark as a pocket. Every sail in the ship seemed to be full of seven devils, and things were coming down from aloft right and left. Somewhere on the port side of the poop, sitting in the waterway, the helmsman was whimpering, "I was preak mine head: I was preak mine head." The ship had broached to, and he had probably been flung across the wheelbox.

All hands were to port, shouting into the night.

As he reached the port mizen-rigging, Cruiser saw a vast bulk of blackness loom out a few yards away. There were glimmers of light upon it, and shouts came from it, as it sheered and surged aft into the blinding of the rain. A reek of hot smoke with a smell of engines drove into his face.

"A big steamer," he said, "and she's been into us hard on our port side."

He yelled at the steamer with all his strength. "Stand by us. Stand by us. Don't desert us." But already the black bulk was gone into the storm.

As it was his maxim never to lose one instant of time in an emergency, he leaped down at once on to the main deck.

There, at the main bitts, among some confused and some frightened men, Frampton, the boatswain, already had the watch at work hauling and singing out at the main gear, now banging itself to tatters above them.

"Where did she hit us, Frampton?" he called.

"Just abaft the boudoir and forrard of the croquet ground," said Frampton, not recognizing him. "Lively now with them clue-garnets."

There was no need for Cruiser to go far to look. There in the waist, almost alongside him, the bulwarks were stove-in for a dozen feet, and the forebraces cut through. He knew at once that the ship had had a death-knock. He flung himself down and put his ear to the deck. There was no doubt there: death was pouring in, just below his ear, in a cataract that nothing could stop. A man running aft fell over him and rose up cursing. Cruiser gripped him and swung him round.

"Get to the starboard fo'c's'le," he said, "see that everyone is out. Then go to the round house. Call them up." The man said "Ay, ay, sir," and stumbled forward (he had hurt his knee in the fall), cursing and calling at once, "O, my knee. Rouse out, boys. O, my knee."

"Not so much bloody knee," Frampton called.

Cruiser ran back to the poop, where he found Captain Duntisbourne standing like a statue, looking down on the main deck from the rail.

"Sir," he said, "the ship is sinking. She can't last twenty minutes. Shall I get the boats out?"

The Captain did not answer: perhaps he was stunned by the shock, perhaps overcome by grief for the loss of a ship so dear to him.

"She's sinking, sir," Cruiser called. "Shall I get the boats out?"

The Captain roused suddenly and blew his whistle. "Still there, fore and aft," he shouted. "Mr. Frampton, Mr. Abbott, the port watch and the Idlers . . . clear away the long-boat. Lively now. Mr. Trewsbury and starboard watch; clear away the starboard boat."

"Ay, ay, sir."

"Handsomely now," Cruiser said. "Get the gear back into her. And answer to your names." All were present, except the man Bauer.

"Bauer," the men called, "Bauer."

"Has anybody seen Bauer?" Cruiser called. "Forward there, and see if he's still in the fo'c's'le: or up there, one of you, on to the deckhouse: once before he went there and never got called."

A man ran forward to the darkness of the deckhouse. "If Bauer can sleep through this," a man said, "he'll be able to snooze in hell."

In all this time, a blinding rain was driving, the gear was flogging and thundering, stunsails in long strips were streaming away to leeward, and pennants and bits of gear were crashing from aloft.

"Lord," Cruiser thought, "will no one show a light?"

He had expected to see a great flare rise from the steamer that had hit them. An old maxim surged up in his mind, 'You must do a thing yourself if you want it done.'

He sprang to the gear of the starboard boat in

that space where he had stowed it the day before. Among the gear, there was, as he knew, a tin of red lights. He found the tin, wrenched off the lid, took one of the lights and pulled the trigger of the igniter. With a sputter the light lit: at once a red glow wavered about the confusion.

"Take a light there," he called to a man. "Light it at the rail. Perhaps the steamer has lost us."

The second light made the scene lurid as a scene in hell, but no answering flare came from the steamer.

"Have you got Bauer there, yet?" he called.

"Hier, sir," Bauer called, "hier, sir."

"What did you think was happening, Bauer, a lullaby?"

"I was asleep on der deckhaus, sir."

"You're awake now, are you?"

"Yes, sir."

"Well, nip into this boat and get the plug in; beat it well home."

Bauer leaped into the boat and at once burst into curses, English and German.

"What's the matter with you, Bauer?"

"Der paint's all wet, sir."

"You'll be all wet, too, if you don't look alive." He leaned over the boat, holding one of the flares. "There's the plug, man: tomm it well home with the maul, there. Let's have a look at this boat's bread-locker."

"I tink Haussen filled her yesterday, sir."

"You think. Let's see. It isn't filled. You, boy, there, Chedglow; nippy now. Take one of these flares and get to the Captain's pantry. Get what food you can. And see that the steward is out of it. Is Coates there? Coates, you were always a champion at finding food. Go with Chedglow and find some now. Get the water-breaker in, now."

"Just as well, sir," an old seaman, James Fairford, said, "just as well, sir, that we got all this boat's gear overhauled yesterday."

"It would have been well if we'd finished the overhaul," he said. "But the bread-locker's empty and the paint's all wet: still, the gear is overhauled."

Up there, on the skids, as he pitched the coil of a fall clear for running, he noticed for the first time that an ugly lop of sea had risen. Lowering a laden boat into such a sea would be ticklish work, as he knew too well. Still there might be time to get an oil-bag to work before they lowered.

"Clutterbucke, there," he called to a steady man of his watch, "Clutterbucke."

"Sir."

"You and Nailsworth there, nip forward to the Bosun's locker. Get two of those big colza oil-cans and job two holes in their bottoms with a marler. Then sling one over each bow. You understand what I want? I want oil on the sea before we lower these boats."

"Get an oil-can over each bow, ay, ay, sir," the men repeated. They ran forward to do it.

"Up here, Edgeworth," Cruiser called, "give us a hand to swing her out. You others, starboard watch, aft with you quick and help pass food forward."

With heaving and crying out, they grappled the wet paint of the boat's side and swung her out all clear for lowering. It was a wild scene that they saw, of red and blue flares, men heaving and hauling, scared faces of men hurrying, the cries of men on the tackles, the seas rising up, gleaming in the flares and tossing by, while the wind screamed in the shrouds and the gear flogged. No more beastly time for abandoning ship could have been found by Fate.

"Stay by her, you," Cruiser said. "Don't let anyone get into her before they're ordered. She feels the oil already."

"Yes, sir, she does," Fairford said. "There's nothing like oil." Indeed already the lop of water about the ship was striking with a dead blow instead of savagely.

"We'll get the boats clear with luck," Cruiser said. "That oil is a godsend. Forward there, Edgeworth, and bring us a tin for the boat."

Cruiser swung himself down from the skids by

a life-line. He had been up there, swinging out the boat for not more than three minutes. In that time a change had come in the feeling of the ship underfoot. He had said that it was the effect of the oil-bags forward, and had hoped to persuade his men thus, but he knew very well that the main and terrible change was not due to the oil, but to the rapid sinking of the ship.

He had often gone over in his mind some of the emergencies of his profession, with the thought "What should I do, or what ought I to do, if . . ." He had thought out for himself plans for many emergencies; mast yards and sails going: ship broaching-to, ship brought aback, or caught by the lee in foul weather, the rudder carrying away: cables parting in a road: and collision in storm, fog, dock, port or at sea. He had thought of a smash such as this. Why, only a few nights before, in a middle watch in the Trades, he had thought of this very thing, of getting out the boats in a hurry. He had ever prided himself on having his boats clear for lowering: yet here he was caught in the middle watch with both boats topsy turvy from the painters.

Fresh water was the thing to take in a boat. The boat-breaker was full: where could he get an extra breaker? He ran to the scuttle-butt, usually kept within a permanent coaming on the port side of the deck, under the break of the poop. It was not now there. He remembered at once that it was among the booms by the main-hatch, being cleaned internally with hot ashes from the galley, before being scraped and painted. One of its hoops was to be renewed and its lid was to be repaired by the carpenter. It should have been finished the day before, but with the light winds and the hands so often at the braces it had been put off till the morrow. Now the morrow had come. He found it lashed to the booms; its top gone, probably to the carpenter's shop, and a mess within it of ashes, sand, canvas, three-cornered scrapers, and rope-yarns. He cut the lashing and tipped the mess on to the deck.

"Here, you, starboard watch," he called. "Stratton, Efans, Jacobson."

"Sir," the voices answered, as the men appeared.

"Heave round on the fresh-water pump here at the bitts. Rinse this butt well out. Fill her, and get her into the starboard boat."

"Ay, ay, sir."

Jacobson at once caught hold of the pump-handle, as the others took hold of the butt. Cruiser could not wait there to see the work done; he remembered the fresh-water buckets always kept standing in a rack at the forward end of the poop. He ran up the ladder and swiftly put five of these into the after well of his boat: each contained about one gallon of rather seedy-looking rainwater: still, rainwater is drink, and drink in an open boat is life. He could think of no other handy tank or water receptacle. There was a small tank built into a locker in the round house, and another, much larger one, built into the fo'c's'le, but it would take half an hour to wrench out either of these. Still, he had filled the boat-breaker the day before; that was nine gallons; the five buckets made fourteen, the scuttle-butt would be another ten: twenty-four gallons. He heard the regular strokes of the freshwater pump handle as Jacobson pumped, and the splash of the water. Looking across from his place on the skid he could see, in the glare of the flares, the carpenter at work on the port boat, apparently smashing something, perhaps the forward chock. Instantly, he thought of another thing that might be done: he dropped himself down and nipped across the deck to the carpenter.

The carpenter was a little old wizened man with a sad face, a drooping gray moustache, and blue eyes that lit up at a joke or a tale: he was said to have been in a big way once ashore, as the master of works in a cathedral, but that his wife had been a bad one. He was plainly just roused from sleep. He wore unbuttoned trowsers, belted about him, a pair of bluchers, and a coat belonging to one of the bosuns, much too big for his little body. A bag of tools was on the skid at his feet.

"Chips," Cruiser called, "is your shop un-locked? I want some tools for the boat."

Chips looked up gravely and sadly: "You'll want the key, Mr. Trewsbury," he said. Fumbling in his hip pocket he produced a key bright from much rubbing on a metal tobacco box. "You'd bet-ter leave it in the door, Mr. Trewsbury," he said. "I think I'll not use it again."

In the uncertain red light, Cruiser thought that there was something wrong with the long-boat's bows. "Anything wrong with her forward there?" he asked.

Chips looked at the deadwood and poked it with his maul. "No, it's nothing gone, sir. It's the mark where the chock came. She's tight," he said, "she's not like one of these liners' boats, all paint and putty."

Cruiser took the key forward. On his way he looked into the round house, where a light was burning. The sailmaker was there, bent at a locker.

"Sails," he called: "Sails."

The sailmaker, an elderly, pale man, who had once been in the Navy, looked up from his task.

"Ah, Mr. Trewsbury," he said, "I was looking out some sailmaker's stores: a fetch-bag for each boat. I'll bring your bag along, and put it in the boat for you."

"Thank you, Sails. That'll come in very handy. Don't stay too long, Sails."

"I've nearly got the bags ready, sir."

Leaving the round house he went to the Carpenter's shop. He unlocked the door, and as he did so got a full shower of spray across his shoulders from a wave that she ducked to too soon. The gleam of the wave ran aft, lifting and dropping all the freeing ports in succession. Cruiser opened the door, hooked it back and lit a match. As he knew, there was a stub of candle in a sconce above the table. He lit this and looked for some tools. A tin bucket, full of shavings for the Cook, was chocked-off in a corner: he emptied this on to the floor and put into it such tools as he could see, a big heavy hammer, a firmer chisel much gone in the handle, a smaller chisel, a saw, and a couple of pounds' weight of two inch nails. As he turned to go, he noticed a wad of oakum on the deck: he took this. He then remembered that a brace and bits would be precious. He rummaged for them, but could not find. 'Chips must have them all on deck,' he thought. A minute later he saw them in clips on the bulkhead and took them, four assorted bits and a big twist-drill.

Once again he turned to go, when he remembered how lost he might be without a vice. There was a little snatch-block-vice nipped to a ledge in the bulkhead; he released the nip and took that. As he went aft with his load he felt under his feet the strange trembling in the deck in the way of the ship's wound, marking the rush of the torrent into her and the panting out of the air. It was unlike any movement that he had ever before felt.

On his way, quick as he was, he glanced into the round house, to make sure that Sails had gone. He found that he had gone after blowing out the light: the reek of the tallow still filled the place; a dwindling spark was still on the wick. After this Cruiser hurried to the boat and stowed the tools in her. As he swung in his bucket, Sails called to him from below:

"I've put the fetch bag forward, Mr. Trewsbury."

"Thank you, Sails."

"There's everything in it you can need, sir; but I hope you'll not need much."

"We're sure to need some, thank you, Sails. Good luck."

"Good luck, Mr. Trewsbury."

"Starboard watch, there," Cruiser called, "forward three of you and get some blankets into her. Yank them out of the bunks. Oilskins, too. Lively with it."

James Fairford was at his elbow. "Mr. Trewsbury, sir," he said, "would we take a few of they rickers?"

"They rickers" were short lengths of light spar, usually the relics of snapped studding sail booms. Captain Duntisbourne always thriftily kept and generally found use for them. They were lashed to the spare spars on deck.

"Three of the light ones," Cruiser said. He stooped and cut the lashings: together they hove out three rickers and got them into the boat. "Get in a coil or so of royal and skysail brace," he said, "I must speak to the Captain."

He went across the poop.

Captain Duntisbourne was standing at the poop rail, burning blue lights for the men on the skids. There was something foul in the upper block of the long-boat's forward fall. A big man, known as Corny, was nipping the davits with his legs, and wrenching at the fall to clear the jam in the sheave. Cruiser noticed the size of the man's smiling toothless mouth: he was smiling, mumbling tobacco and swearing, all at once, while the Boatswain Frampton, at the boat's stern-sheets, lifted in gear handed to him from below.

"Starboard boat all clear for lowering, sir," Cruiser said.

"Very good, Mr. Trewsbury."

"Can I bear a hand here, sir, with my watch?"

"You'll need all your watch, I think, Mr. Trewsbury, to get the gear into your own boat, strewn all over the deck as it has been."

"Shall I take the chronometers, sir?"

"Will you kindly take yourself to hell out of this?"

"I still have hopes of the other place, sir; accompanying you."

The Captain uttered something between a snarl and a grunt, stamped out his now dying flare beneath his foot, and at once ignited another, still staring impassively at the long-boat's forward davit, where Corny still clutched and cursed. Cruiser stepped swiftly to the open companion, put in one hand, took the made-up Red Ensign, stepped to the rail, bent it, toggled it, ran it up to the peak and broke it out there. "We'll go down colours flying," he said. From the feel of the deck beneath him, he judged that that might be at any minute.

The Captain still stood there, his right hand lifted with the flare, his left still steady on the flare-box.

'He'll give no more orders,' Cruiser thought. 'I'll take the chronometers.'

He went into the chart-room, calling, as he entered, "Steward, Steward," and "Puss, Puss," for the two cabin passengers who might still be there. A light was burning in the saloon, which was otherwise deserted: the Steward's cabin was empty. The clock was still ticking at six minutes to four. All that eternity through which he had lived had lasted twelve minutes.

Someone (he supposed it would have been the two lads, Chedglow and Coates) had opened the hatch into the lazarette. It was still open, in the middle of the saloon. A candle was still burning there.

"Chedglow, Coates," he called. "Are you still there?" There was no answer: they had gone. As he looked down into the stores, he was shocked by the roaring wash of the water coming into the after hold. "She's not long for this world," he muttered. He took the chronometers, a North Atlantic chart and the ship's log: going rapidly to his cabin he took his sextant, Raper's Tables, some blank paper pads for working out sights and his box of dividers and protractors. Going out with these, heavily laden, he collided with the two lads, Coates and Chedglow, who were charging down the companion, singing.

He saved the instruments from a fall. "What are you up to?" he asked.

"We're getting food, sir, as you told us."

"On deck with you," he said, "the ship's sinking. Take this sextant, Coates: see you don't drop it. Did you see the cat anywhere?"

"Yes, sir: I caught her once, sir, but she got away on deck."

"We'll probably want the cat for fresh meat before many days are past." But this thought he kept to himself.

Cruiser swung into the boat and handed in the instruments. There were several boxes there which shewed him that the boys had foraged well. When the chronometers had been stowed, he clambered out. "Coates and Chedglow," he said, "you've been up and down in boats a hundred times. Get in here and tend the life-lines and see no one unhooks the forward fall. These are red lights. Each of you burn one till further orders. Starboard watch. Is the starboard watch all present, Fairford?"

"All present, Mr. Trewsbury."

He saw that the water-breaker was in its place, and shook it, and thanked God that he had filled it the day before.

He went back to the Captain on the poop. "Starboard watch all present, sir. May we bear a hand with the long-boat, sir?"

The Captain slowly turned and surveyed him, without answering, then leaning forward, still holding aloft the flare, he called, "Swing out, there, Mr. Frampton. Get your boat over and your men into her."

The jam, or whatever it had been in the sheaves of the fall, was now gone. Cruiser saw Corny clearing kinks out of the fall, so as to be all clear for lowering. It occurred to Cruiser that in the last five minutes he had heard Corny call seven different things a bastard; the davit, the purchase-block, the sheave, the fall, the gunwale of the boat which had knocked his shin, the belaying-pin welded on the davit which had barked it and now the kinks in the fall, against which he kicked with his naked foot,

saying "Ye damn white Manila bastard." The nose
of the boat swung out: there seemed to be some
hitch in the getting out of the stern; a momentary
hitch. Anxious faces shewed in the glare; Cruiser
noticed the steward, an old, white-faced man, staring with haggard eyes and mumbling. Cruiser
spoke again to the Captain.

"If you don't want the starboard watch, sir, am
I to shove off?"

The Captain looked at him, there was a kind of
pleasure in his eye; he did not answer. Instead of
answering, he took a step away from Cruiser and
called "Mr. Frampton, you will leave that boat if
you please, and take charge of the starboard boat,
and push off in her."

From the after davit of the long-boat there
came an unexpected answer from the much-tried
Mr. Frampton. "You can shove the starboard boat
down your Sunday pants, Captain Duntisbourne.
My place is in this port rattle trap, and I'm going
in her if I sail to Hull or hell. . . ."

Some men tittered at this; they started to titter
before Mr. Frampton had finished what he had to
say. But before he could finish, the ship gave a motion of shaking that was plainly a death throe before her plunge. The men at the starboard boat-
falls, without waiting for any order, lowered away
handsomely: the men about the port skids swarmed
up and got into their boat. Captain Duntisbourne

turned and walked aft, still holding aloft the flare.

"Captain Duntisbourne," Cruiser said, following him, "will you not get into your boat, sir?"

"Do you command this ship, Mr. Trewsbury?"

"Certainly not, sir."

"Let me at least thank God for that," the Captain said, "my holy topsail, yes."

At this, there were cries from the starboard boat now in the water, of "Mr. Trewsbury, Mr. Trewsbury." Coates, holding a red flare was on the skids calling, "Mr. Trewsbury."

"I'd better get to my boat, sir," he said. "Good luck, sir." He knew that without him, the boat would have no navigator. He walked quickly across the poop and leaped up to the rail. As he did so, the lad Coates slithered down the forward fall. Cruiser caught the life-line and lowered himself down into a boat that was leaping up and dropping away in wild water. The two lads tended the tackles and held their red flares aloft: two men with boat hooks were fending her off and having hard work to do it.

"Get out your oars, there forward," Cruiser called, as he shipped the tiller. "Cast off the after hook, boy. For the Lord's sake, boy, mind how you do it. You'll brain someone. Down port oars and shove her off: back a stroke starboard oars. Cast off, forward, Coates. Mind your heads with the hook there."

The hooks were flung clear as the boat rose up, and in an instant the boat was tossed away, in a spatter of spray. "Back together," Cruiser said, standing in the stern-sheets. He looked at his watch: it was now one minute to four. As the boat rose on the next wave, his head came to the level of the bullseyes of what had been his cabin. He noticed them as dim rounds of light from his still burning candle: he thought that not twenty minutes before he had been asleep in his bunk there.

"Back her clear of the stern," he said. "Back. Back. But easy all. Oars a moment."

They were now dropped astern of the sinking ship. As they rested on their oars, Cruiser put by the tiller, and lit another red flare. Up above them, only a few fathoms away, was the ellipse of the ship's stern, with the black gauntlet carved in high relief over the words

Blackgauntlet.
London.
Ever First.

"She's down by the head already," James Fairford said.

"She's going to dive," Cruiser said. "Give way together. What's wrong with the long-boat?"

The boat's head swung round to port: they pulled under the stern, and saw the run of white water streaking red from the flares. The long-boat, in the light, full of men, was still at the davits.

"My God," Cruiser said, "why don't they lower?"

It may have been that he saw more than they did, as a looker-on will; it may have been that the fall had jammed in the forward sheave again; or that Captain Duntisbourne had had some fancy of his own. Cruiser shouted with all his strength, "Lower away the long-boat falls there."

Even as he shouted, the after end of the long-boat dropped a little, and a man slid down a life-line into her. On the same instant the ship bowed suddenly forward, as in a big 'scend: a spray lifted high along her rail as she dipped to it. She lifted her bows a few feet, dipped them again in what seemed slow time: and then with horrible speed flung herself over on the lowering boat. The red flares quenched. The men in the starboard boat saw the fabric of the spars lean swiftly and more swiftly with a rattle and splash of falling and flying gear. They heard the masts and yards flog the water as they struck it. As they smote their smack upon the sea, the ship, now sunk, righted a little and plucked them partly upright again, and then went down like a stone, sending up into the night, as she went, a gurgling moan unlike any noise they had ever heard.

Cruiser and the others with him were as men stunned.

As the gurgling in the toppling of the water above her ceased, there came a sighing rush, as a rain squall slid in a wall of grayness upon the boat and quenched their flare. Wind was within the squall. They had to grope in the darkness and the storm amid the clutter and the wet paint for gear under which they could lie-to. It was most bitterly cold, blowing hard from the south. Cruiser knew, as he shivered, that this was now the storm that had been threatening, that it was now on them and might last all day.

It must have been nearly half an hour after the sinking of the ship that they had their next stroke of luck. There came a relenting in the rain, so that they could see a little, dark as it was. All were keeping a sharp look-out for survivors, and calling at intervals, "*Blackgauntlet,* ahoy." Presently the lad Percy Chedglow called, "I think there's somebody hailing, sir."

Cruiser took a flare and lit it. "Shout, all," he cried.

"Ahoy there. Whereaway?" they shouted, hoping against hope that the steamer which had sunk their ship was hailing for them. A faint cry came from the water, not far from them: there was no sign of any ship. They pulled towards the voice, peering into the night ahead.

"Whereaway? Whereaway?" they cried.

Cruiser passed the flare forward: a voice cried "Help me." In the dark water shot with red mottlings from the flare they saw a man's head: the men in the bows leaned over and gripped him; others helped. There was a scrambling struggle, and the man was dragged on board.

"Who is it?" Cruiser asked.

"It's the Cook, sir," Fairford answered. "Cheer up, Doctor, you're safe, old son. Here's our good old Doctor, boys. Are there any more of you around, Doctor?"

"Dammit, boys," the Cook answered, "it's a wash-out. A fair wash-out." He collapsed into the bottom of the boat with a shuddering of cold that seemed to shake the teeth in his head.

"That's all right. That's all right, Doctor," Cruiser said. "Take the tiller here, Chedglow, till we get the Cook warmed up a little. Chafe the other arm, Fairford: and you two chafe his legs. We'll soon get his circulation going again. But look out, all, for someone else, and keep on hailing."

"Perhaps I might help a little, sir," Nailsworth said, coming aft. He busied himself over the Cook, until the shuddering ceased to shake him; then the

Cook pulled himself together somewhat and re-sented attention.

"There's nothing the matter with me," he said. "But I tell you, it's a fair wash-out." He pulled out a small black wooden pipe from a pocket and stuck it in his mouth and sucked it. "That's what it is," he repeated. "A wash-out: and I'd got a pair of shackles I was working for Dose . . . Is Dose here, by any chance?"

"No, Doc," a man answered gently. "Not yet: but we'll pick him up all right, soon as it's light."

"It's almost light now," another man said. "Then we'll soon see anybody: and that sea-cow that horned us, too."

"Can anybody give the Doctor a fill of to-bacco?" Cruiser asked. "A smoke all round would be a good thing. But go easy with the matches."

"We'll go easy with the matches, sir," an old seaman, named William Kemble, said.

The day was long in coming on them. It came at last, with a wild heaven blotting into rain and a confused ugly sea. They had lain-to under a rag, waiting for the light. They were all wet and chilled through from the rain and the sprays. Cruiser had but to glance at the sky to see that worse was coming.

There was no sign of any ship.

"Do you think, sir, that the ship that ran into us sank?" Chedglow asked.

"No," Cruiser said. "She hit us with her strongest part in our weakest part: then she went on."

"She must have known what she'd done, sir?"

"Yes: she knew."

"She must have been damaged, sir."

"She didn't blow off steam. And if she'd been flooded forward we must have seen her by now. She may be fifteen miles away by this time: far out of sight in this weather."

"If you please, sir," a forward look-out hailed, "there's a body ahead there."

All roused to look. A body was lifted by a wave ahead and tumbled over by it. An oar had been secured to its wrist by a clove hitch of spunyarn. The oar was lifted and tossed on to the body; it rose again with its blade in air, and the body seemed to tug it down.

"He's alive," James Fairford said. "Who is it?"

"He's a big man, in a white singlet. But he's dead: he's face down in the sea, man."

"Who is it?"

"Give way a stroke or two with the forward oars," Cruiser said, "and salve the oar with him if you can."

"It's Corny," one man said.

"No, no, that's not Corny."

"It's Mr. Frampton, sir," James Fairford said.

"Py chee," Bauer said, "it vos der Bose. He vos dead as der oar, py chee."

They got him on board with much difficulty, for he was a big man. They cast loose the lashing on his oar, and laid him down in the stern sheets.

"We may be able to bring him round," Nailsworth said. He worked on him for more than half an hour, first with one method then with the other: he could not restore his breathing.

"He is dead," Trewsbury said. "I'm afraid he's dead."

"Yes, sir," Nailsworth said, "I'm afraid no man can help Bosun Frampton."

"He was a fine seaman," Fairford said, "and a big strong man. He was the weight-lifting champion of the English Navy at one time."

"Yes," Chedglow said. "Once when we were in port he took an oar in his teeth, and told Coates and me to hold on to the ends, and he lifted us both off the deck with it: he was strong all right."

"It was a treat to hear him swear when things went wrong."

"He was lipping the old man just before she went over," Coates said.

"Yes," Cruiser said, "and if he had obeyed the old man he would have been in charge here now." He stood up and stared carefully at the surrounding sea.

"There's no other body in sight," he said. "We're not likely to see another. There are some odds and ends floating about which we had better salve."

They spent the next half hour salving the floating wreckage: very little of it was of any use: they picked up

One teak wheel-grating.
One sail-maker's fid.
Two pins from the fife-rail.
Two fresh-water buckets.
One handspike.
Seven bunk-boards.
A corked bottle containing half a pint of vinegar.
A wash deck broom (straw).
A wash deck broom (coir).
Three unstropped, unsheaved blocks.
One unstropped snatch block (wood).
Two rickers, one seven, one ten feet long.

"Hold on, sir, I see a cask," Fairford called. It was a dingy old cask almost submerged. They pulled to it, and examined it: it was on the point of sinking when salved. It had once stood at the foot of the forward 'tween decks ladder, and contained nothing but a little straw and some "prayer book" pieces of holystone: they turned it adrift again.

"That seems to be everything we're to have," Cruiser said, as he scanned the water.

"There's a body out there, a point on the lee-bow, sir," the look-out called.

"It isn't a body," old Kemble said, "it's got a brass band on it. It's the scuttle-butt."

His eyes were reckoned the best there, and he proved to be very nearly right: it was the harness cask. They got a line on to it and hove it carefully aboard. Inside it there were a few grisly looking pieces of salt beef, weighing in all a little less than twenty pounds.

"That's the best find yet," one seaman said.

"You won't want so much salt beef," old Kemble said. "After a week in this boat you'll give all the salt beef in God's earth for a spoonful of cool clean water."

"Ah, go on with you."

"Hold on a minute," Cruiser said, as a thought occurred to him. "Where's the scuttle-butt?"

"Not here, sir," several men said.

"Not? It was to be filled and put aboard. Didn't you fill it, Jacobson?"

"Yes, sir. I filled it."

"Didn't you put it in the boat?"

"No, sir," Jacobson said evasively.

"It was leaking, sir," Stratton said.

"Captain Duntisbourne, sir," Efans said, "if you please, sir, Captain Duntisbourne said she wass to go in the long-poat, yess, sir."

Efans was a little, dark Welsh seaman, with very bright black eyes.

"Did you put it in the long-boat?"

"No, sir, the men of Mr. Appott's watch, indeed, they took the putt, sir, to the long-poat, yess."

"All leaking?"

"Yes, sir," Stratton said.

Cruiser looked at the three, Jacobson evasive, Stratton defiant, Efans bold, and knew that they were lying.

"Did anybody see Mr. Abbott's men taking the scuttle-butt to the long-boat?" he asked. Efans and Stratton had: and gave the names of the men: no other man had seen them.

"Did anybody hear Captain Duntisbourne give this order about the scuttle-butt?" Only Jacobson, Efans and Stratton had heard him: no other.

"Odd, isn't it?" Cruiser said, "that the only men who heard Captain Duntisbourne were the three furthest from him? I told you three to fill the scuttle-butt and put it in this boat, and you didn't."

"We had to obey the Captain, Mr. Trewsbury," Stratton said.

"It was a bit of a weight, wasn't it?" Coates asked, "to get the whole full scuttle-butt on to the skids and into the long-boat?"

"No, no," Stratton said. "We handed up the handy billy, they made it fast to the davit-head, then we slung the butt, and up she went with the tackle like a rocket."

"I thought Efans and you said that some of the port watch took the butt?"

"So they did, sir, with the tackle, when we'd brought it under the skids."

"Did you help bring it under the skids, Jacobson?"

"No, sir," Jacobson said, blushing.

"It was only Efans and you, Stratton?"

"Yes, sir."

"My God, you're two champion liars then," Coates said. "Just before we cast off, I shinned up the life-line from the boat to call Mr. Trewsbury. I lit a flare on the skids to call him, and I saw the scuttle-butt just underneath me, by the fresh-water pump there, and wondered why in blazes we hadn't taken it. You never moved the butt from the pump and you know you didn't. You three frauds went off to sneak rum, I'll bet."

"Well, you'll pay for it in thirst," Cruiser said. "The only drawback is, that we shall pay, too. That is ten good gallons of water, which I thought we had, wiped off the slate. What's the good of trying to think for fools like you? Get aft to the helm here, Stratton, and steer. You Efans get forward and stand a look-out. I don't blame you, Jacobson, quite so much: and you aren't quite such a liar; but I'll stop a whack that's coming to you as soon as I know what whacks there are."

Stratton took the tiller, Efans relieved the look-out: they looked from eye to eye in the hope of sympathy and support, but received none. Old Kemble spoke what all felt.

"You three Lord's mistakes will very likely be the death of us."

"Death, hell," Stratton said.

"Death for us," Kemble said. "But I promise it'll be hell for you first."

"Yes," some others said, "it shall."

"Hold on all," Cruiser said. "Listen to me. Are you satisfied, fore and aft, that we have picked up everybody and everything now remaining of the wreck?"

The men looked at each other, till Fairford, speaking for them, said: "We shan't find anything more, sir. She's taken the rest with her. We're satisfied of that, sir."

"We will bury Mr. Frampton, then," he said. "Four of you come aft and get him overboard."

They lifted the body along to the taffrail. All who could stand, in the tumbling boat, stood. Cruiser took off his cap, and said, "I have no prayer-book and do not know the proper service. You all knew Mr. Frampton here, and how well he knew his work and how he met death doing it for the sake of the port watch. I pray God bless his soul. Amen."

Some of the men said Amen; the Cook wept.

"We therefore commit his body to the deep,"

Cruiser said, and at that they lighted the body overboard.

"Get the oars out and get way upon her," Cruiser said.

They pulled for a few minutes into the teeth of the storm, to get clear of the body: but they saw it for a long time after that, rising and falling.

"Way enough," Cruiser said, "and oars a moment. Lay in your oars. Get the mast stepped there: handsomely now."

When the mast was stepped and secured, he said, "Pay attention to what I have to say.

"We're here in an open boat in mid-Atlantic. Our nearest port is certainly Fayal in the Western Islands, about seven hundred miles from here. It's blowing hard and will blow harder, but the wind is fair, and I propose to run for it.

"You know very well that we are on the busiest Trade route in all the seas and may be picked up within a few hours. If not, we are in the range of the prevalent westerlies, and may reasonably count on making Fayal in ten days' time.

"But you don't need to be told that you'll get nowhere in an open boat unless you bear a hand and step lively. You know the rules: watch on deck, keep on deck: watch below, keep below. You know the rule; obey orders.

"I am in command here. Mr. James Fairford has been your boatswain: he is now your mate. He is Mr. Fairford, henceforth, remember. Mr. Fairford, we'll pick watches, if you please."

When they had picked the watches Cruiser entered them in his Log.

"Survivors of the ship *Blackgauntlet*, at sea, in the starboard boat, Cyril Trewsbury commanding, bound for Fayal in the Western Islands.

Starboard Watch.	*Port Watch.*
Cyril Trewsbury, Master.	James Fairford, Mate.
Percy Chedglow, Apprentice.	John Nailsworth, A.B.
David Coates, Apprentice.	Johan Jacobson, O.S.
Nathaniel Clutterbucke, A.B.	Stephen Tarlton, A.B.
Thomas Rodmarton, A.B.	William Kemble, A.B.
Ewyas Stratton, A.B.	Peter Edgeworth, A.B.
Karl Bauer, A.B.	Llewellyn Efans, O.S.
Joseph Perrot (Cook).	Purchas MacNab, O.S."

When the watches had been logged, Cruiser spoke again.

"Before I send the watch below," he said, "I've got to overhaul the stores, and to tell you that we've got sixteen men on board, with nothing for them to eat and drink except what you see, which is little enough. These stores and this water will be issued as though we shall be twenty days getting to Fayal. We may be picked up, we may be there in a week, but we may not be there for three weeks: and we shall act accordingly. That is a nine-gallon

breaker. I filled it from the tank yesterday. Thank
God I did.

"It's raining now: and you have each probably
had a drink and a bite this morning. We shall catch
some rain, I hope. A lot of what you catch will be
mixed with spray, but you can rinse your mouths
with it, even if you can't drink it. There's a bolt of
small canvas forward there. Rouse it out, Mr.
Fairford; see if you can't rig a rain-catcher from
abaft the mast into these buckets. They've been
afloat, but we can rinse the salt out of them.

"Four of you there, Tarlton, Nailsworth, Kemble, Bauer, rouse aft that breaker and its chocks
and set them down aft here."

The men turned-to, and brought the water-
breaker aft, and chocked it securely.

"Well, that," Cruiser said. "Now about food.
As you know, we were overhauling these boats,
smartening up for London River. Their bread-
lockers were emptied yesterday and scraped clean.
They should have been refilled; but they weren't;
what with going to the braces . . ."

"We got some bread, sir," Chedglow said.
"Coates and I got quite a lot."

"Let's see it."

Chedglow went to the after-locker, opened it,
and hauled out two rather mouldy partially filled
sacks.

"And you had the sense to put it in the lockers,"

Cruiser said. "Who'd have thought it? It would have been ruined if you hadn't."

"Please, sir," Chedglow said, "Kemble put it in the lockers. We just dumped it and went to get more."

"I thought there must be some fly in the ointment. Well . . . Get me some of that canvas. I want a screen to keep the sprays off this while I get it into the bread-tank."

They screened him with canvas as he removed the bread, biscuit by biscuit, from the sack to the tank. Like all the biscuit in the *Blackgauntlet*, it had been nearly a year in store: it was softish, inclined to flake away from its heart, and when it did so, it revealed short, fat grubs of the colour of earth-worms, packed within it. Cruiser counted the bread aloud: there were 87 complete biscuits, four midshipman's nuts and perhaps three pounds of scraps in the first bag; 94 complete biscuits, eleven midshipman's nuts, and five pounds of pieces in the second bag: perhaps just over fifty-three pounds of bread in all.

"Fifty-three pounds," the man, Bauer, said. "You boys, why not bring more?"

"We brought more," Coates said. "Naturally, we brought more and put it in the long-boat."

"And you did well," Cruiser said. "You did very well. Has anybody else brought any bread?"

"I have, sir," old William Kemble said. He un-

packed from about his person, and from between
his shirt and the skin, nearly five pounds of biscuit.
No other man had any. The biscuits were put into
the tank.

"You won't get fat," Cruiser said. "You will
each have about the half of a pantile a day, or a bit
more. Is there anything more?"

"Yes, sir," Coates said. "We got some things
from the Captain's pantry, and would have got
more, if the Steward hadn't been so rossy."

The things were those small tins and boxes lying in the stern-sheets. Cruiser checked them carefully. They were as follows:—

One unopened	7 lb.	box of cabin raisins.
One half empty		box of cabin raisins.
One full	5 lb.	tin of currants.
Three	2 lb.	tins of bully beef.
Four	1 lb.	tins of jam.
One		tin of sardines.
Two small		tins preserved milk.

"Hear all," Cruiser called. "This is all the food
we have on board, so far as we can tell at present.
It will all go into the bread-tank here.

"Your allowance will be about the half of a
pantile, and an ounce of raw salt beef, or beef
bone, and three raisins each a day: one small spoonful of jam each, once a week, and a quarter panni-

kin of water each, twice a day. The milk and the sardines will be kept for anyone who may fall sick. As I take it that you have all breakfasted, I shall not serve you any whack of food till mid-day, to-day.

"Remember, that your lives depend on this water and food lasting till we reach Fayal. You'll be hungry and you'll be thirsty, but you'll get your bare whack and no more. This tank and breaker contain our lives. Don't let me have to remind you of that."

"Yes, and Mr. Trewsbury tells you the truth, let me tell you, and don't you forget it," old William Kemble said. "I've been in a boat once before: and we chewed cringles and obeyed orders and some of us were picked up alive. But I remember the *Saldanha's* boat, they quarrelled for the water: and they all was killed or died, but one . . . My God, I saw him after. He'd use to have been a merry fellow, playing on a jew's harp. When I saw him in Sandy Point, he looked like a dug-up corpse. He was all gone black in the face and mealed away: my God, yes."

"Thank you, Kemble," Cruiser said. "I'm glad you spoke. I'm not going to have quarrelling for the whacks here. So turn over all your knives to me. They'll go into the bread-tank till we make Fayal."

"That's right, Mr. Trewsbury," Fairford said.

"I say the same, all hands. You won't be working aloft here: you won't want your knives. Turn them over, right now."

The men looked inclined to growl, because their knives were their tools, almost the marks of their professions, but after looking from face to face, for a leader to refuse, they drew their knives and dropped them into the bread-tank.

"Thank you," Cruiser said. "I'm glad I hadn't to ask twice. Now this bread-tank will be shut till noon. Get sail on her."

The boat was an eighteen-foot clinker-built ship's boat, with good breadth of beam for her length. She had spacious forward and after lockers, five thwarts for rowers, and a mast-step for a short mast, which set (on occasion) a small storm-jib, and (usually) a single dipping lug, fitted, according to the practice of the Min River Tea Company, with two reefs. This lug, with the two reefs in it, was now set. Cruiser took the precaution of rigging a preventer stay and back-stay before the sail went up.

They had been in the boat, what with waiting for daylight and searching for flotsam from the wreck, for nearly three hours. It was now almost seven in the morning of a wild cheerless day of wind and sea. All were wet through from rain and sprays, very cold and depressed, thinking of ship-mates drowned, and of their own little belongings lost. As the paint in the boat was wet, they were all marked and barred with it. When they sat or leaned anywhere they stuck. As nearly all of them were unused to the motion of a boat most of them felt rather seasick. The paint stank, and the boat, being in the water for the first time since she was built, after three weeks in the tropics, leaked like a sieve, besides taking in from rain and sprays. A hand was busy bailing in the stern-sheets throughout Cruiser's stock-taking.

When Cruiser had worked out a course and got the boat upon it, there was a visible improvement in the doleful faces.

"I want a tobacco muster," Cruiser said. "If men will bring their tobacco into a common stock, it shall be paid for when this voyage ends."

There was, however, no need to bring tobacco into a common stock: no man had brought less than two pounds (Kemble had nine) except Chedglow, who did not smoke. Cruiser told all hands that they might smoke whenever they chose, except when steering or on the look-out.

"But bring all your matches into store," he said. "We may be short of matches. Put them in the water-tight compartments, fore and aft, where the flares are stored. And the officer of the watch will serve them out. But try to light your pipes from each other's pipes: you can do that with ropeyarns, if you try."

However, at the match muster, he found that they had twenty-seven dry boxes, and eleven damp boxes of matches, which was rather better than he had hoped. He stored them all carefully, and then proceeded to an inventory of the boat's stores.

As the boat was now under way, he called all hands for another address.

"We're under way now. We shall get there; don't fear. The main business on board will be to catch rain. You are all sailors. You have all heard of men in open boats: thirst is the real enemy, not hunger. Remember that you can do a lot to check thirst by splashing your face and arms and chest with sea water. But whatever you do, don't try to drink sea water. That brings madness and death. Don't think that you can rinse your mouths with it, even. When you get your little whack of water twice a day, try to make it last as long as you can. Hold it in your mouths a long time. I hope that we may get a lot of rain: but there'll be spray with most of it.

"It's going to be no easy job to steer this boat. One hand will have to come aft to tend the sheet while another steers. And as she's jumping around like a monkey on a stick, you'll not see your course in this little compass, half the time.

"One other thing. We are in a fair way. There must be a look-out all the time. The look-out who sights a ship shall have an extra whack: say three raisins. The man who sights land shall have ten. The man who sights the ship that picks us up shall have a plug of tobacco from each of us.

"The watch, Mr. Fairford's watch, may go below now. It won't be much of a watch below. Presently, we may be able to rig up something. Anyhow, think this, that you're alive and the rest of the crowd are gone. Go below the watch."

They went below; that is, they lurched and stumbled over the thwarts into whatever spaces they could get into. They could sit or lie or crouch on the bottom boards in a little water, or lie heaped on thwarts and locker tops, in cramped positions, flicked by flying sprays, and spirted on, from below, by jets flung upwards at leaky seams. Still, they were sailors to whom sleep was the blessing of life. They had slept under even worse conditions, on deck off the Horn or in the English Channel in the winter. They disposed themselves to sleep now, without much success: the motion of the boat, with her jerks, sudden dives and sheers, was still unaccustomed to them.

Cruiser spent the hour of his watch in devising a safe stow for the chronometers and sextant in the after-locker. There was no chance of any sight that morning. He worked out the *Blackgauntlet* position at the time of her sinking as 32° 40′ N. 39° 3′ W. He found that the boat under way in that wild water was leaking like a running brook at each seam. He told the men that the seams would soon "take up," and hoped sincerely that they might. He turned the watch to lashing the rickers to the thwarts, covering the fresh-water buckets with canvas covers, and devising canvas water-catchers, leading like funnels from the mast to a bucket. One hand was on the look-out, one steered, one tended the sheet with the helmsman, and one passed his time tapping oakum into the worst of the seams.

They were running free in a confused sea that was in the main a following sea, but not running true to the wind. The boat was going uneasily in slow climbs, swift-running dives, and pauses in the hollows. She went strangely silently, Cruiser thought, remembering the racket in the *Black-gauntlet* when running. Instead of the wrenching, never ceasing stretching strain of the fabric, the whine of the wind in the rigging, and the roar of the beating, drumming gear, the little boat toiled, swooped and panted, with little splashes, little thumps and spirtings, and an ever present seething of wave bursts close astern. Cruiser had not much experience of handling a boat at sea. The following seas looked grim to him: he knew that if one caught the boat and lifted her stern a shade too high, it would roll her over end for end. However, a brief experience shewed him that it did not happen, that the boat was always on ahead, going down the valley, when the top broke above, though sometimes, down in the valley, the sail would almost be becalmed. He had a little while to take stock of her, this little, crowded, eighteen foot boat, finding a way somehow in the toppling and confusion of wastes of water: going up, up, up, seething in a smother, pausing, rushing down a gliddering hill, with spray drenching down over their shoulders, then pausing again, sidling, edging, as it seemed, to one side or another, then trying it again, going on up the hill ahead. The swoops, and the hiss and rush and power of the great waves made his heart stand still at times, then the pluck and the cheek of the boat reassured him; and the vitality of the wind took hold of him till he felt confident that he would bring his command through. He was the Master of this company. His heart was sore enough as he thought of what the voyage would be, but he felt that he could do it: these fifteen men depended on him. Most of them were older and several of them were better seamen than he, yet they were his sheep, he was the shepherd, and without him they were but dead men.

He sat at the lee tiller for a few minutes, with Ewyas Stratton who was steering: and an ugsome business steering was, with these mad seas romping up astern, and sprays flying, and the little boat-compass card tilting out of sight and swinging hither and yon. Every now and again, perhaps once in twenty minutes, a rain squall swept them, so densely that sometimes Cruiser could not see the mast nor the sail; nor anything but a dim figure in the bottom boards near him, spitting out spray and rain and baling the well with a dipper.

Ewyas Stratton was a 'hard case'. He was a man whom Cruiser had disliked from the first. He was a fair-haired young man, with evil blue eyes, and a mouth that seemed always to be sneering. He was aged, perhaps, twenty-three, and had been at sea for several years, but was not a good seaman. He did just as much as he had to do, and no more. He was a man of some social standing: he could write a good hand and spoke good English, but here he was, an A.B. with no wish to be an officer, and no great interest in being an A.B. He held his own and more than that in the fo'c's'le, yet made no friends there. He was insolent in his manner to officers and shipmates alike: ever ready to defy and to rebel: and prone to sarcastic comment. He was one of those born neither to obey nor to command, but to be evil to the commander and the obeyer alike. He was strongly built. Perhaps there was nothing in life that he had much wanted to do, except to shoot rabbits and hit his father on the jaw, and both these things he had done. A rumour had spread through the *Blackgauntlet* that he had three rows of teeth. There was something in the lift of his ugly upper lip that suggested this.

"She's not making much of a course," Cruiser said.

"She's a sight better fun, sir, than that black gauntlet that's gone down the well."

"There was too much style about the *Black-gauntlet* for you," Cruiser said. "Pentonville new gaol is more your mark."

Stratton looked at Cruiser, wondering whether it would be worth while to retort: on the whole, he liked Cruiser, and thought his answer not amiss. 'Mr. — Trewsbury comes the sarcastic,' he thought.

"This is a wetter job than hoisting a leaky scuttle-butt, isn't it?" Cruiser asked.

"A sight better fun, sir, than any other job on board her. I'd steer her all day for a plug of tobacco."

"You may have to steer her all day without any plug of tobacco," Cruiser said.

Again Stratton looked at him. 'Mr. — Trewsbury is coming on,' he thought. They were silent together for a little while, the three intent on their jobs, the sheet-tender eyeing his sheet, Stratton shaking the sprays from his head (he was bare-headed), Cruiser trying to estimate how much of the course was being made. A rain squall, which had been blotting out the sea astern, came down in a gust, and at the same moment a big vicious sea seethed up underneath them, and broke into cataracts on each side. A high spray leaped and collapsed on them with rain. It was not much more of a shock than had been smiting them since they made sail, but it was a little more that snapped the tie at the yard, and brought the sail down. Nothing but the readiness of Stratton and the swift leap of Cruiser, Kemble and the lad Chedglow, saved the boat from broaching-to.

When the yard was retied, Cruiser returned to the con. Water was streaming from everyone; there was no dryness anywhere in the boat save in the lockers. The tongues of all played about their lips sucking in the rain and spitting out the spray too often sucked in with it. Stratton was wetter than any man there. He wore only an old dungaree shirt and a pair of dungaree trowsers old in themselves yet patched with something older. Cruiser wondered what the man's father and mother would think if they could see their son. Stratton was a hard case indeed. Cruiser knew that those old dungarees were the only clothes he had had in the *Blackgauntlet*.

"What did you go to steal," he asked, "when you left Jacobson at the pump?"

Stratton paused a minute before answering.

"Tobacco, sir."

"Did you get any?"

"I only got one plug, sir."

"Anything else?"

"No, sir."

"Why not tell the truth, Stratton?"

"That is the truth, sir."

"Are you a clergyman's son, Stratton?"

"Yes, sir."

"Yet you only stole one plug of tobacco, though you were stealing hard for ten minutes. I should have thought you'd have done better."

"The spirit was willing, sir, but the luck was weak."

"The luck was willing," Cruiser said, "but the spirits happened to be where you couldn't find them." He rose from his place as something occurred to him. "One bell, there," he said, "call the port watch."

A few minutes later, he made it eight bells and called all hands to muster.

"Stratton will stay at the helm and Efans at the look-out for a while," he said. "I want all hands on deck. I have to hold an enquiry now into the loss of the *Blackgauntlet*. We were all in the watch below when the collision occurred; except the Cook, who was an Idler, and also below. But was anybody here on deck when the ship ran into us?"

"I vas sleep on deck, sir," Bauer said.

"Were you awake?"

"No, sir."

"No other of you was on deck?" He looked

from face to face: all shook their heads or said
"No, sir."

"Was anybody here awake at the time of the
collision?"

"I was awake, sir," Clutterbucke said. "I was
awakened by the rain on the deckhouse: a very
heavy squall. I was just dozing off again, but not
asleep, when I heard the Spieler, the big German
in Mr. Abbott's watch, who was the look-out,
bang the bell and shout 'Light on port beam.' The
crash came before he finished, I thought: a sort of
double crash: one, two, like a gun with two barrels."

"I thought there was a pause between the
crashes," Cruiser said. "Three or four seconds.
What do you others think?"

"Yes, sir," several men agreed.

"I don't think there was much pause, sir," Kemble said. "But we were asleep at the first shock and
awake for the second. She hit us twice."

"I felt that she hit us hard, and made us heel,"
Nailsworth said, "and that when we rolled back
we hit her."

"That's near enough," some of the men agreed.

"She hit us the first time," Coates said, "whether
she hit us or we hit her the second time doesn't
much matter. But the second whack was a damn
sight further aft than the first, that I'll swear to."

"Anyhow," Cruiser said, "she struck us hard,

while we were in a rain squall, somewhere forward of the port main-rigging?"

"Yes, sir; by the fore-brace-bumkin. All the port fore-braces were cut through."

"And the two ships struck again as they ground clear. Now I want to know about the ship that struck us. We were on a N.N.E. course."

"No, sir, W.N.W.," the man Tarlton said. "I was at the wheel till eight bells in the middle watch."

"The ship was becalmed, then," Cruiser said. "Not lying any course. The wind came soon after midnight from about S. x E. and freshened all through the watch. Here's Mr. Abbott's log slate. She was running nine or ten knots on a N.N.E. course when the smash came. I would have even said that she was doing eleven. The ship that struck us must have been on some course between East and South. If we say South East, we shall probably not be far wrong. Who saw the other ship?"

"I saw her, sir," James Fairford said. "The knock she gave us was right on my front door. When I got to the deck (it was raining skysail yards then), she was just backing clear of the main rigging. She was a big ship, high up above us, with no navigation lights, and black as a Sunday hat. There was a sort of a dim light in two fo'c's'le bullseyes: and a sort of binnacle light on her bridge. There were foreigners yelling on her, all yelling at once, just like foreigners. I yelled out 'What ship is that? Stand by us,' I said, 'don't back away.' Somebody on her bridge shouted some foreign nonsense. And her bells were going like church parade to her engine room. But I had to see the watch all out, sir. I didn't see her again. She seemed to me to be a big ship, very high in the bow, and painted black."

"Did any other man see her?"

"I did, sir," the Cook said. "I came out on deck with Jim, sir, Mr. Fairford that now is. I saw a bit of her side swinging away from us. I saw a sort of glow above her funnel. But we were swinging apart, and things were raining down from aloft. I dodged under cover again."

"I saw her, sir," the lad Chedglow said. "I ran up on to the poop at the first smash: I was scared, sir. I saw her on the port quarter for just a second. She was black and long and had two or three patches of light."

"Do you mean flares?"

"No, sir. A sort of glow at her funnel, and a sort of glow over her binnacle."

"She didn't burn any flare?"

"No, sir, I'm sure she didn't. Then Captain Duntisbourne came beside me and burned a blue light, and that dazzled me. I lost sight of her, after that."

"Did any of you hear anything from the other watch of what she was?" Cruiser asked.

"Yes, sir," several men said.

"If you ask me, Mr. Trewsbury," James Fairford said, "I saw more of her than anyone. I was out on deck, right alongside where she hit us, within about fifteen seconds. The look-out was on the fo'c's'le, and the watch on deck were all at the break of the poop standing by for a call. I was on the spot before any of them. They were all flung galley west and didn't know what had knocked them."

"You saw no sign of a name on her bow?"

"No; not a letter."

"Which bow was it that you saw?"

"Her port bow, sir."

"Were our bulwarks stove-in when you saw them?"

"Yes, sir, for nine or ten feet. But you'll remember, sir, that blocks and tacks and booms and pennants of all sorts were flying down from aloft, and rain was pouring. I didn't get what you might call a calm view of things."

"You said, Clutterbucke, that the look-out called 'Light on the port beam'."

"He did, sir."

"As though he saw a light."

"He shouted as though he were scared stiff, sir. She hit us right on top of his yell. He may not have seen any light, but shouted 'Light' when he meant 'ship'."

"What happened to the look-out?" Cruiser asked. "Did he go aft?"

"He wasn't forward, sir," Clutterbucke said, "when we got the oil-bags over the bow."

"Was that the Spieler?" Tarlton asked. "Yes, sir, the Spieler went aft. I saw him passing stores into the long-boat."

"Since you had the best view of the ship that hit us, Mr. Fairford, would you say that she was on a S.E. course?"

"Yes, sir, pretty much S.E. But going fast as we were . . . Yes, sir . . . it must have been S.E. there or thereabouts."

"When you saw her last, Chedglow, was she lying by or moving? Perhaps you couldn't tell?"

"I think she was moving, sir; but perhaps it was we who were moving. She was very dim in the rain, sir."

"Did anybody hear her blowing off steam?" He looked from face to face. He was the only man there who had served in a steamer: they did not understand what he meant.

"You didn't hear steam being blown off?" he repeated. "A long, loud, coughing, drumming roar?"

"No, sir. Nothing of that," they said.

"I think we may take it then," he said, "that

she wasn't sunk, and that she didn't lie-by for more than a few minutes before proceeding on her course. I conclude that she was some foreign ship bound from a North Atlantic port to the Cape."

"I'll bet they're watching their forward bulk-head," Coates said.

"Perhaps not," Cruiser answered. "A steamer has enormous strength forward. She may not be damaged at all."

"Why didn't the dirty hounds lie-by and help?" Coates asked. "They must have seen our flares."

"They were all off their heads, like a lot of foreigners," Fairford said, "all jabbering at once."

"Damned dirty hounds," Coates said. "They're at work in their damned saloon at this moment, I'll bet, cooking their damned log together. 'Hit submerged wreck and damaged bow-plates: proceeded under reduced steam.' Then they'll put in a faked time, and that'll be that."

"Rather a lot of damns about it, Coates," Cruiser said. "We may be able to trace her presently. Another point that we ought to enquire into is why the long-boat didn't lower and get away from the ship. I saw that she'd a jam, or something of the kind in her forward fall, but they'd cleared it three or four minutes before she sank. What else went wrong with her? Can anybody say? Why didn't she get away?"

"Yes, sir," the Cook said. "The fall had swollen

and jammed in the sheave, and then the davit jammed in its socket."

"That wasn't the real reason," Stratton said, from the helm above them. All turned to him, to hear what more he would say: he said nothing more: lifted his eyes to the sail and spat the spray from his lips.

"Go on, Stratton," Cruiser said. "What was the reason, in your opinion?"

"Discipline. The taut hand, etcetera."

"Yess, py Cot, she wass Cot's truth," Efans said, with swift support.

"How?" Cruiser asked.

"Those poor fellows, or silly swine in the long-boat, whichever you like to call them, were waiting for orders, just as we were. And who were to give the orders? Mr. Sunday School Abbott, just out of his time, just done pinching raisins, and the intellectual Captain, who'd have died fifty times rather than give the order to abandon his precious command. For the matter of that, this boat wouldn't have been lowered if I hadn't stepped in. I gave the order and saved all the lives here. Anyone with half an eye could have seen what was ailing the Captain. He wanted all hands to sink with him, to sail his precious ship in Hell."

"Py Cot, yess," Efans said, "he wass all for all hands tying, look you."

As it happened, the thought had occurred to

Cruiser, that Captain Duntisbourne had been unable to bid the crews abandon ship, and had in fact determined to let all drown with him. Still, even if it had been the case, which no one could now prove, he was not going to accept that way of speech from Stratton.

"I was going to enquire who lowered this boat," he said. "Since it was you, I'll log you for it; as I'll log you for disobedience with the scuttle-butt."

"Will you log yourself, too, sir?" Stratton asked. "Mr. Frampton was put in charge of this boat."

"I am in charge of her," Cruiser said, "take care you don't get reminded of it."

Stratton hesitated a moment, whether to let the boat broach-to, and wondered for a moment whether he would tell Cruiser to go to hell. Then he reflected that the time was not ripe; that he could have his fun later in the day.

"Certainly, Captain Trewsbury," he said.

"Does anybody know what jammed the long-boat's after-davit?" Cruiser asked. "Do you, Perrot?"

"No, sir; I don't."

"What did they do to clear it?"

"Mr. Frampton, sir, got a bar from the deck-capstan, and he and Spieler forced it. That made it turn."

"Why didn't you lower then?"

"Waiting for orders, sir."

"What were they saying round you?" Cruiser asked.

"They were all scared stiff, sir, saying 'God's sake, boys, lower; we shall all be drowned. What in hell's keeping you?'"

"You were waiting for Captain Duntisbourne?"

"Yes, sir. And he neither came nor let us go. Mr. Frampton shouted at him, 'Are you coming in this boat, Captain Duntisbourne, or are you thinking of swimming?' We all shouted, 'Come along, Captain Duntisbourne,' but he didn't come. Some of us said, 'Cut the falls, boys. Let us get clear; we'll salve him later'. But Mr. Abbott kept saying 'He'll come in a minute,' but he didn't. Then Mr. Frampton went aft and tried to get him to come, but the Captain shook him off; and Mr. Frampton came back swearing; he said 'That damned sea marine won't speak or shift: he wants to go down in her.' And some of the men said, 'Well, we don't. Let go the falls, Joe. Let him drown, if he's a mind to.' (You see, some of us still called Mr. Frampton Joe.) Then Mr. Frampton said, 'I'm damned if I won't, too, and let him sink or swim.' And he did let go, or start to let go. Then somebody came slithering down a lifeline. And someone started singing 'Wait for the waggon, and we'll all have a ride'. And the next thing, the whole ship came toppling down on top of us."

"Can you remember anything after that?" Cruiser asked. "A squall came down as the ship went over. We could see nothing and do nothing."

"I'm not likely to forget the rest, sir," the Cook said. "It was a fair wash-out."

"Let's hear it. And try to remember anything you saw or heard of the others."

"I tell you, sir," the Cook said, "it was a fair wash-out, like being run over by a funeral. First thing, I was in the water, with things falling on my head and ropes all round me. Somebody clawed hold of me and dragged me down, and somebody got me by the mouth. I fought and kicked to make them let go. I'd heard of being 'sucked down' with a wreck, and I thought I was for that. I don't know how far I went, but it seemed I should burst. So I said to myself, 'I *shall* burst if I don't do something, and that'll be a fair wash-out.' So I struck out and I kicked somebody, I know. Then after a time I felt I was coming up: and up I came and got a breath, and felt the rain on my face. So when I got some breath, I called '*Blackgauntlet.*' Presently something hard came sidling right along my back, and that turned me sick, for I thought it was a shark, but it was one of the spare spars. I tried to get on to it: it kept rolling over from me; but at last I got support from it. It was pouring rain. At last a voice said, 'Is that you, Doc?' It was that man Harry; 'Pots', they called him, because he'd been a pot-boy down Wapping way; the lad what said he ate a calf in forty-eight hours against Bix of Millwall. So I said, 'What, Pots, this is a fair wash-out,' just like that, see; and he said to me 'Whitechapel High would be a bit of all right.' And I said to him 'Get across this spar, Pots,' I said, 'that's the only all right here,' just like that, see. So he got to the spar and said to me, 'Where's all the others, Doc?' just like that. And I said (I didn't want to frighten him and make him lose heart), I said, 'They'll be all along presently, sure to.' And he said, 'No, they won't be along, Doc: the others won't. They're all drowned.' So I said, 'No, Pots, no: you'll be laughing at this with them when they pick us up. Think what a laugh there'll be, old Pots being astride a spar with Doc.' And he said to me 'A bit of Monty's eel jelly would be a bit of all right. Whitechapel High of a Saturday evening, what?' And I said to him, 'We'll have a bit of Monty, you and I, Pots, as soon as we get ashore.' 'No,' he says to me, just like that, see; 'No,' he says, 'I shan't ever see the shore again. I can't hang on to this spar,' he says, 'I'm a London man, not a herring,' he said. 'Why, Pots,' I said, 'we've all got to be herrings in a wash-out like this.' 'Ah,' he says to me, 'you've got that shape skin, perhaps; but I'm too cold.' And he just let go and was gone.

"And I hung on for a bit longer, giving a call or two. Then presently, I thought I heard somebody hailing *Blackgauntlet*, so I hailed again. It came being near the end of me, for I lost my hold of the spar and couldn't reach it again. And though I hadn't thought much of it when I'd had it, I did feel the comfort of it when it was gone. I nearly went to visit poor old Pots when you got me and pulled me in."

"You may reckon that you weren't born to be drowned, Doc," Cruiser said.

"You may just about reckon that," Kemble said.

"Poor old Pots," Clutterbucke said. "He could sing, too: 'the Lavendered Bed' and that."

"I don't believe he ever ate that calf," Rodmarton said.

"You've heard the Cook's account," Cruiser said. "He was at the long-boat from the time we mustered till she sank. There were jams in the long-boat's gear. . . ."

"And why?" Stratton put in from the helm. "Why were there jams in the long-boat's gear? You, Captain Trewsbury, were responsible for the gear of the boats. Why weren't they both all clear for lowering?"

"Yess, by Cot, why not inteet?" came the parrot cry from Efans.

"You know Captain Duntisbourne's standing orders about the boats, Stratton," Cruiser said. "You were by me when he gave them. Take this as a second warning. You'll get no third."

Fairford struck in here. "You all know that Captain Duntisbourne would never have the boat's covers off till we cleaned ship."

"Not one captain in twenty will," old Kemble said.

"Hold on here," Cruiser said. "We're enquiring into the loss of the long-boat. She was delayed by jams in her gear, but she could have been lowered if Captain Duntisbourne had given the order. They waited for the order: they waited for the Captain, and neither came. They waited too long. Do you agree to that?"

"Yes, sir," several men said. "If she had lowered when we did she'd have been safe. She could have lowered."

"It's my pelief," Efans said, "that that Captain Tuntispourne wass the murterer look you, of fine mans, much petter than him."

"Your beliefs aren't asked for," Cruiser said, "keep them to yourself till they are.

"You know very well, all hands," he went on, "what a fine seaman Captain Duntisbourne was, and how proud he was of his ship. He had little rest, certainly no proper rest, from the day we left the Min River. Naturally, from the want of rest, and the strain of a calm, and the longing to make a passage, he was not himself last night, as no one knows better than myself. That was plain enough, in the middle watch, long before the collision. He was always a peculiar man, and the strain of the passage had made him almost mad. I believe that he worshipped the *Blackgauntlet*. When she was struck I believe he determined to go down with her. You have heard the Cook here telling us what Mr. Frampton said only a minute before the *Blackgauntlet* sank, that Captain Duntisbourne wanted to go down in her. I'm sure he meant to.

"If we reach port and come to a Court of Enquiry, I shall say that Captain Duntisbourne was overstrained and unbalanced and did not give necessary orders. The crew waited for orders, the necessary orders were not given, or not given in time; and twenty good lives were lost as a result.

"As to the ship: nothing could have saved her. Even if we had had a collision mat as big as a small house all ready on deck we couldn't have got it over in time. The hole was too big.

"If you have views about the officers and the ship, remember, that if we reach port you will have a full opportunity of stating them, if you are asked for them; but the Court's first aim will be to get at the facts. Your views may not be wanted.

"Now before I send the watch below, I want to check this boat's stores." He raised his voice on the last few words, so that there could be no doubt that he was heard fore and aft. He raised his voice with intention, and got from it an indication that he wanted: Efans, the look-out, glanced meaningly and as though with enquiry at Stratton who was steering. Stratton's sullen face shewed no change and gave no sign, save that he bowed a little more doggedly to watch the leaping compasscard.

Cruiser caught Fairford's arm and whispered into his ear: "Keep an eye on them forward there, while I check these after-lockers. Watch the fellow Efans."

Fairford gazed at the wild sky without changing a muscle, and replied, "I'll be ready, Mr. Trewsbury: but I think the worst of this is north of us."

Cruiser turned to the boat's after-lockers.

The first locker was the tin-lined bread-locker, which now contained the bread and other articles of food, except the beef. The second locker contained two two-gallon tins of colza oil, two boat-lanterns, two wicks and burners, an unopened tin case of matches (1 gross), a case of blue lights, and a box of self-igniting red flares.

On the port side aft were corresponding lockers, numbered 3 and 4. Cruiser gave orders for the beef from the harness cask to be put into Number

Three locker. When this was done, he ordered the rain-catchers to get the cask swilled out.

"It will be thick with brine," he said, "but in time that will go, and it will serve as a rain-catcher."

Number Four locker contained the stores put there by the sailmaker, a sailmaker's canvas fetch-bag, a flat-pointed marler for wire-splicing, a roll of No. 6 canvas (nearly twelve yards), and seven hanks of sailmaker's twine. In the corner of the locker, below these, were a tin jam-pot containing slush, a ball of spunyarn, three small blocks, a hank of amberline, some nettles, seven small thimbles and nine small jib-hanks stopped together with yarn.

"God bless old Sails," he said. "Look, you men, at what old Sails found time to get for us."

"He was always a one to have things on top and to hand," the Cook said. "He done us well."

"He was a fine man, the Sails," Kemble said.

Cruiser climbed forward to the forward lockers; he noticed that Efans had shifted his position. He opened Number Five locker. It contained the boat's collapsible drogue or sea-anchor at present stopped up with yarn, two ten-fathom lengths of one-inch hemp-rope, not in good condition, two hand scrubbing-brushes, much the worse for wear, (which he handed over to the men who were cleansing the brine from the harness-cask), and three fish lines on frames, with hooks and spoons.

"Strong enough for cod, them hooks," old Kemble said, "but the lines have all the heart out of them: they've been stowed wet."

"Bend one of the hooks to some spunyarn," Cruiser said, "and pay it out astern; we may get a bite."

Rummaging in the extreme corners of the locker, he pulled out a much weathered piece of yellow soap, three small fragments of holystone, an old rag, and a tin-lid that had once contained 'gumption', or oil and crushed bath-brick, used for the polishing of brass.

In Number Six locker on the top were the tools which he had brought from the carpenter's shop. Below these were the boat's spare mainsail and a little storm jib. There were five lengths of rope, each about five fathoms long, newly cut from the *Blackgauntlet's* upper mizen braces. There was a bunch of galvanized iron boat-crutches, with spunyarn laniards. Besides these he turned out one three-cornered scraper, two old iron dippers with perished handles, a bully-beef tin secured to a stick, two spare tillers and a spare rudder, also a brass steering yoke with fine white lines, for use in port, a boat-flag, a boat-ensign and staff (to ship in a gudgeon in the after-sheets) and a roll of red Chinese straw matting, which had perhaps once been spread in the stern sheets on state occasions.

There were also two dirty little scraps of blue Chinese silk-embroidery, which had been used as rags to wipe paint-brushes.

"That is the lot then," Cruiser said, to Efans, who was just beside him.

"That wass the lot, sir," Efans said.

"No other locker, is there?"

"No, sir," Efans said.

"Except the cable-locker that you're sitting on," he said. "Just shift till I look there."

"There wass no things there, except caples, look you," Efans said.

"Shift, till we see," Cruiser said.

Efans shifted to leeward from the chain-locker, which was in the boat's eyes, beneath the shackle for the stay and the cable-leads. Cruiser as he put a hand to the locker, glanced aft at Stratton, who was still steering, with a scowl on his face. As he opened the locker he saw two little boat killicks, lying unshackled upon a jumble of chain.

"Nothing much there," he said.

"No, sir," Efans said.

"Something else, though," Cruiser said. He reached down into a recess on the port side which was less filled with chain than elsewhere. One by one he pulled out three bottles of brandy; bottles 7, 8 and 9 from the cabin dozen.

Cruiser held them up to the general view.

"Who put these in here?" he asked: nobody answered.

"They were in the cabin case last night," Cruiser said, "they were put in here since the collision. Who put them in? Did you, Efans?"

"No, Captain Trewspury."

"Did you, Stratton?"

"No, sir."

Groping further, Cruiser pulled out a box of cigars, which had been upon a shelf in the cabin. Captain Duntisbourne had kept them there, in port, for the entertainment of merchants, shippers and visiting captains; they had lain there ever since.

"Did you put these here, Stratton?"

"No, sir: neither the bottles nor the cigars."

"You're a champion liar then," Coates said; "I saw you putting them in as I was calling Mr. Trewsbury. I had a flare lit just over your head, and saw you stowing them and knew you'd been up to no good. Only I thought they might be your own whack-pots, so I didn't mention them."

"I know nothing about them," Stratton said.

"De hell you don't know notings about dem," Bauer said. "I hear you say to Efans: We'll claim de forward places for sleep and sneak a trink in der dark. I got corkscrew, you say, in my pants pocket."

"Have you a corkscrew, Stratton?"

"Not now, sir," Stratton said; with a swift movement he dropped something into the sea.

"What kind of shipmate do you call yourself?" Cruiser asked. "Here was poor Cook, very nearly drowned, nearly dying for want of stimulant, and you had this brandy stowed away and never said a word about it. You'd have let him die here, rather than give up the chance of getting drunk yourself. It would do you two good to be towed overboard in a line."

"It's nothing to get excited about," Stratton said.

"I'm not getting excited," Cruiser said. "If we were to get excited about it, it would be a bad day for you. Two dirtier hounds never breathed. However, Cook shall have a nip now."

"You haven't got a corkscrew now," Stratton said.

Cruiser did not answer. He took from his pocket a general utility tool, containing corkscrew, knife, blade, fork and spoon. He uncorked No. 7 bottle, and called hands aft to splice the main-brace. Beginning with the Cook, to whom he gave a double allowance, he gave each man a small spoonful of neat brandy. "Stratton and Efans will go without," he said, "they don't believe in sharing." The lad, Percy Chedglow, refused his brandy, having promised his mother never to touch spirits. Stratton and Efans glowered and looked wicked.

"Like kids at a Sunday School treat," Stratton said.

"And don't you wish you were in it?" Cruiser said, as he stowed the bottles with special care in the bread-locker.

"If you'd been in the Navy, Stratton," Kemble said, "as England may thank God you aren't, you'd have had four bag for that, across your stripped back, as I wish to God you'd had."

"If you'll give me a plug of tobacco, Efans," Tarlton said, "and keep well to leeward of me, I'll let you smell my breath, since you're so fond of brandy."

"You wass funny mans, by Cot," Efans growled.

"Get below the watch," Cruiser said.

"Am I to be relieved, sir?" Stratton asked.

"No, you're not," Cruiser said. "You and Efans will keep as you are."

The men of the watch below arranged themselves as comfortably as they might in whatever spaces they could find, in the sheets and between the thwarts. All were of course long since soaked to the skin, and all became wetter at almost every moment, from sprays from the following seas, and the frequent deluge of the rain squalls. The boat drove on, not really going fast, but seeming to do so from the violence of her motion, her abrupt jerking climbs and seething gliddering rushes.

What shocked Cruiser, though he kept his feelings to himself, was the discovery that he was now dealing with the sea. Hitherto, he realized, he had dealt with the wind. In all his previous sea-service the wrestle had been with the wind, to use it and master it. In all his past at sea he had been conscious of the power and fury of the wind, and had found exhilaration in the roar of a great gale ringing and shrieking in the rigging. Here, though it was blowing hard enough, there was no sense that the wind was the enemy. The real enemy was the seething leaping and appalling water so close at hand. All that waste of tumult was the enemy; and alert and on the clutch and on the pounce. Devils surged up abaft from it, and flung out engulfing arms that curled; little devils ran under the boat and knocked and flung up fingers through the seams; and the teeth of other devils flashed out at the straiks or over the gunwale. As far as the eye could see was a dimness of tossing drab angry devils with grabbing and gleaming tusks and talons, with drift cut off sharp from the wave tops and flung flat with the scoopt scud; with strange sheers and scurries and dives and glides in the boat, which somehow seemed to find her way, guided by the hand of the savage at the helm. There was a strain on the leaning shoulder of the water-darkened sail, then a pause, then an urge, then a seething of white along the gunwale and a tipping over of more spray, and curses from the drenched men who were trying to sleep, and the drenched man baling.

——In the stern sheets, the sheet-tender was busy beside the baler, whose work was only slowly lessening, as the seams swelled or were patched. It was now nine in the morning: the crew had been in the boat only five hours, but already they were feeling the strain of being in cramped positions, unable to walk or sit comfortably, or stand or stretch. They were all jammed together and half a dozen of them were seasick. Forward, old Kemble, Tarlton and Edgeworth were quilting together the few blankets on board into a communal bed to cover the bottom-boards. Efans was crouched above them, looking-out. MacNab stood with Jacobson at the mast, working the rain-catcher. The watch below were ducked down to windward each sleeping for a few minutes uneasily, then waking from the pain of the position, and rousing and shifting and cursing.

Cruiser had given word for the two lads, Coates and Chedglow, to berth aft, as members of the afterguard: it was a poor privilege, to try to sleep in the open well, in range of the baler, against the edges of the after-locker and the breaker. Cruiser had no doubts about Coates, who was a rough and tough customer. Chedglow was a delicate-looking lad, who was nick-named Mary Ann. However, there was nothing that could be done to make his lot easier to him: nor would the boy have allowed it, for he had a proud spirit.

Without saying a word, Cruiser stepped gingerly forward and removed the boat hatchet from its painted canvas case against the chain locker. When he had brought this aft, he removed the similar hatchet from its case in the stern sheets. Both tools were thick with wet paint. He wrapped them in the old clouts from the lockers and stowed them together with the knives in the bread-locker.

"Just as well, Mr. Trewsbury," Mr. Fairford said, "just as well to have everything out of harm's way." He glanced at Stratton as he spoke. Stratton smiled with disdain and spat and muttered something.

"No chance of a sight," Cruiser said, "I shan't get a sight to-day."

"No, sir," Mr. Fairford said. "It won't clear to-day."

"The boat's straining a bit."

"First time she's been used, sir. She'll take up. The lower straiks are taking up well."

"Keep a hand busy with oakum," Cruiser said. "I'll whack out the bread and water at eight bells. We'd better keep the breakfast at the end of the morning watch: dinner at the end of the forenoon watch; and perhaps supper in the dogwatch."

"Very good, Mr. Trewsbury: we shall get so little that we shall be thankful for it at any time."

"I daresay we shall be," Cruiser said. "But still I'm confident. We shall get there, or be picked up."

"O, yes, sir." Mr. Fairford paused as though there were something that he wished to add.

"What is it, Mr. Fairford?"

"Beg pardon, Captain Trewsbury," he said. "But I've had experience of harness-casks. You'll never get the brine out of this one, no, not in years, any more than you will out of the pickling rooms on a pig farm. It will only be wasting rain, trying to rinse it."

"I was thinking that," Cruiser said. "But I'm glad you confirmed it. The cask's only in the way, then; we might as well heave her overboard."

"Yes, sir."

"Two of you empty the harness-cask, and heave her overboard."

"Ay, ay, sir."

Cruiser watched the cask bob away aft, and go rolling over in the top of a comber. When it was too late he thought that perhaps the cask would have made a good sea-anchor in case of need.

He turned to Mr. Fairford.

"Well, I'll turn in," he said. "Be sure you call me if the sea gets worse: we may have to bring-to."

"I hope not, sir."

"I hope not, too: but it looks pretty foul to windward."

"A real bag of dirt, sir: though I think the worst is to north of us."

"I wish I could think it," Cruiser said. "It seems to me to be coming on." He did not wish to argue the point, but snuggled down, so wedged between the bread-locker and the water-breaker that he would be roused by any attempt on either. He was wet through and cold, but certain of enough fatigue to drug him to sleep. In a minute he was very heavily asleep.

However, no one slept long in that boat. It was a part of her discomfort, that no one could wake in her without waking others. Whenever one of the watch on deck moved he was certain to tread or trip upon one of the watch below. Whenever one of the watch below moved he was certain to knock against others. There was a good deal of movement in the crew, as it happened, for seven of them (five of whom had never been seasick before) were violently seasick. They were used to the big rhythms of ships; the little sharp jerks of the boat upset them. Every now and then one of these sufferers would rise from his crouch, lurch swiftly to the side, disregarding all in his way, and be sick. Then after the paroxysm he would cling there in his misery, cursing the boat and fortune.

After ten minutes of being knocked and trodden on, and twenty minutes of heavy stupid sleep, Cruiser woke from pain in his limbs. He shifted uneasily in the puddle and slept again till pain in other limbs woke him.

Rousing up a little, he heard Tarlton talking in a low voice to Nailsworth. "We'll be picked up to-morrow, John, so I don't mind this just for one day."

"We ought to be picked up," Nailsworth said.

"I don't see it," Stratton growled. "Why should we be picked up?"

"Well," Nailsworth said, "all South-Spain ships pass where we pass, going or coming, and just where we are now we cross the routes from the Eastern States ports, so that we stand a double chance."

"Of course we'll be picked up," old Fairford said. "But for this coming on so thick we'd have been picked up by now, I daresay."

"How many ships have we spoken since the Line?" Stratton asked.

"None."

"What about your double chance then?"

"We haven't tried to speak with any," Nailsworth said. "We've sighted nine or ten ships, or more; I've seen nine or ten myself."

"Picked up," Stratton repeated. "Picked up and carried by a loving father, like in the hymn."

Cruiser heard one of the watch below, it sounded like Coates, growl out that he wished folk would remember that the watch below were trying to sleep. The voices stopped at once, and Cruiser was able to doze away into a stupor; he slept for another twenty minutes, when poor old Mr. Fairford, going to be sick, trod on his hand and woke him thoroughly.

He sat up, eyed the sky, still resolute and wild with storm, saw that Stratton was still scowling at the flying compass card, and keeping something of a course. He noticed Fairford, recovering and angry, and the boy Chedglow, rather white and scared, sitting up awake beside him.

"Go to sleep, Chedglow," he said.

"I can't sleep, sir."

"This will soon pass," he said. "Try to sleep."

He himself rolled over and slept again for a few minutes, and so passed his watch below, until at six bells, he ached all over and could stand it no more. He stood up in the attitude of crouched readiness which was the nearest that one could get to standing: he stretched himself and noticed that nearly all the watch below were awake. Chedglow, however, was asleep in the well at his feet, roughly covered in the quilt that the seamen had stitched. Edgeworth was in the well, baling.

"It's half your life to be out on a boating party, Edgeworth," he said. Edgeworth was an oldish

English seaman, with something the look of a walrus from long, drooping moustaches. He had been forty years at sea, and some years (altogether) in the gaols of seaport-towns up and down the world. He was dressed now in the only clothes he possessed, a pair of cotton trowsers and a cloth waistcoat without sleeves. He grinned at Cruiser, and said that he would as lief be in a boat as in a ship, he couldn't see that it made much difference.

"Is she taking up at all?" Cruiser asked.

"Yes, sir; she's taking up nicely. There's not more than half what was coming into her in the morning."

"Were you ever in a boat before, Edgeworth?"

"Yes, sir, once, in a sort of way. I was taken off a wreck by the *Lizard* life-boat, twenty-two years ago. We went on to the Manacles in thick weather with snow. I and five others were in the mizen-rigging for a day, but three of them were dead when the boat got to us. We were coming home from Havana, with copper-ore, in a barque called the *Sapphire* of London, one of William Jewel's *Jewels*.

> *'William Jewel*
> *Pin rail gruel,*
> *Pound and pint*
> *And use you cruel.'*

However, I learned some sense from it, for I lost all my clothes in her, and I had some good clothes that voyage. I've never taken clothes to sea since; and never will. You spoil more than you earn."

Cruiser marvelled at the man: he was one of the choicest seamen in the China Trade: well over sixty, hardened and battered by every kind of service, from piracy and slaving in early West Indian days to the bombardment of Sebastopol and the China Tea race. Perhaps it made no difference to him, what kind of service he took, as long as there was rum of some sort, in abundance, somewhere, for some time, after it.

"Well, the longer you're in the boat the bigger your pay-day will be," he said.

"Yes, sir. I like a long passage," Edgeworth answered. "The more days the more dollars."

Cruiser cast an eye over his crew: they were all looking the worse for wear. He himself was aching all over, but thought that in a day or two the boat would be more bearable, less wet and uneasy, and they themselves might become accustomed to the life. Still, he would have given much to be able to walk ten yards, and something to be able to say so; but these longings had to be kept within.

"Seven bells," he called at last. "Come aft to dinner, the watch below." As the men mustered, he took two biscuits from the locker, divided them into exact quarters and served out a quarter pantile to each man. "This is your dinner," he said. "Make it last as long as you can by chewing it over and over."

They did their best to make the bread last, but an ounce of bread cannot last very long.

"You fellows bolt your food," Cruiser said. "You must go at it in a different spirit. Pretend that the sight of it is one course and the smell of it another. Spin it out more. Look at me. I haven't eaten half of mine yet."

"Ah, sir," Coates said. "We've all got that waking-up brown taste, and ate to get rid of it."

"You'd do better to smoke to get rid of it," Cruiser said. He turned to Chedglow, about whom he had begun to be anxious.

"Well, Chedglow, this will be something to write home about. The letter will go from Fayal, by the mail-steamer which takes us probably. It will reach your people the morning before you do, about twenty-four days from to-day, or sooner: that isn't long to wait, is it?"

"It seems a good deal to us now, sir."

"Ah, it'll pass," Coates said. "Time always passes: it's all the damned thing has to do."

"Not so much 'damned' in your remarks, Coates."

"I wish someone would clump me a sock on the ear," Coates said, "whenever I say damned. I got into the way of it when I was a boy [he was then seventeen] and half the time I never know I'm saying it."

"Hear, there, fore and aft," Cruiser said. "Anyone hearing Coates use the word damned, is to clout him on the head."

"Ay, ay, sir, we'll clout," the men said. "We'll . . . well, teach the young . . . not to . . . well, swear."

"Eight bells, there," Cruiser said.

The watches mustered and the wheel and lookout were relieved. Stratton was released from the tiller. Though he scowled and pretended to be fresh even he had had plenty.

"I hope you enjoyed your trick, Stratton," Bauer said. Bauer was a pale-faced, rather evil-looking young German, with slick mouse-coloured hair and a big mouth. He was short and very broad. He had shifty eyes of the palest possible gray. Cruiser suspected that he was a man of some education who had come to sea for some pressing reason, to avoid the police or military service. Both these reasons had weighed upon Bauer, but his reason for remaining at sea after his first escape from Germany was love of pleasure. After every voyage he had a sum of money, from twenty to seventy pounds, to spend on pleasure. He endured the year or two at sea for the sake of the week's spree at the end. Stratton owed him one for his betrayal about the brandy.

"I enjoyed the trick very much," he said. "Aft at the helm I couldn't smell you stinking Dutch-men."

"Now you sleep forward," Bauer said. "And get a nice trink of brandy mit your corkscrew." Stratton did not answer this, but received and ate his allowance of bread with Mr. Fairford's watch. He had steered for five hours, but it was now his watch on deck. Cruiser put him to baling.

"Come aft, the watch below for fresh water," Cruiser said. "Get ready the canvas screen two of you to guard against sprays flying into the breaker. Hear there, fore and aft, you're going to have the half of this tin pannikin of water, each, twice a day. Make it last in your mouths as long as you can, for this is the only whack you'll get to-day."

Very carefully he opened the wooden screw-bung of the breaker under a stretched canvas screen, and dipped the pannikin into the water. "Mr. Fairford first," he said. "Here you are, Mr. Fairford," he said.

"And I'm very glad to have it," Fairford said. "I've been looking forward to this drink ever since we left the ship. I've had a good gollop of water running down my face all morning, but about nine-tenths of it was salt. Here's Fayal, boys." He waved the pannikin to the men about him, lifted it to his lips and took a mouthful. Cruiser was looking at him at the moment. He noticed that Fairford's face changed suddenly. Fairford held the pannikin carefully, made for the boat's side and spat his mouthful into the sea.

"What's the matter, Mister?"

"Your pannikin must have had salt water in it."

"No: it was dry when I took it."

"It may have been dry, sir, but it was all salt. The water in this pannikin is salt from it."

"It may be brackish, Mister."

"It's too salt to drink, Mr. Trewsbury. Taste it."

A sudden terror came over Trewsbury. He took the pannikin, and sipped. Mr. Fairford was right: the water in the pannikin was salt.

"But I drew it from the breaker an instant ago," he said. Swiftly leaning, he dipped two fingers into the bung-hole of the breaker, and put them to his lips. Beyond all doubt the water in the breaker was salt water.

"What on earth is this?" he asked.

"Is the water in the breaker salt, sir?" Mr. Fairford asked.

"Salt as the sea," he said. "Taste it."

"No doubt of it," Fairford said, after tasting. "You try it, Kemble." Old Kemble came aft to them, tasted and shook his head. "That's sea-water, sir. The breaker's full of sea-water."

"My God," the men said. The Cook added, "That's a fair wash-out, that is."

"I tink," Bauer said, "I tink der sprays soak into der preaker and make der water salt."

"You tink hell," Edgeworth said. "Go and tink of beer and tell me when you've got some."

"Come aft, all hands," Cruiser said. "Our water supply is salt. We've got nothing on board that isn't more or less brackish from sprays. This in the breaker is pure sea."

He paused a moment: then began again: "You, Tarlton, and you, Rodmarton, you cleaned this breaker yesterday with ashes, in the forenoon; you brought it to me at the fresh-water pump, just before I went to take the sun."

"Yes, sir," Tarlton said.

"What then?" Cruiser asked.

"You pumped fresh-water into it while we rinsed it clean, sir," Rodmarton said. "When it was all rinsed clean you pumped it full, and screwed in the bung, and rolled it this way and that to see if it leaked anywhere. Then you opened it and tasted the water."

"That's right," Clutterbucke said. "I saw you, sir, and you said, 'Tight as a drum and sweet as a nut.' And it was true, sir, for I took a drink from it when you went on to the poop to take the sun."

"Well," Cruiser said. "That was only twenty-four hours ago, and now the water is sea-water. You can't take a drink from it now. How in the wide earth has it changed?"

"Der sprays soak in," Bauer said.

"If the fresh-water couldn't soak out the salt couldn't soak in," Coates said.

"What did you do with the breaker?" the Cook asked Tarlton. "When you'd filled it and that?"

"Stood it down among the booms," Tarlton said, "with all the other boat gear, while Mr. Abbott's watch did the painting."

"Down among the starboard booms?"

"Yes, of course: it was the starboard boat, wasn't it?"

"My holy sailor," the Cook said.

"I don't know what you're holy sailoring about."

"It was young Mr. Abbott worked that quiff on you, sir," the Cook said.

"How?" Cruiser asked. "And when and why?"

"In the first watch, he done it," the Cook said. "You were on the poop, sir, keeping watch. He'd just come below all mucky with paint and hot from sweating the braces. He said to me, 'Doctor, can you give me some hot water?' just like that, see. 'No,' I said, 'I can't, sir: my fire's out and kettle's empty.' I could see he was in a tear about something."

"Our lamented Captain had expressed displeasure with his trim of the yards," Stratton said.

"Take care we don't express displeasure with you," Cruiser said. "Go on, Perrot."

"Well, Mr. Abbott said, sir: 'If I can't have a hot wash, I'll have a cold; if this parish mud-flat sinks for it. I'm not going to split my spleen in her,' he said, 'sweating the yards all ways for that poop ornament in the deck-chair, and not have a wash when I come below.' And then he went straight to the booms, took the breaker, and poured it all into that canvas bath he had; and had a bath. Then, when he'd dried himself, he filled up the breaker with salt water from the wash-deck-tubs."

"That was the splashing that I heard then," Cruiser said, "just before it came on thick. I heard him splashing and wondered what it was, but couldn't see."

"I marvel he bothered to fill the breaker," Fairford said.

"If he'd only left it empty we could have filled it," Cruiser said.

"We all saw him having his bath, sir," old Kemble said. "We didn't know what water he was using, nor what it was going to mean to us."

Cruiser turned to two of his watch. "Start this salt water overboard," he said. "Get it overboard by the dippers."

When it was empty he said, "Get it rinsed as soon as you can with rain. We'll hope to get the salt out of it, and then fill it with rain. Now let us see what water we have."

He had put into the boat five buckets of fresh-water from the poop, containing in all perhaps six gallons. In the excitement of men getting into the boat, and pitching gear into her, one of these buckets had been knocked over and emptied. Later in the morning, a second had received a full splash of spray before a cover had been devised for it: the contents were now brackish. They had of this brackish water about one gallon and a quarter. Of the water practically free from spray, whether that originally in the buckets or saved during the morning from the rain squalls, they had about six and a quarter gallons. Cruiser reckoned that it would be two pannikins full in each week for each man.

"That is all the water we've got to live on till we reach Fayal," Cruiser said. "The only water we can count on. We've had a good rain to-day and may have more. And as you've all been at free pump with the rain to-day I can't serve you any water from store. You'll have no whack of water till to-morrow morning.

"It's my fault in a way that you have no water. I ought to have made sure that the water in the breaker was pure. But as I had seen it filled only yesterday at noon, I took it for granted that it was. I couldn't have supposed that Mr. Abbott would have played that prank.

"I ought to have seen that Stratton, Jacobson and Efans filled the scuttle-butt as I ordered. I left it to them and they left it to the marines. I went to get instruments: they went to steal rum. If I'd stood over them, we should have had water, but neither chronometer nor sextant. Through Mr. Abbott's prank and their disobedience we shall go pretty short."

"Yes, Stratton," old Kemble said. "We'll take it out of you three with a stretcher, you and Efans and Jacobson. You've not been in an open boat before; you don't know what thirst is yet: none of you knows: but you will know before you've done with this hooker: and when you know be sure that we'll lay it in to the three responsible."

He was a big, lean, fierce old man, with cold, blue, pitiless, hawklike eyes, a face drawn tight over the bone, a hooked nose, and great whitish gray fluffy moustaches, standing out from his face like yard-arms. There was no finer seaman afloat.

"You mark my words now," he said, knowing that all were marking them. "This Mr. Trewsbury has tried to look after you better than most would have done. He's had sense. He's thought for you. But you can't think for fools and against Fate, that's sure. Now I've been in an open boat; off Cape Horn. It was Christmas time, which is summer there. I was towed out of sight of my ship by a whale we were fast to. I was harpooner then. There was seven of us. We'd nothing with us; just the lines and lances and what we stood in.

"We were four days before we got ashore some-where on the East of Cape Horn and eleven days living there on shell-fish and sea-weeds and trash. But the thirst before we got ashore was the thing that killed us. We chewed buttons, and the eyelets from a sail we had. But we used to look at each other and think, 'My, God, that fellow is full of blood and I could drink it.' The third day, the day before we got ashore, a young fellow said he'd as soon die one way as another: he drank the sea; and he did die: it made him mad first. It was hot, still weather the first three days, and the alba-trosses knew that we weren't going to live: they came all round us and they came at us. I hit three of them, but I couldn't kill. There was always one behind me when I hit at one in front. I was in a boat once before for part of a day in the Gulf of Mexico, and the sharks came round us, rubbing along the boat and heaving her up, but they were nothing to those birds. And after we got ashore, two others of us seven died. They were raging mad and drank a lot of a pool we found.

"We had a boat-steerer, Jack Handsome we called him, I never knew his real name. He said animals never drank when they were mad with thirst, but got into the water and let it soak in for a while before they drank. He persuaded us to do that, but not those two: they drank quarts and quarts, and their stomachs were all dried out and couldn't deal with it, so they died.

"I'll get through this and so will you: but only if you help the men who are thinking for you like Mr. Trewsbury and Mr. Fairford.

"There's a big crowd in this little boat. Stratton, Efans and Jacobson will be the first we'll ask to make room."

"Mein Gott, yes," Bauer said.

"Hell you will," Stratton said. "You were both glad of the brandy we thought of for you."

"Yes," Kemble said, "and we'll be glad to give you three the basting we've thought of for you; and we'll give it what's more."

"How were you taken off Cape Horn, Kemble?" Cruiser asked.

"A Government survey-ship party found us, sir, and took us to Sandy Point, the four of us: and there I went bull-whacking and fighting the Indians for a time, but I soon got tired of shore-life, it's all so shut-in.

"I was out after Indians once, sir: they'd been driving away cattle and taking women, and another man and I got lost. Jim, the other man's name was; he'd got no memory; but he knew of a plant that grew there, a little thing like dandelion, with a tough root. It was sour to taste, but it took away thirst if you chewed it. I wish we'd a few piculs of it here."

"I wish we had," Cruiser said. "Go below the watch."

They went below, to such momentary eases as they could find, stretching in the wet under the thwarts, or sitting crouched now on one side now on the other, jabbed at by spirts from beneath, and dowsed by sprays from over the gunwale. Stratton was baling: Coates tending sheet; Rodmarton steering: Cruiser sent Chedglow forward to look out. They had rigged a small canvas dodger forward, which made a screen for the look-out man. There was nothing for the look-out man to see but wild water under a flying heaven; still it was the easiest job that he could put Chedglow to do. The rest of the watch stood by to catch rain to add to their six and a quarter gallons.

Cruiser could see that all were scared at the scantiness of their supply and at what old Kemble had said. He thought that he would speak a few words of cheer to them; then he decided that he would leave the words of cheer till later. "If they get really scared," he thought, "they'll take what I have to say to them." He did not like the thought of the next week, with those few gallons of water. He looked from man to man of the crew, and his heart leaped at their fineness: Fairford, that quiet, steady, stalwart seaman, always so neat in his dress and in his work, who always grew quieter, steadier and more stalwart as things became worse: old

Kemble, a tower of strength, whose experience had
made him a believer in authority under all conditions: Edgeworth, a hardy old tough, very de-
pendable at present, but perhaps one who might
fight for his own hand later: Rodmarton, the very
handsome young seaman steering, whose devotion
he had somehow won: Clutterbucke, the strange-
looking fair-haired man, the visionary who saw
things (and was thought a little mad by the
fo'c's'le), whose sense of duty was passionate and
religious; a man to be depended on to the death:
Nailsworth, the grave, thoughtful man, with the
steady eyes, about whom there was some mystery,
and some certain mark that he had once been something very different from an able seaman. Ah,
what had Nailsworth been, and why had he come
to change? Some great sorrow had gone over him
with its wave, perhaps, and had taken out his life,
leaving only a desire for hard work and constant
change. He was a grave, silent fellow, who never
spoke of his past, always did his work well and
always could be trusted. Sometimes Cruiser had
surprised him into little gleams of interest, from
which he had come to wonder whether Nailsworth
had ever been a doctor. He remembered how
Nailsworth had worked over the bodies of Mr.
Frampton and the Cook. He knew that he could
depend on Nailsworth utterly.

The Cook was likely to be a trustworthy man at

anything except cooking. He was a shrewd, humorous, little man of the streets, who had come to
sea "for the sake of the slush", so the fo'c's'le said.
That at any rate was a reason, and he himself
could give no other.

Tarlton was a tall, very handsome man, with a
wild, humorous eye and dare-devil manner. In
port, or anywhere ashore, he was probably up to
any mischief at any time. It was said that he had
once locked the clergyman of St. Nicholas Church
in the belfry and had then taken the service himself; and he had certainly waited for and thrashed
Bully Captain Banca for killing his chum in the
Seagull. "Bully B." had never gone to sea again:
Tarlton had marked him for life.

At sea Tarlton was a very handy active seaman,
ready and strong, and with astonishing agility. In
the boat he suffered more than most of them; being six feet four with nowhere to put it.

Coates was a short, tough, thick boy, some seven
years older than his age (17); foul-mouthed often
without knowing it; and ever ready to speak his
mind. Chedglow was a charming-looking lad who
seemed to have no business there save to call up
the protective sense in those who had it and the
destructive sense in those who hadn't. All these
three were loyal to the core.

Efans, Bauer, Jacobson and Stratton were not
a pleasant four; he was glad to feel that they were

divided. The last man, MacNab, was a young Scot, who had worked his way to the gold-fields in Australia and after failing to prosper there was working his way back to be a school-master in Glasgow. He was a wooden-faced young man, with a limited tenacious brain and a habit of arguing which had driven the fo'c's'le frantic. So far he had not argued in the boat, having been bruised rather badly by falling gear a minute after the collision. No one knew of this however, he kept it to himself: and men thought him cowed, whereas he was resolutely enduring.

At the moment, as Cruiser saw, he was whiter in the face than the rest of the watch below and also more uneasy in his attempts to rest.

The three men, Bauer, the Cook, and Clutterbucke, were together on the midship thwart at the job of rain-catching. A technique of rain-catching had been perfected during the forenoon. Three men sat on the midship thwart, facing aft watching the heaven: they were allowed to smoke as they watched. When a rain-squall came blinding down they stood up and stood by. One of the three prepared to take off the canvas cover of a water-bucket, and the other two raised the water-catcher, or triangular canvas sheet which sloped from the mast into the bucket below. Those who held the catcher watched for any violently flying sprays, and at a warning from them the bucket-watcher dabbed the canvas cover over the bucket. The worst of the sprays were kept out, but the air was full of spray. The wind was now a full gale above a big sea, and the fine flying drift only ceased to be salt on the lips in the heart of the wilder squalls. Cruiser watching their skill knew that the sea was rising, and that in spite of the covers some of his precious water would be splashed from his buckets by the leaping of the boat.

The boat was running under the tiny rag of her double reefed sail, which she was finding as much as she could manage. Cruiser had served a part of his time with a driver, who had once said to him, during a middle watch, "Never shorten sail if you want to make a passage. Canvas is weaker than masts and stays: it'll blow away before they will." He thought of this now, and of how that old driver had stood smiling at the break of the poop, with his ship half under the sea, holding on to his topgallants, while his scared crew were standing by the halliards, praying.

He thought: "I suppose I ought to heave-to. If it gets any worse I must heave-to. The question is, have I left it too long? Heaving-to in a boat like this, in a sea like this, is going to be no lamb's wool."

The thought of the six and a quarter gallons decided him. The boat was on her course, and making a couple of knots an hour. His duty was to keep her going if he could so as to lessen that waterless distance. He knew instinctively that all in the boat were for driving on. The tradition had spread through the China fleet that wind must never be thrown away. He looked at his sail and the well stayed boat-mast, and the straining sheet so often dipping and dripping: the gear was holding. Then he watched how the boat seemed to show a life of her own, with a will and a way of her own, as she slipped away from the collapsing comber top, sidled down the seething gully, lifted above the smother, and went on, while the human heart stood still. Watching her for a little while he was convinced that she had a life and that he could trust to the luck of it. "She'll do it if I trust her," he said to himself.

He looked suddenly to his right and found that Mr. Fairford was sitting up from his rest watching him. He knew at once that Mr. Fairford was in doubt about this running on, lest the boat should be run under.

"Can't you sleep?" he asked.

"O, I've had a bit of a rest, sir," Fairford answered. "But it seems to have come on worse since I turned in."

"There's worse coming," Cruiser said. Fairford seemed to understand from his tone that he was not to worry and that the boat at present was not to heave-to.

"All right, sir," he answered. "If you want us, you'll know where to find us." He settled himself down again as an old sailor will, but Cruiser noticed that he did not sleep. However, Kemble and Edgeworth both slept: and this fact was comforting up to a point. Yet, as he knew, those two desperate old hard cases had decided that the sea offered only two things, one at a time, sleep and duty, that each would be taken hard when its turn came, and that when the voyage ended there would be some drunkenness and then the sea again. Those two would give no symptom and show no worry till emergency forced it.

"How are you getting on with the water, Perrot?" he asked.

"It's not much good, sir," Perrot said, "trying to rinse this breaker. There's as much spray as rain in most of these squalls. It's like the River Jordan what flows into the Dead Sea, Shakespeare."

"Heave round at it," Cruiser said. "You'll get some pure rain at the end of each squall."

"Ay, ay, sir." He bent to his task and added to Bauer under his breath that "it would be like the Irishman's pie; mainly pie."

Cruiser looked forward to the bows. Chedglow was looking very sick and faint there.

"I'll get that child below," Cruiser thought. He gingerly edged his way forward to him and found the boy shaking with cold.

"Well, Chedglow," he said. "This is great fun, isn't it? A boat-cruise in the North Atlantic. Have you seen any ships?"

"No, sir, not yet, sir."

"Well, you go below and turn in aft there, I'll stand look-out for a while."

"I'm all right, sir, really I am."

"Yes, I know," Cruiser said, "but I want to come here as a matter of fact, and there isn't room for the two of us."

"Couldn't I help bale, sir?"

"No. I want you to turn in, Chedglow. You're the youngest here and I must look after you."

"I can stick it, sir."

"Why, I know you can, and I see you doing it, but lay aft and try to sleep. You'll be twice the man after a bit of a rest."

"Well; thank you very much, sir."

"If you find a soft plank don't mention it to anyone but me. I'll save it for my own bunk."

"Very good, sir."

"And don't put your feet through the garboard straiks."

"No, sir. Thank you, sir."

When the boy had gone Cruiser roused out the boat's painter, which was of good hemp one-inch rope, so nearly new that the stretch was not out of it. Like most ships' boats' painters, it was a full twenty fathoms long, and spliced into a shackle in the stem. Cruiser drew the splice and secured the end by a round turn and two half hitches to the forward thwart. He then roused out the drogue or sea-anchor which was a Wensley's patent, like a big shut umbrella with ribs of oak batten and a cover of No. 1 canvas. He cut the stops of this. He had examined the drogue the day before and knew that it was in working order. He bent its cable to the painter's-end, and could not fail to notice that ten of his crew were watching what he was doing.

"Heave round there," he said. "Get to it."

Creeping aft again, as it was now four bells, he caused the helm and look-out to be relieved; Bauer took the tiller, Rodmarton relieved Stratton at baling, Coates went forward from the sheet to the look-out, and Stratton took Bauer's place at water-catching.

As he had some misgivings about Bauer he remained by him at the helm for half an hour "while he got the hang of her". He disliked Bauer, as one who was rather loud in the voice for such gifts as he had to offer to the world. He did his work well enough, but had given Cruiser the feeling that in the real emergency, if there were one, Bauer's help would not be there. Bauer was now not mutinous but nervy. He kept glancing back at the following seas which were grim enough.

"What are you looking back for, Bauer?" he asked. "There are no German police there."

Bauer licked his lips and smiled an evil smile.

"Dose seas," he said. "Dose seas, sir; I tink dey pretty bad."

"If they get us," Cruiser said, "they'll sink us. But if you watch your tip and don't play the silly ass they'll not get us. Do you want to be sunk?"

"No, sir."

"Don't look back then."

He kept Bauer intent upon his course: for a while all went well. The gale was steadily darkening and worsening: the gusts of violence coming more closely together and from the same southern point, that told him that the worst was not yet.

"Knock off that water-catching," he said. "Strike all the fresh-water buckets into the port afterlocker here."

When this was done he put the three water-catchers to the job of seam-caulking with oakum, rope yarn, and strips of canvas. He took a hand with them at this. He did not mention it to anybody, but decided that the boat was straining more than she should be in her upper straiks. Below the water she was now reasonably tight: up above she seemed to be worse. He discovered presently that the teak rubbing-piece which made her outboard upper straik had warped away from the gunwale.

He could see daylight here and there for six inches together in several places. Now and then a spirt of water shot through these. He mended up the worst of them, others formed elsewhere. He thought that this was a signal which had better not be neglected.

"Mr. Fairford," he said, "I'm going to heave her to when we get a good smooth. Will you go forward?"

"Certainly, Captain Trewsbury. Shall I call all hands?"

"If you please."

All hands, except Edgeworth and Kemble, had been long awake expecting a call. Cruiser knew from their faces that they thought he had run her too long, and that now their only chance was to continue to run. He had taken a risk for their sakes and had knocked a few miles off that grim seven hundred still against them. Now perhaps it would be proved that he ought not to have taken the risk. "It'll be sad if I'm only to keep my first command for eleven hours," he thought. Then he looked at those fifteen men, his crew and yet his fellows, with the thought that they were one united will to live, and that not all the fury of Heaven and smashing of the sea could prevail against that will. The boat, too, his little command, with the loose straik and the stink and smear of paint, straining mast and spouting chinks, she, too, was alive, and would find her way alive.

"I'm going to heave-to," he called, when the hands had mustered. "Though I hate to lose the wind. Kemble, you come aft to the helm with me. Edgeworth, go forward with Mr. Fairford, and stand by the drogue. Nailsworth and Tarlton make an oil-bag with one of our colza-oil tins, but don't prick the tin at the bottom: prick it a third of the way from the top; we've very little oil."

"Very good, sir. We understand."

The necessary work did not take as long as it seemed to take. All hands knew the difficulty of heaving-to in that wind and sea. It would be wrong to say that they were scared, perhaps three of them, Bauer, Efans and Chedglow, were scared, yet able to disguise it. The others were eager for it to be over, and critical of Cruiser, either for not having done it at eight bells or during the fore-noon, or for trying to do it now when it was too late. There were nine critics: all the middle part of the crew. The two officers and two old leading seamen had the job on their hands which was enough for them to think about.

"I beg your pardon, Captain Trewsbury," old Fairford said. "But did you think of putting an oil-bag on your drogue?"

"No. Is that a good dodge?"

"I was shipmates one voyage, sir, with a man

who'd been a lot in the Tyne and Baltic trade. They would lie out the storms in the winter, he said, with a sea-anchor on a good span, and an oil-bag on the anchor. He said it was good."

"Try it," Cruiser said.

"Very good, Captain Trewsbury."

A minute or two passed wearily by.

"Oil-bag all ready, sir," Nailsworth reported. "Shall I prick it and put it over?"

"Yes. Put it over aft here."

"Prick her and put her over aft, sir; ay, ay, sir."

A couple of minutes passed, during which the sting seemed to be drawn from the water.

"For a sick child or a sick sea, you can't beat castor oil," the Cook said.

"If you'd give the sea some of your cooking," Stratton said, "that would make it want to lie down."

"If you and Balaam's Ass was in Parliament to-gether," the Cook said, "you and he would just make a pair."

"Stand by there, Tarlton and Clutterbucke, to smother the sail when I give the word. Stand by the halliards, Rodmarton. Let go cleanly when I call."

"Ay, ay, sir."

Cruiser watched for a smooth, which seemed a long time in coming. Waves came in sets of big ones together; after about a dozen big ones there seemed a promise of smaller ones. "Let go your sea-anchor forward," he said, and on the instant eased down the helm and let her go on her perilous path.

She ran down a gliddery valley towards a pit and sidled away along the slippery side, and lipped a salt side full, which put them over the shoes in sea. A power unseen hove them up suddenly: and old Kemble at the helm said: "My God, look at that, sir," and jerked with one hand at the water alongside. Cruiser glanced, tense as he was, and saw there alongside a shark, seemingly as long as the boat, floating below the surface. It looked as though it had risen expecting a meal. In another instant the boat was round steadying to her drogue, and half a dozen hands in the waist were smothering and making fast the sail.

"Get to it and bale," Cruiser said. At the splashing of the baled water the bulk of the shark dimmed a little and then dimmed away entirely with no perceptible motion.

"I'd like to get that fellow on the snout with a whaler's spade," old Kemble said. "They talk about wolves, but they're nothing to sharks."

"If we see him again," Edgeworth said, "it'll be a sign that somebody in this boat is going to die. I've known a shark follow a ship eighteen days for a man. The man was well when he first came, but the shark knew. He was about that ship all the time, always the same shark, for he'd got a dark patch on him where he'd been rubbed or bitten. We all said that he'd come for someone: so he had. He'd come for a man who took sick suddenly with thirst and was all the time drinking: I never saw a fellow drink like that. Then he died.

"Before we buried him we tried to catch the shark, but he kept away. When we buried him we put some stone-ballast in with him to carry him down quick. We couldn't see the shark anywhere at the time, but the instant he was in the water he came up and took him: the same shark. And it was plain that he'd come for that man, for we never saw him again after that. We'd an Indian working in the galley who said the shark was his evil deeds come for him; but I don't see how that could be."

"You don't often find sharks alone," Cruiser said. "There'll be others about, so keep your hands inside the gunwale or you may get them snapped."

The boat rode to the drogue easily when they had baled her out, the watch was relieved; the port watch coming on deck made all things snug for the night. Cruiser insisted on rigging a spare sea-anchor in the shape of a log ship. Three lashed rickers made a frame, and canvas was nailed across them. He bent on to it a spare line which he flaked down in the bows, all clear for letting go.

"That patent contraption may be all very well,"

he said, "but it's been a long while in store and may not hold."

When this was done he unshipped the tiller and rudder and shipped in their stead, in case of emergency, a thole-pin steering oar which was part of the boat's equipment.

When this was done the night was beginning to close in. There was no sign of any bettering in the weather; it promised to be a night of storm. Cruiser tried to think only of the good things in their condition: that they were alive, in a sea-worthy boat, with some food and drink, that they had made some thirty miles of easting, and had lain-to without mishap. Yet he did not feel happy. Where would they be if they had to lie-to often? And what was going to happen about water? And how was he to bring cheer to all these men when he had no cheer within himself? He was not cheerful: he was as wet and cold and cramped as any of them, and had worked harder and had had more disappointments.

He thought, "This is so beastly a night that I must give them something to cheer them: not brandy, they had a nip of brandy, and once a day is all we can afford of that. We might perhaps each have three raisins."

Three raisins with the pips in them can be made to last a long time. He contrived that all hands should compete to see who should make a raisin

last the longest: they got through an entire hour
thus: and were still sucking or chewing raisins
when Fairford suggested that as it was the second
dog-watch they should have a sing-song.

As it happened he had a good tenor voice and
many songs which the crew had not yet heard. He
sang very touchingly the ballad of "The Fair
Pretty Maid"; and then at the general request his
own favourite of "We Met, 'Twas in a Crowd," in
which all hands could join in the refrain of:

> *"And thou wast the cause of*
> *This anguish,*
> *My mother."*

The tune had been for many years popular, the
sailors had long known and loved it: what did the
words and the meaning matter? The song made
all of them forget their troubles in a delight which
all shared. They were warming up to the singing
of it a second time in unison when one of the two
men forward, keeping the anchor watch, gave a
loud cry. Cruiser leaped up, thinking that the
drogue's painter had parted. He had only time to
sing out, "What is it?" when he saw for himself
what it was, and all hands saw and said, "My
God."

Ahead, to windward, they had been accustomed
to seeing the slow hills of the sea lumping up,

collapsing at the top, advancing and roaring and seething by. A big sea was running, to themselves so near to the surface it seemed much bigger than it would have seemed from a ship's deck.

Now out of the darkness of the storm ahead, such a sea was lifting as they had never seen. The first sight of it was to them as though a low range of hills was moving bodily forward; then the effect changed in their minds to that of a line of crags. It was dark, toothy at the top with fangs, like the body of night below, and moving with a life of its own from somewhere. All there had at once the dreadful feeling that it was alive. How high it was they could not guess, but higher certainly than any wave that any of them had ever seen. It was not like a wave: it was like the Judgment Day advancing, wolfing up all the sea into its power and licking out the sky with its tongue. Cruiser could only gasp to himself, "My God, that's got us." But he had two thoughts: one for his crew, one for his boat. He cried, "Hold on, all," and contrived to get to the steering-oar, and hove on it, to keep her bows on to it. It seemed to them that it crackled as it advanced as though it were breaking the air to shreds. It sent out fore-boilings and up-bubblings that broke and wrinkled about them; all the sea seemed to know beforehand of it and to laugh and to writhe. No one of them doubted that it was the end. Perhaps it was the end of the world as well.

"Heave out that spare drogue," Cruiser called.

Dreadful as it was they could not keep their eyes off it. Marching swiftly as it was it seemed that it would never come. Cruiser felt oddnesses, unevennesses and hardnesses rubbing under the boat's keel and plucking at it: all the sea's surface went stiff suddenly with eddies: his oar-blade seemed to plunge in steel springs. A power slued the boat to one side: he let it take her: when it passed, he hove on his oar and forced her back. She moved her snout towards it. He bent with all his strength to hold her there. She bowed down: then instantly, the mountain was on them: they were going up, up, up, the darkness which was a living thing growling and snarling at them and moving with a force and speed so awful that Cruiser caught a joy from the instant. He shouted to the boat, "Good old girl: you'll do it yet."

The boat went up, up, up into a hush: then rose so that Cruiser could just gasp to himself, "She'll toss us end for end." He saw the two forward hands crouched in the bows high up above himself, as it were on the top rungs of a ladder about to fall backwards. Then the air and the boat were both forgotten, being changed suddenly and utterly into a rush and blinding power of water, trembling below, furious above, and a weight on the bodies, pressing down.

This passed. Cruiser knew that he was not dead, but that the boat very nearly was. She was full of water and trembling on the brink of collapse.

"Get to it. Bale her," he cried. "Take anything you can and bale her."

They had three buckets, three dippers and a fetch-bag with which to bale. The men had these out and at work at once. No one in her thought that they could save her: she was full to the gunwale, they were over their waists in water, and the boat moved under them as though about to go bodily down. All the teak rubbing piece of the gunwale was torn loose, and her three topmast straiks were spouting like freeing ports: this and her buoyancy chambers had saved her.

"A few more like that," Cruiser said, "and we shan't have a dry rag left on board."

"No, sir."

No one was badly hurt, yet all had something to show for it, a bruise, or cut or scrape. However, there was the boat to bale; that kept them working hard for more than an hour, by then it was eight bells and pitch dark: all were very weary and depressed. They had no light save the baleful glimmering of the sea-bursts: all the rest of their world seemed now to be swallowed up in the storm; the loose straiks were working and grinding; the drogue-cables kept surging and yanking; there was a weeping leak coming in at the stem, and no sign of mend in the weather.

"Mr. Fairford," Cruiser said, "we must frap this boat and stop this working."

"We shall be like St. Paul, sir."

"Yes," Cruiser said. "And I wish we were coming to his island at dawn to-morrow."

He got out what rope they had to spare, and by the help of his best men passed four good frappings right round the boat, and were thankful indeed to find that this checked the working of the plank. Somewhere about half-past nine, Cruiser felt that the boat was as safe as he could make her. Though the baler had to bale rather more than in the day-time he found that he could keep her free.

"Go below the watch," Cruiser said.

At this point Stratton spoke: "We've had a pretty tough time here, sir, to-night," he said. "What would be the matter with a spot of brandy?"

"I'm in charge of the brandy," Cruiser said, "I'll serve it when I see occasion."

"It's very hard, sir, on a lot of poor men, that you don't see occasion now."

"I'm not going to argue the point, Stratton," Cruiser said. "Either you'll go below now, without another word, or you'll spend the rest of this watch on anchor-watch."

Stratton thought it wiser not to speak another word: he got down into a nook muttering something about the rest of the crowd being a lot of curs who wouldn't stick up for their rights, would they, hell, but left it all to him.

Cruiser had a few words with Mr. Fairford before he turned in.

"She's easier now," he said, "I believe she'll do, if we don't get another like that. Did you ever see a sea like that before?"

"No, never, sir, and I hope I never will again. But the sea is full of surprises: some volcano under the sea started that one."

"Before I turn in," Cruiser said, "I'll have a look at the lockers. They're supposed to be water-tight, but with such a sea as that right over us, one can't quite tell."

"No, sir."

It was very easy to tell at once by opening the lockers. The port after-locker in which their scanty fresh water had been stored was full of salt water. The starboard after-locker was nearly as full: their drinking water was gone and their provisions were ruined. Cruiser baled out both lockers with his own hands, thinking that the day had dealt him some ugly strokes and trying to think what they would do on the morrow. He knew that old Fairford beside him was overcome.

"I think the worst of this is gone," he said. "We are sure to get some heavy squalls from the west as it clears away. You must look out for them and catch some rain."

"I will, Captain Trewsbury. You may be sure. Is the bread all pulp, sir?"

"Salt paste, most of it."

"It seems to me, sir," old Fairford said, very solemnly, "that we're very much in the hands of Almighty God."

"We can't do better," Cruiser said.

"I suppose some bits of it could be soaked out and ate, sir?"

"We'll try that in the morning as soon as it's light. Why, look, it's clearing to westward."

The wildness in the heaven was both dark and near like a thing pressing down upon them. Now ahead of them suddenly a loophole of more distant heaven blew clear, so that those watchers could see promise of light, and then light itself, some western star very bright indeed among that darkness.

"It will clear now," Cruiser said. "But it will still blow hard from the west before it's done with."

"Shall I get sail on her, sir?"

"Not with the sea as it is," Cruiser said. "No, we've got a crazy boat and mustn't strain her. We must just lie-by and wait for it to moderate. Keep a sharp look-out for any more seas like that big fellow."

"You bet I will, Captain Trewsbury."

"Right. I'll turn in then. Remember, the flares aren't wet."

"Right, sir."

Cruiser was weary and out of heart as he tried to compose himself to sleep. He heard the general growl and curse of his crew as they shifted in their pain and misery. He heard Perrot saying to somebody:

"Nothing to eat and drink on board this hooker, just a nice fried nothing for breakfast with a bit of crisp air. Lor! that's a bit of all right: and a cut off the nought, with some nothing stuffing, that's the menu for lunch: and, Jane, we'll have the same cold for tea, please. That's the orders for our butler."

"Chuck it, Doc," somebody growled: perhaps it was Rodmarton, "it's a damned sight more fattening than the muck you've been serving."

After this the crowd was silent, except for an occasional oath as someone shifted in his pain, or as someone relieved the baler at the well. There was always the noise of the dipper scooping into the well, scraping up water and splashing it into the sea. The hiss of water was always in their ears. The boat was noisy in her tread on the sea. Her two cables worked in their leads. Every now and then Mr. Fairford would go forward to make sure that they were not chafing or to help the anchor-watch to freshen the nip. Whenever this happened he had to clamber under or over the frappings and always trod on somebody. The night was loud with the exasperation of the sea; under her shrill cry was the growl of the comment as men cursed the boat, the wet, the pain, the night, the storm or Mr. Fairford.

Midnight brought Cruiser on deck again to a sea if anything worse than it had been, being now more confused, as the wind had shifted to true west, blowing a full gale.

"It's blowing itself out, sir," Mr. Fairford said. "There's a star or two almost all the time."

"Poor chaps who've been sodden in a stinking barge all night would give all the stars for a drop of brandy," Stratton said.

"If you'd think a little of how your life's been spared," Mr. Fairford said, "you'd not talk of brandy."

"And a very true word, sir," Clutterbucke put in. "Good tackle."

"I don't know that my life has been spared," Stratton growled.

"O, yes, it has," old Kemble said. "There's a

patch of a field in Russia some place, or out Dan-
zig way; maybe it hasn't been cleared or ploughed
or planted yet; but it will be, for hemp: and when
that hemp's been hackled and spun, and put on
the winch, and rubbed down and been gone back-
ward with, you'll learn what it's been spared for.
Hemp and the sea are two things what take each
other's leavings. I've known three men like you,
what died of hempflammation in the throat.
You've got just their look, and you'll make a
fourth, mark me."

The middle watch dragged itself on without
much change for an hour, when in a very heavy
squall they contrived to rinse some buckets and
catch about four gallons of water. As this squall
drew to an end it unrolled a starry heaven, the
horror of darkness passed off into the east, and the
constellations shone again. Cruiser tried to "take
a star," but could not get an horizon. While he was
wedging himself up for this observation, he felt a
sudden knock of the sea on her starboard side. It
was only one knock among the many that runs of
water dealt her, but after this one old Edgeworth
woke from his sleep, calling the boat some un-
necessary and ill-chosen names.

"What's the matter, Edgeworth?"

"Give us something big for a mat, sir," Edgeworth said. "This hija de puta of a straik's all
adrift like a shifting back-stay."

A running brook of water was coming into the boat where he had been sleeping. He made a sort of mat with a rag of blanket and tamped it in with a sailmaker's rubber. After this he chinsed up the edges with lesser rags. Water seeped in still, but the worst of it was stopped.

"This boat is one of those contractor's jobs," Edgeworth said. "They build boats for a firm and send in anything that'll stand on a skid. They think the boat won't ever be used: and if she is, no one will live to say anything. All the fastenings on this side are just rotten punk wood."

"If you'll make a boat," Cruiser said, "that will lie three years on skids and cross the Line twice a year, and then stand what this boat's stood, with sixteen men in her, not leaking any more than this one leaks, I'll eat her."

"Ah, sir," old Edgeworth said with a grin. "An old sailor like me has to curse the ship he's in. We don't mean nothing by it half the time." He composed himself to sleep in the same spot and was very soon asleep again.

As Cruiser could not take his star, he put away his sextant, and longed for the sea to go down so that he could get under way. There was no sense in complaining: that they were alive was the answer to all complaints. Keeping alive was going to be a problem. He had almost no food nor drink: the boat seemed as crazy as a packing-case and only held together by his lashings: he could not strain her much without knocking her to pieces. Coates was in the well with him sucking a pipe and swearing to himself as he went over his amorous memories, of which he had many.

"What is the joke, Coates?" he asked.

"I was thinking of a time at Pagoda, sir, before you joined us. Did you know a chop and chow joint, sir, Mother Bomby's, where the reefers went?"

"No."

"Well, sir, the reefers go there: we could usually get cakes and candied plums and things when we had any money. There were a couple of yellow China girls serving there. We got one of them to pretend that she was in love with Mr. Stratton. We wrote out a love-letter which we pretended came from her, and we got the girl to give it to Percy here to give to Mr. Stratton, which he did.

"Of course Mr. Stratton never suspected Percy of any prank and he believed that the letter was genuine. It said: 'Me poor China girl: me die for love of you. Me love you all the time. You come see me, Mother Bomby, me lovee you vellee dear. You watch till me put white thing in window, then you knock at door. Me let in.'

"You wouldn't believe it, sir, but old Mr. Stratton dressed himself up to kill in a boiled shirt and that yellow necktie that he had; and he came ashore day after day and walked about the back of Mother Bomby's joint, looking for the white in the window. We got the girl to look out at him sometimes and cast sheep's eyes at him and shake her head."

"I hope he found you out in time and belted the life half out of you."

"No, sir, he never suspected. He thought she loved him, but that Mother Bomby was watching her too closely. He asked us sometimes about the girl: we always said she was a good straight girl, but seemed to have something on her mind."

"Why didn't he go boldly in and see her?"

"No, sir, he couldn't have done that. No certificated officer would ever go to the reefers' joint. So there he was with his mahogany face and coir-broom-whiskers and general reek of rum, and a tall collar and yellow necktie parading up and down like Danny's billygoat. Chaps called him 'the rutting stag'. It was a joke at the time, but I'm sorry, now that old Strattie's had that block on his head."

"Rather a dirty trick to play on an old man, wasn't it?" Cruiser asked.

"I don't know, sir; he asked for it."

"Steamer's light on the starboard quarter, sir," the look-out hailed.

A gleam of hope shot up in Cruiser: he rose to

his feet and stood unsteadily in the tumbling boat to examine the light. It shone out and was blotted from him and blinked and was again gone as the boat or the seas leapt or dropped.

"A steamer's light, sir," Coates said. "Two miles away coming right down on us. Shall I call all hands, sir?"

"No," Cruiser said. "Hold on a minute."

"I'm sure it's a steamer's light, sir."

"If you're sure, you needn't say so," Cruiser said. He was determined that he would always hope, but never permit himself a false hope. Chedglow was at his elbow, also staring.

"Well, Chedglow, what do you think?" he asked. "Is that a steamer's masthead light?"

"I do hope it is, sir."

"Do you see any gleam of a sidelight?"

"I thought I did then, sir, both sidelights."

"It will have to be both if she's to be on a course to help us."

"Couldn't we burn a flare, sir?"

"Not till I see a sidelight. She'd never see it."

By this time the watch was up, staring at the light.

"She's a steamer," Perrot said. "It's a great life they lead on board steamers: there's hot pipes you can hang your wet socks on, and a whistle you can play by pulling a string."

"There goes her port light."

"Go on with your port light."

"I knew a man once," Perrot went on, "what sailed in steam. He said they'd a free pump all the time condensed by the engines. And the Captain 'ad cold 'am for tea."

"If that's the very ship," Rodmarton said, "it'll be a bit of just right."

"That's not a steamer's light, it's a rising star," Cruiser said after they had watched it for a few minutes. The men were slow to admit it; presently they saw that he was right. In the clear sky that followed the passing of the storm Cruiser noticed two or three others before his watch was out. Each one gave him a few moments of hope and of anxious watching, each presently rose clear into the sky.

At four o'clock the watch was relieved. The wind was now blowing a full steady gale out of the west, with a clear sky, and a promise of fair weather.

"I'll lie by till daylight," Cruiser said. "The sea may be a bit less confused then, and we can have a look at the hull before we get sail on her."

"Very good, sir," old Fairford said. "She's come through the night very well, sir, considering."

"Yes, considering."

There was nothing more to be done at the moment. Cruiser looked round the boat and saw the heads of the watch on deck all alert, and the boat's bows rising and falling with a grinding and chopping noise, and the sprays gleaming as they flew off on either side. The light of the false dawn was whitish aloft, "taking the shine out of the stars". He felt gladder than he could say for the blessing of light and the passing of the gale. All the men about him, however seasoned to the sea, were feeling cold. They had now been a day in the boat; and how much worse their lot was now than it had been twenty-four hours before.

"Still, we're alive," he thought. "And the port watch are dead, whatever that means." He wondered what it did mean.

He saw that Chedglow was fairly snug; and then wedged himself into a nook. Being exceedingly weary he fell into a deep sleep, like a death, from which he woke in an hour, so cramped and stiff that it took some minutes of pain to get movement into neck and limbs. He rose and stretched and took a look at the sea. The false dawn had died leaving the heaven dark and shot with stars. The sea was still high, though it seemed to be steadying to the wind.

"I'll wait another hour before making sail," he said.

"Very good, Captain Trewsbury."

Before curling down to sleep again he looked out over the starboard quarter at the beginning of the dawn, and at once shouted, "Sail-ho." As he shouted the look-out man sang out,

"Sail on starboard quarter, sir."

All hands were up on the cry full of the wildest hope.

"Trip the drogues and get them in," Cruiser said, unshipping the steering-oar and reshipping the rudder. "Get the sail on her."

They ran in the drogues to an overhand chorus:

A handy ship and a handy crew,
Handy, my boys, so handy;
A handy mate and a second mate, too,
Handy, my boys, away O.

They ran up the sail to a similar ditty of:

Away, haul away, boys, haul away together,
Away, haul away, boys, haul away O.

With the brightness in the sky exhilaration had come to those weary men: hope was now quick in them.

Old Fairford came aft when the drogues were stowed; the boat was standing towards the sail, which was now plainly in sight, little more than a mile from them.

"A fine full-rigged clipper, sir," old Fairford said.

"Burn a flare, Mister," Cruiser said. "Go on burning till she sees us."

The ship was coming down on a soldier's wind under a press of canvas. Her royal masts had been sent down, probably in the storm of the night before, but she carried full topgallants and her fore topmast studding sail. She was making probably twelve knots an hour in what seemed a succession of staggering pauses followed by lifting thrusts forward. She seemed to bow down till her bowsprit was deep in smother and her eyes submerged, then after a check amid the bubble she would rise and rise and clear what seemed like half her length all shaking with running water and surge herself forward still rising and rolling till the power of her fabric bowed down again.

"Quick, the flare, Mister," Cruiser said.

"The flares are wet, sir; that's the third. Ah, here's one."

There came a sputtering from the little torch, sparks flew from the end of it, then the red glow burned true, so that all the haggard faces became transfigured, and the broken boat was as a thing of ruby bringing spirits across the sea of death.

"Pass the flares forward. Burn them forward," Cruiser called.

In an instant a second flare was burning, making

such a glare on the sea that they could see fishes rising at it thirty yards away. A flight of flying fishes came into it as they fled, they streamed across it like scarlet darts. The ship was dimmer to them from the glare. She made no sign of having seen them. She held her thundering course.

"Shout. Hail her all together," Cruiser said. "She's to leeward; she may just hear."

They shouted together: "Ship ahoy. Ahoy there, you. Ship ahoy."

"There she comes. She sees us. She's coming to the wind," Rodmarton cried.

"She doesn't see us," Kemble said. "She yawed a bit perhaps."

"Another flare there, quick."

They burned yet another flare. This time a flight of fishes confused by it fell aboard the boat and flapped and fluttered in the well. The ship had now crossed their bows, without any sign of having seen them.

"It's a bad time to be seen by a ship," old Kemble said. "The look-out's been relieved: and the watch has knocked off for coffee. The mate's having coffee on the poop, and the only man who could see us is the man at the wheel, and you can see he's got his hands full."

"I wish to God we'd a rocket, sir," old Fairford said. "A rocket or two would catch the eye more. Men in a ship are always looking up, and men ashore generally looking down. Those fellows are looking aloft."

"They're not looking at us," Cruiser said. "They haven't seen us. But burn another flare, Mister."

"I'll bet dey seen us," Bauer said. "But dey want to make der passage and not split der sails."

"Because you're a dirty skunk," Edgeworth said, "it don't follow everyone else is."

However, Bauer had spoken to some willing listeners. As the ship dimmed away from them the disappointment broke out in growls against the unknown ship, that she had seen them and must have seen them, but had not chosen to stop for them. Cruiser thought it wiser to check them.

"A boat is never easy to see," he said. "Even in broad daylight a white boat is hard to pick up at sea. Before dawn with a big sea running the chances are anything against our being seen."

"Dey must have seen der flares, sir," Bauer said.

"Hell with your 'must,'" Kemble said. "I've told you, if you'd ears to hear, why she didn't see. You Dutch square heads can neither see nor know. I was shipmates once with a man who was on the raft from the *Carradale*. He said they had two wefts flying and twenty men hollaing and praying, yet a big ship went past them just before dawn, within two cables, and never saw nor heard. Hell with your 'must.' There's vapours at sea, in the air, that will hide anything; and jobs on board that will keep every eye in the ship; and there's the fortune of the sea, too; what we all signed for and have to take."

"Pick up the flying fish and bring them aft," Cruiser said. There were eleven flying fish.

"Delivered at the door just like the milk," Perrot said.

"Lash an oar to the mast there," Cruiser said, "and bend a weft to the blade. Someone aloft in her may see it."

They did this, and looked longingly after the flying clipper, now far to the south of them. There was a bare chance perhaps now that the sun was almost up that someone aloft in her might sight the boat; but would he report her? And if he did, would she fling away the wind and a sail or two to come to them? Cruiser felt that she would if the weft were reported, but thought that the chance of the boat's being reported was remote. He knew that the only men likely to be aloft in the ship were the lads, overhauling buntlines: and that if a lad saw them he would not guess what they were. He would probably come down and say that he thought he saw some floating wreck; and would then be told that he wasn't paid to think, but that if he saw any more he could have it for his breakfast.

The sun came out of the notched and tossing skyline. He brought brightness and warmth and cheer to those sorrowful seamen. When they had given up all hope of being seen from the clipper, Cruiser brought the boat to her course: and turned all hands to take stock and repair damage. The two officers and the four best seamen, Kemble, Edgeworth, Tarlton and Clutterbucke, set to work at once upon the planks. With some nails well placed and a few transverse battens and patches of wood, they repaired the worst of the damage. They were guided by old Edgeworth's advice not to try to do much.

"If you go hammering too much at one of these old rattletraps," he said, "you'll mar more than you'll mend." They saw enough of the boat's condition to make them trust his instinct. The boat looked in a sorry mess. All the new paint in her was smeared and soiled till it looked like a skin disease, and odd patches and pads stuck to her here and there at the worst of her leaks. The sea was running high and bright and blue under a bright blue windy heaven. It was a glorious morning full of cheer. The boat drove through this like an unclean insect.

"My God," Edgeworth said, "we're like a travelling workhouse ward."

"Get to it, then," Cruiser said. "Get out those

scrapers and scrubbers from the forward locker and turn to, the lot of you, to clean ship."

While they cleaned ship he examined the supplies. The bread was ruined. He roused it out in little packets and spread it to dry, but knew that even if dry it would be so salt as to be useless for food. Most of the raisins were in boxes not yet opened; the sea had soaked only those in the open box. These salted raisins he handed over to Coates and Chedglow to wash and re-stow. They washed each raisin in one pannikin of rain and rinsed it in another and whistled as they worked to show that they were not eating any. The beef was no salter than it had been, they still had the medical comforts and this little bounty of the flying fish. For water they had four gallons of fairly pure rain and no prospect of more at present. In all they had one quart of rain a man to last for how long? Possibly twenty days, Cruiser thought.

"Breakfast, all hands," he called. "Fresh fish for all."

With the fresh fish, which could not keep, he gave them a fragment of biscuit each from the midshipman's nuts which had not been spoiled; to this he added two raisins apiece from those that had been washed. Then he added a measure of brandy to a half pannikin of water and doled it out in a spoon, one spoonful at a time, till all had had at least a flavour and a fragrance in their beings.

"That's all you'll have till tea," he said. "It'll be hot to-day. We shall all be thirsty. I want you all to splash yourselves with sea-water, and wet your heads and necks and chests constantly; that'll help your thirst. And chew buttons and these thimbles and cringles. Whatever you do don't drink salt water."

"Any man what drinks salt water," Kemble said, "ought to get a dozen with a stretcher. And I'll see he does, too."

There were no growls from the crew at this: they were downhearted from the passing of the ship and scared at the spoiling of their stores. Cruiser sent the watch below and took some fairly good sights. The sea and wind were high, but falling, and the boat was now on her course and making at least two knots an hour on it, under her double reefed sail. He took a trick at the helm while Rodmarton tended sheet.

"It's not so bad, sir, now we've got the sun," Rodmarton said.

"We're having our share of luck," Cruiser said. "What did you think the ship was this morning?"

"One of those Australian clippers, sir. I'd never seen her before."

"She was a fine ship," Cruiser said.

"She wasn't as fine as the *Blackgauntlet*, sir. As I lay awake last night I couldn't help crying for the *Blackgauntlet* going down like that. I'd

been in her two voyages, sir; and never knew anything like her. And the Captain was so set on winning the prize; and we had such a chance of it too,
sir, till we lost the Trades. We must have been
leading when she sank."

"There or thereabouts," Cruiser said.

"And I'd a box of cigars on our winning too,
sir, with my brother Joe."

"What is your brother doing?" Cruiser asked.

"He's a second boatswain, sir, in the *Bird of
Dawning*, what they call the *Cock*. They have two
boatswains over each watch in the *Cock*."

"Your brother will get the cigars and his ship
runs a chance of the prize; a fine ship, the *Bird
of Dawning*, except that I can't like that long
poop."

"She used to carry passengers, sir. I was in her
three voyages with my brother Joe. I was under-
donkey man, helping work the donkey-engine,
but I wouldn't stay in her when Joe was a second
boatswain, not to be ordered about by my own
brother."

"I should think not," Cruiser said. There was a
silence for a minute, then Rodmarton asked:

"What would you be fancying, sir, of all the
ships in the race now that we are out of it?"

"There isn't much to choose between half a
dozen," Cruiser said. "I've not been in the China
Trade and do not know the ships nor their cap-

tains, except Captain Winstone, now in the *Caer Ocvran*. He was mate over me in one voyage. Knowing him, and having seen the *Caer Ocvran*, I should say that she would win this year."

"I was in the *Caer Ocvran*, sir," Rodmarton said, "for one passage before the *Cock*. I was in her under Captain Whodd. We were dismasted in the North East Trades; we lost all three top-gallant masts; so we lost some time by that and it was a very close thing that year and we finished fourth, so we might have won but for losing the spars. She did win last year, beat us on the post, when we had it in our pockets. I say the *Black-gauntlet* for a gale of wind, the *Cock* for all weathers, and the *Caer* for wet. She is like a half-tide rock, running or reaching."

"There are two other ships," Cruiser said. "The *Natuna* and the *Min and Win*; either of those might win it. Of the two, I should say the *Min and Win*. You may remember how she slid past us when we were becalmed off Anjer that time."

"Yes, sir, they say that her Captain can get steerage way on her with a pair of bellows."

"And what do you fancy," Cruiser asked, "out of all these, now that we're out of it?"

"The new ship, sir, the *Streaming Star*."

"She's a beauty for looks," Cruiser said, "though the real beauty of these clippers always seems to me to be below the water-line. But you've got half a dozen ships all built on the same lines and rigged with almost the same sail plan. The captains and officers are just about equally good; and the ships are stowed by practically the same stevedores. Then they sail on the same tide and get the same weather; one gets a stray slant here and another there, one loses this and the other that. Usually they come on to soundings on the same tide and the rest is either a bit of snatch or a bit of luck. Still, I was getting to love the game till we lost the Trades, and it's hard to be out of it."

"We might be picked up by one of them, sir. We're going right across their track. A new watch of men would give the ship that picked us up an extra chance, sir. We might be in the winning ship still."

"Let's hope it," Cruiser said. He watched his course for a while, then he said: "One great cause of success is a Captain suiting the ship and knowing her. The luck of a ship often dies with her captain and the same way with a Captain, he may be a wonder with one ship and fail with the next. But Fortune is like the plunge one takes at a dive, it will carry you through if you put enough into it."

"Well, I never had enough Fortune to say, sir," Rodmarton answered, "but I hope for the best. And we've all had a good gollop of Fortune, being alive now. When we get ashore I'm going to a church before I go to any pub or dance-house or any place. I feel grateful and I'm going to show it."

The talk dragged on, about ships and points of seamanship and Rodmarton's girl and ambitions. He had two girls it appeared, one blonde, the other brown, and had ambitions about both, but could not decide. Cruiser told him that one of them would decide for him, and was inclined to bet against the blonde. Presently, he gave orders to shake out a reef, and then the second reef; the boat ran on now swiftly, and the hearts of all rose to feel her moving. Cruiser watched his crew as he steered. He had a man in the bows looking out, Chedglow in the well baling for a few minutes in each half hour, for the leaks were now well in hand, and the other four men of his watch doing odd jobs about the defective seams or rigging up a sun screen. The sun was now high in heaven: all hands, who had been cold and sopped only a few hours before, were now longing for coolness. A few men of the watch below had hung their clothes to dry on lines between the forestay and the gun-wale, they themselves sprawled naked on the mat on the bottom boards trying to sleep, but they were not sleeping. All without exception were rest-less, cramped and uneasy, shifting about to avoid pain but unable to avoid it; and all longing for a chance to stand erect, walk even ten yards in any direction, leap and stretch and lie down flat, after drinking cool clear water out of a stream; indeed any water was beginning to be desirable. All the faces in the boat had the gaunt, haggard and hollow-eyed look of high and hard endeavour, which keeps some hope of an end in the agony of trial. The sullenness on Stratton's face, that had been savage the day before, was now dogged. Bauer, whose face had been a mixture of evils the day before, now was mainly sullen and furtive. Cruiser knew that if any trouble began among them it would begin from those two. At present they had no following, but distress or greed will give any rebel a following. Distress and greed were with them and growing.

Now the talk became general about the chances of being picked up. On the one hand a big ship had come close to them, then, on the other, she had gone by without seeing them. Both parties had a good deal to say; the depressed party, headed by Stratton, said that even if they were sighted they would never be picked up, because all ships passing would be either making a passage and unwilling to stop, or homeward-bound, short of provisions, and unable to take them on board.

"You talk like the Father of Lies and the Father of Folly," Cruiser said. "I've known a sea-captain who jettisoned a hundred tons of cargo, for which he might lawfully have been forced to pay, in order to make room for shipwrecked emigrants. Our Service has generous, fine fellows in it."

"Like the men who put the *Blackgauntlet* down and then went on," Stratton said.

"Chuck it," Tarlton said. "Chuck it. If you must talk in this heat and drought, talk about beer or women or some other cheerful thing."

The talk about being picked up, flagged, began again, and then died. It grew hotter and hotter and thirstier and thirstier, and the liquid bright water looked so cool.

Some of the naked sprawlers, roused up from their discomforts, went to the side and splashed water over their heads and chests.

"You look out that you don't blister," Cruiser said to them. "This sun will skin you alive if you aren't careful."

After a pause he ordered them to put on their clothes, so as not to get all blistered. The clothes added a good deal to the derelict look of the crew, being all barred and smeared with the contacts of wet paint.

Wind and sea died down together throughout the watch, and as they died the power of the sun grew. They drove on in the glitter of great seas from which the danger had gone. They drove silently, save for the creak of the gear and the babble of the talk of the water beneath them. They themselves talked little; their mouths were all foul from the bad night, and to the foulness thirst was being added: most of the watch on deck were now chewing buttons and trying, as Perrot told them, but without much success, "to believe that they were melons."

It was a scene of great beauty through which they passed. The sea rose blue and glittering bright and no longer foamed down upon them. As far as they could see were rising and falling brightnesses of water, blue in the main, violet in the hollow, and of an intense pure green at the burstless crests. Up above was a sky so full of light that its blueness seemed pale, and low down upon its paleness were the little and lovely clouds of the Trade Winds. There was no life in sight in all that beauty, save theirs, as they drove on, resolutely athwart it. To Cruiser steering there came from that fact an exaltation that he was the master of this vastness, that his will and imagination would bring this little frail, patched, leaking, spotted scarecrow of a crowded ship's boat, safe across the pathless sea to a haven. He looked at the sun and he looked at the sea, and said to them within his heart, "Perhaps I'll do you yet."

He was by no means sure of it. He had been sure of it a day before, now their chances were down by at least two-thirds. Still they had a third of their chances left, perhaps the best third, when all was said, they were all still alive.

"If God were going to kill us," he thought, "He would have drowned us with the others. He wouldn't play with us with hope as a cat does with a mouse." It was an odd thought, but it comforted him. Yet even with the comfort there came thoughts into his mind of men who had been "tortured by hope", men who had almost escaped from execution or prison or disaster, and had had leaping hearts perhaps, before being dragged back to despair and death.

He called to the men of his watch to strike the oar with the weft upon it, and to set up in its stead, properly stayed and guyed, the boat's boat-hook with a red ensign upon it. "This is a crack ship's boat," he said. "We will go in style, and it may help us to be seen."

The men were strangely clumsy at the job; he realized how much better Mr. Fairford's watch was. Fairford, as an old seaman, had picked old seamen, he, as a young man, had picked young men, and had now, as a result, a very poor team to drive—"three blind ones and a bolter". He had to call Bauer to the helm and do most of the job himself. When he had done it he wondered whether the men's clumsiness had been due to want of training, want of practice in boat-work, and general personal fecklessness, or whether thirty hours in a boat had already taken the best out of them? He did not like this last thought. Bauer was only good at routine, and useless when emergency upset routine, he had not expected much from Bauer. Perrot was the ship's cook, not a sailor at all; he had no right to expect anything from Perrot. Stratton and Coates were the worse for wear, he decided, already a good deal the worse for wear. As he prepared to take the sun, he thought that it would be a wise thing to get all the big jobs that might still have to be done on board prepared for while the men had strength and wit. "Perhaps by the time we reach Fayal," he thought, "we shall be so weak bodily, that we shan't be able to hoist the yard if it carries away, and so weak mentally that we shan't be able to shape a course."

Still, he kept a stiff upper lip and made Coates and Chedglow work out the sights independently. He found Chedglow, who was usually quick at working out the position, unable to get a result. Coates, who was always stupid at figures, made some bad mistakes; however Cruiser saw where the mistakes were and was satisfied that his own figures were roughly right. They had made just twenty-two miles in the twenty-four hours. Perhaps thirty miles of their seven hundred were now wiped off the account, only six hundred and seventy remained; and two men of his watch were the worse for wear and Chedglow near to breaking down.

"Coates," he said, "do you feel sure that you could take a sight?"

"No, sir," Coates said, "I'm sure I couldn't. I never can remember the corrections."

"You'll have to remember them if you're going to be an officer. And you'll have to remember them now. You're the only navigator on board here. Suppose I were sunstruck or taken by a shark or washed overboard by a sea like that big fellow yesterday, you'd be responsible for getting the boat to Fayal. What do you propose to do?"

"O, I suppose I'd get along, sir, fudging a day's work. I can do Dead Reckoning."

"Dead Reckoning will reckon you into death, Coates, in a job like this. You're not aiming to hit a continent too big to miss, but a small island, and a mile either way may mean death to all hands. You're playing a difficult hand and have no margin for folly nor for inexactness, but must calculate to the half second. Turn to here now on this sextant with me." As he saw some vexation in Coates' face, he added: "I know it's your watch below, so is it mine, but you owe it to the ship's company, so do I."

He took Coates for an hour over the corrections of the sextant. Fairford and Edgeworth watched them with wonder and admiration.

"You'd better learn too," Cruiser said to them.

"No, sir," Fairford said. "I could never remember those little things. A fellow tried to teach me once in the *Belted Will*, he'd been a Master too, but lost his ticket. I never had the brains nor the patience."

"You, then, Edgeworth."

"No, sir," the old man said. "You can't teach an old dog new tricks. If I'd my time over again, like these young fellows here, perhaps I'd go to school and pass, but I guess I'd be the kind of a fool I have been," he added. "I was as like Barney's bull as his own brother, and that was my ruin and always will be."

When the sextant lesson was over it was nearly four bells. MacNab, who had been forward on the look-out, was called aft to relieve the helm. Cruiser had had an eye upon MacNab ever since they had been in the boat, he had seen him white-faced and silent, utterly unlike his usual self, and had put it down to shock and scare. He had noticed him at odd times during the day, with many misgivings, as one of the first likely to collapse, and had had his misgivings raised by noticing Nailsworth's eyes upon him more than once.

"I believe that Nailsworth has been a doctor," he thought again, "and sees something very wrong with MacNab."

At the attempt to take the tiller MacNab

flinched with pain, tried a second time, and with grim lips forced himself to it for a couple of minutes, while Cruiser watched him closely, and then said, "If you please, sir, I can't do it. I've got such pain."

"Hell, you've a pain," old Fairford said, all the boatswain in him suddenly flashing out. "Take and steer or you'll get a worse pain the same as the cat give the monkey, so I promise you."

"Hold on, Mister," Cruiser said gently. "He looks pretty sick. Take the helm a minute, Tarlton." Then, when MacNab had stumbled clear of the steering place, he said, "Where is the pain, MacNab?"

"I got a kind of a welt, sir, from some skysail gear that came flying doon juist after the collision. It caught me a rare skelp and knockit the wind oot o' me. Then when I was sliding doon intae the boat I slippit doon and hit maself against the edge of yon thwart in the same place. I'm sae sair and stiff I can barely lift my airm. Every time I have turnit aboot I have hurt it mair. Every clout is on the claur. If I could hae a wet bit rub with yon thing Arnicky I'd be all richt, sir."

"Might I have a look at him, sir?" Nailsworth asked.

"He might have broken a rib," old Fairford said, musing.

"Well, come on here, MacNab, sit down and let's have a look at you."

"Can you tell if he has broken a rib?" Cruiser asked.

"Yes, sir," Nailsworth said, "I could tell and I could set it after a fashion."

"I can tell if his rib's broken," Fairford said. "I've been shipmates with broken ribs before now."

Very very gently and skilfully Fairford stripped MacNab's shirt and felt his side.

"I've known men," he said, "had their ribs knocked loose inside their chests all flying about like shifting backstays. And when they tried to do anything, the broken ends ran into their lungs."

Nailsworth with deft fingers felt MacNab's chest. "Your ribs are all right," he said, "but you've a bad external bruise on your right side. What hit you there?"

"Something that hit me a queer wee dunch."

"It's your collar-bone that's broken," Nailsworth said. "I could set that, Captain Trewsbury, if I could have a broad strip or two of blanket."

They cut some strips and Nailsworth bandaged him.

"You've done well, MacNab, not laying up till now," Fairford said. "And not complaining, for you've had some pain, I'll bet."

"It's naething to lie-up with, sir," MacNab said. "I could stand look-out, sir."

"Lie up for to-day anyway," Cruiser said.

When he had finished upon MacNab, Nailsworth went back to the job he had been doing with the others of his watch, of shaping a spare mast and yard out of the rickers, and fitting the standing gear to it. A moment before he had been a general practitioner called in to set a fracture, now he was again an able seaman, "one of the crowd," putting an eye-splice into a piece of old brace for a stay.

"Where did they learn you doctoring, Dee?" Kemble asked him. The nickname "Doctor Dee" had followed him from his last ship.

"Oh," Nailsworth said, "at some classes in London when I was a boy."

"You seem to do it pretty good."

"O, boys learn easily, if they learn at all," Nailsworth answered. He turned the conversation lightly into a question of the job in hand, so that Kemble and Edgeworth started arguing about tapering a splice and asked no more about doctoring.

Cruiser lay down to rest for the last remaining hour of his watch below, but before he slept he called Nailsworth to him and whispered into his ear. "I suppose MacNab should have special rations?"

"Well, sir, could it be managed?"

"Yes. And this boy, Chedglow, there?"

"He's young, sir. If we can keep him hopeful

he'll be all right. A week after this is over he'll pick up and forget that it ever happened."

"Thank you, Nailsworth."

Cruiser splashed his head and chest with sea-water against thirst. Like all the men on board he was very thirsty. It was intolerably hot in the boat, nor was there any escape from the heat save the splashing with water and sitting afterwards in wet clothes, letting them dry upon the body. The splashing with sea-water was a temptation to all. Those who splashed had mouths foul with thirst and malaise: they longed to rinse their mouth with the cool sea so clear and bright. Both Cruiser and Fairford repeated their orders that no one was to rinse his mouth with sea-water.

"If you start doing that you'll swallow some and only make yourselves thirstier. Clout anybody doing it hard over the side of the head."

Cruiser settled down to try to sleep for a while. He remembered how his old top-captain had once said to him: "Ah, my son, an officer's life is not all jam." He had often longed for command, now he had it. Presently he asked himself if it were not all a dream, or whether they were not all dead and in hell? "Nothing so easy," he said to himself, "this is life, and hell is pastime to what life can do. And in this particular little patch of life I am Providence and Wisdom and the power responsible and without me they'll all go into craziness and quarrelling and death. But I'll bring them through, or most of them. It's not going to be easy though."

It was too hot and he was too thirsty to sleep, and the men near him were too uneasy: they were always starting up with growls or moans to splash water over their heads. No one in that watch below was sleeping at all. All were glad to be done with the pretence of it and to come on deck at 4 P.M. for their dogwatch.

All on board were so wretched from heat, thirst and discomfort, that Cruiser called them to tea at half-past four instead of waiting till the usual time. He began by telling all hands that MacNab had a broken bone and that Chedglow being the youngest on board was less able to stand the racket than the rest of them, and that these two would receive double rations. Both the two protested against being favoured in any way. Most of the rest of the crew were silent; three or four shewed by their faces that they thought it hard that the useless members should be better fed than the rest. Bauer made what he considered to be a joke.

"We fat you up, Chedglow, for when we kill and eat you."

"If you make another remark like that, Bauer," Cruiser said, "all hands shall scrub your mouth out with sand and canvas."

"Tea" was a particle of raw salt beef, a particle

of biscuit, three raisins and a spoonful of water each. Some of the men had the fancy to make little puddings of their allowances, crushing beef, bread and raisins together.

"This'll make our bloods rich," Perrot said. "We'll come out in boils like Nebuchadnezzar, living high like this."

"It's fine for the thought, they say," Kemble said.

"Tea" was a cheery meal; they made it last a long time, and enjoyed it, for it came with the drooping down of their enemy the sun, who now fell away into the west, which reddened to receive him.

He was just stooping to the horizon in a clear sky with every promise of steady weather in it when the look-out man hailed with "Sail-Ho". Instantly all turned to stare in the direction to which he pointed.

Almost dead to windward from them and on the extreme verge of the sky was the grayish minute smudge which they knew to be a ship under sail. They knew that in that clear light she might well be three or more miles away. How she was heading they could not tell, she might be running towards them, she might be on any course; only the brightening of the skyline at the evening's lessening glare had made her visible to them. They watched her with longing for some minutes while

Cruiser tried to make up his mind what to do. He was very much fagged and found it hard to think. Some of the younger men watched him crossly, evidently expecting that he would at once alter course towards the sail.

"I shall not alter course towards her," he said. "We have a fair wind for Fayal, which is a certain hope. We're making five knots an hour at the moment, dead on our course. We're miles from that ship and can't tell how she's heading. It will be pitch dark before we can even tell that, and how are we to find her in the dark? At best she is heading towards us. If she is heading towards us she'll be near us with this wind in an hour and we'll burn flares; if she's heading away from us or in any other direction we can't hope to catch her and I won't try. But unless there be a real chance of being picked up I will not alter course. Fayal is our real chance, so don't come urging me to alter course every time you see a sail on a skyline. A boat can't go traipsing after a ship, as you well know."

The sun dipped down; almost at once a sombreness took the sea, and the colour dimmed in heaven. The men in the boat were all silent: nearly all the younger men rebelled against his decision, with the bitter feeling that he, their Captain, was condemning them to the boat when with a little pluck and luck they might be on board a ship by midnight. In a few minutes the little smudge on the skyline was one with the darkness of the sea and no man saw her again: the boat went rippling on, almost in silence, save for a little creaking, a little moaning and a little gurgle of water under her foot.

The night promised to be very fair, with a dropping wind and a sea lapsing from a swell into a calm. Cruiser had the first watch and took the helm, with Chedglow as sheet-tender. He and the lad talked together in low voices as the boat ran on across the swift black night.

Soon the stars came out in their thousands, shining all over heaven and shaking brightness in the sea. Then as the darkness made their burning the more intense, the light of phosphorescence grew in the sea, till the boat was clearing herself a way of fire. From time to time the flying fish arose in flame and glimmered, and fell in flakes of flame. From time to time a rising star, looking like a ship's light, raised hope in them till it lifted clear into the sky. A drenching dew cooled them as they sailed. The discomfort of the heat and some of the ache of the thirst were gone, but not their memory, that was there in all minds with the thought that "To-morrow they will be with us again much worse than they were to-day."

Another thing which was now maddening all hands was the discomfort of the cramped quarters; no one there could be comfortable: all ached and were bruised in every limb. All were cross from the continual touching of their fellows; no one could move without touching someone. All, except the two old men of the sea, Kemble and Edgeworth, whom the sea had hardened to something that could stand her, were restless and almost fevered from lying cramped. All thought "if only I could walk," "if only I could drink". All thought "It may be three weeks before we can do either, shall I last so long? Will any of us last so long?" Cruiser knew from the fact that he asked himself these things that all there were asking them. Three weeks. Why, they might be becalmed for three weeks; what would the boat be like then?

"Are you going to follow the sea, Chedglow?" Cruiser asked.

"No, sir; not after this."

"Don't be too sure," Cruiser said. "You'll be glad of this after it is over. This is a real thing, and somehow few people get anything real into their lives."

"What do you call real, sir?"

"Real?" Cruiser said. "When you've got nothing except just your bare life and you're up against destiny or death. When you're up against your Fortune, whether it goes for or against you."

"Were you ever up against it before, sir?"

"Yes, once, on a lower topsail yard, when we all thought the mast was going. It was a steel yard, buckling like a whale-bone, I don't know now how the mast stood. If you go ashore after this, you'll wish you'd stayed on and had some more of it."

"A steamer's light on the lee bow, sir," the look-out reported.

They turned to examine the light; nearly all the uneasy crew roused up to watch.

"It's another star," someone said.

"It's not a star then," Stratton, who was look-out, said. "When I see a ship's light I make sure that it's a ship's light before I report it. I'm not like some I could name."

"Well, I tank mein Gott dere's difference between us," Bauer said.

"She's a steamer," Cruiser said. "Look, there's her starboard light."

A tiny speck of green shone out below the moving white light and moved with it; a couple of tiny lesser lights appeared.

"She's a mail steamer; a South American mail steamer, heading towards us. Boys, we're in luck."

"Get the flares ready," Cruiser said.

They waited, watching eagerly for some moments, while Cruiser calculated that they were nearing each other at the speed of one mile in four minutes, and that they had been nearly three miles apart when the light was reported. He also longed for a case of rockets; ah! why had not the boat been stored with rockets? The unknown ship drew slowly nearer with a growing brightness in her lights. Soon the lights in her ports shone out in a long line and Cruiser pulled the trigger of a flare: it was dead, it did not fizzle.

"Light it in a dipper with some matches," he said, as he took another. The second flare also was dead. "Light that too," he said, putting it down. "Are all these flares damp?"

"This one is damp: it won't burn, sir," Rodmarton said. There was not much time to lose. Cruiser took out flare after flare and pulled the triggers of their igniters; one, for one instant, flickered but did not ignite. The truth was plain, the flares were all perished; they had but seven left.

The ship strode slowly past them. It is barely possible that the man on her bridge saw the little gleam of the matches kindled in the dipper; if he did he put it down to some effect of phosphorescence in the sea, and continued to think of the girl whose photograph was in his breast pocket in his oilskin tobacco pouch. Soon the ship had passed, so that the swell of her beam shut out her navigation lights. The ports in her steerage shone out, and as they came into sight a flare sputtered red in the dipper.

Perhaps some little portion of its chemical content was dry and ready to burn, perhaps they

might have made a real flare from it and caught
the attention of the ship's doctor, who was smoking
a cigar on the after turtle-back, thinking of one of
the lady passengers.

Unfortunately, when the mass caught fire and
began to burn red, Nathaniel Clutterbucke in his
excitement emptied more chemical upon it from a
somewhat damper flare which he had torn open.
Whether it were the mass or its dampness that did
it was not certain: in any case the new fuel put out
the fire that had begun nor could they kindle it
again.

Some of them cursed the steamer for not keeping a proper look-out: others cursed the man who
had put out the fire: luckily for Clutterbucke no
one save himself knew who had done this: he
kept quiet about it.

"I had got the stuff to burn," Rodmarton said.
"It was lighting up lovely, when someone put it
out."

"She's gone," Cruiser said, "she won't see us
now. To miss two in a day is bad luck."

Stratton, out of earshot in the bows, muttered to
his crony Efans that it might also be bad manage-
ment.

"Dese tam steamers," Bauer said, "dey know
noddings about look-out. Dey go tam-slam: you
look out of der way, we not mind you." He said
this, meaning to turn "opinion" against Cruiser,

who was known to have served in steam. Efans picked up the intention and carried it a little further.

"They neffer get real sailors in steamers, neffer; look you," he said. "No sailor wass to go in a tin pot, like mother's poiler."

"A damned sight better sailors than you'll ever be," Kemble said. "I tell you, Efans, I'm thirsty, because of you and your friends and the scuttlebutt. When next it rains, I tell you, you shall catch me three good drinks before you touch a drop; and four if you make me talk any more. A doctor would give as much as five shillings for you, to make people sick with what had ate too much."

This ended the discussion about the steamer: the men relapsed slowly into their discomfort; they muttered each a little to his neighbour and shifted about and chewed on button or bit of metal, then shifted again and cursed, and now and again slept for a few minutes.

The middle watch found them thus: the boat moving quietly forward, at about four knots, on a sea that was running in a long lazy subsiding swell, hardly broken anywhere. It was cool in the fresh dew of the midnight. There was little gratefulness felt for the coolness. Bauer, who usually was the first to growl at what could not be remedied, said that "We get what we want when we wants der oder ting. We want der sun now when we was colt: we want der dew to-morrow when it was hot."

"You want a damned gag in your mouth at all times," Kemble said. Already the ship's company, under the strain of life, was beginning to form parties: those for and those against the recognized authorities: discipline was still strong on all of them, but how soon would discipline begin to crack under the strains that were coming?

"The breaking strain is probably still some days away," Cruiser thought. "But in this kind of life, who can tell? At any minute something may make this unbearable."

He saw that MacNab was fairly comfortable, and Chedglow cheered, then turned in, so that his body guarded the precious water. He slept in an uneasy broken way, with hideous and very vivid dreams, which seemed to him to be all fore-tellings of disaster. It was as though spiritual vultures were flying after him, and following the boat, ready to tear at any soul that death might bring to them. "You are all going to die," these shapes of dream were saying. "We shall get each one of you, one by one, and have you with us for ever."

Others of the crew were afflicted in the same way, especially Chedglow, who woke twice with loud cries of terror. Being wakened, they complained of their dreams and being haunted. They began to feel that perhaps death may rove with a troop of harpies, and pursue and catch and kill. Cruiser sometimes woke up, or nearly woke up, certain that fearful shapes were following in the boat's wake. When he so roused from unconsciousness, something that did not quite wake up remained upon him, and in this state of being conscious, yet held by something not himself, he saw horrible faces in the wake and at the gunwale. Then suddenly he would be himself again released from the clutch of dread: he would gasp with relief, and look up at the stars in all their majesty of beauty: star upon star, planet beyond planet, wheeling up out of the sea and marching across heaven. Looking at the stars, he knew that He who established the heavens was stronger than these phantasies. He would lie looking up at them and marvelling at them until he would doze off into another nightmare. The wind that had almost died began to freshen at four bells and blew true from W. x S.

He roused out before his watch below was through in order to take some observations: then having checked his position he lay down again, till it was time to come on deck for the morning watch. Just before he was called, he had a strangely vivid feeling that someone much greater than a human being, and altogether good, was trying to convince him that all would be well. It was not human, it did not use human speech. It was a spirit of blessing, such as guards, watches and befriends, very beautiful with all attributes of mother and saint and beloved; so beautiful that for some moments on waking he stared at a planet with a feeling of gratitude that was the deepest emotion he had ever felt.

As he "came on deck" to take over, he noticed a change in the eastern heaven where already dawn was beginning to prepare. He had a thick brown taste in his mouth and an ache in every joint, and yet his bliss was so great that he could have cried from joy. As he called the muster and dismissed the watch below, he found it hard, not to promise all hands some special issue at their breakfast. He checked himself. "You must be as hard as adamant," he said to himself, "over water and food. You can give them kind words, but not stores: no, not if they beg you on their marrowbones."

His watch took place where they could, Coates steering, Chedglow on the look-out and Rodmarton tending sheet. There was no doubt that the wind was freshening and the sea rising under its impulsion. The boat's pace had increased through the middle watch till she was at her full pace of five knots. She was moving with increasing liveliness as the following sea rose to lift her: as she began her antics, so did the caulkings driven in with such care the day before begin to work loose. Little flicks and spirts of water flew into her from seam and cranny. By two bells of Cruiser's watch, he had to put a hand to bale.

"Going to blow fresh, sir," Clutterbucke said.

"It'll help us along," Cruiser said. "A hundred miles on our course will be a very good thing."

The watch below did not count it a very good thing: the spirtings of wet kept them from sleep: they growled and cursed at her as they shifted from place to place. Presently, before it was full daylight, there began a grinding noise forward in the way of the mast-step: the straik of the gunwale was working loose from the knees there, owing to the strain of the mast. The foot of the mast was both splintering and slipping.

"She'll work herself as loose as George's cow," Perrot said. "It's a big strain, a mast like this."

"We must strain her," Cruiser said. "We daren't lose a fair wind."

Tarlton turned out from his watch below. He had been a sporting man, runner, jumper and boxer, till something had happened; no one quite knew what. It was thought that he had arranged a fight, had blown the proceeds in a spree, and had then left the dry land for a time. He was a resourceful sailor, with a Berks accent. "Sir," he said, "I think I can fix this she-cow from milking, if you'll give me leave to try."

"Certainly try," Cruiser said. "Use what gear

we've got, and if you do it I'll give you a plug of tobacco."

He set four rickers athwart the boat just forward and just abaft the mast: got these bowsed well taut with under-girdings, and then with frappings made them nip the mast. Then with sawn pieces of ricker he made a strong tenon for the mast-foot. Clutterbucke bore a hand at this last job. It was a great success; it made the mast stronger, it secured the mast-foot, and checked the play of the straik. "Well done," Cruiser said, that's a fine sea repair."

"That's finished her for the time, sir," Tarlton said, "I got nippy with ropes and that, going round with the fairs one time, knocking chaps out on piece." He took his plug of tobacco and went below.

By this time, the colour was flaring to the mid-heaven for morning. They had before them the prospect of a bright hot windy day, full of tumbling and of flying water: no chance of rain, but every chance of extreme discomfort whether from the sun or from the spray. When the sun was over the foreyard and the sights had been taken, they breakfasted, on an eighth of a biscuit apiece, and two teaspoonfuls each of water. After this, all hands smoked, except Chedglow, and found some satisfaction in champing the pipe-stems. No sail was in sight, even on the crests of the rising seas they could see nothing, but the familiar toppling blue brightness, and no cloud over the Lord, the sun.

Cruiser went below at eight bells, still having in his mind a feeling that something would soon happen, that would be a change. It was not a hope: he had schooled himself not to hope, lest the disappointment should be too bitter: it was an inner certainty that something was preparing. Before he lay down, he saw that Nailsworth made an examination of MacNab, who was sick and feverish from pain and restlessness. He gave MacNab two spoonfuls of brandy and a half pannikin of water. It was not a popular mercy. MacNab was disliked by all hands for his wooden stubbornness in argument upon impossible propositions, as well as for being sick in this emergency. Cruiser, as he gave the extra rations, was well aware that many of the others grudged them.

"What about it, Efans?" he said. "You look as though you wanted MacNab to die."

"He wass a sick man, sir: not aple for duty. Why should he have prandy and trink, and we none, look you?"

"Because I say he shall. If you'd been keen for duty, there would have been drinks for all and to spare."

Old Kemble roused up from his work of caulking to speak his mind to Efans.

"We'd be doing a Christian deed to cut your tongue out, Efans, and use it for fish-bait. We might not catch fish, but we'd be spared your Taffy's jaw at least."

When the little breeze had died down, Cruiser asked Nailsworth quietly, what he thought of MacNab. "None too good, sir," Nailsworth murmured, without any change of face. "He's getting no rest, and is bound to have pain whenever he moves. If we could give him some comfort he would rest: but we can't. Still, he's young. Youth's half the battle and more."

"Thank you, Nailsworth," Cruiser said.

MacNab knew well that he was the subject of the talk. He rose unsteadily and said, "If you please, Captain Trewsbury, I can come on deck and stand men's look-outs."

"Lie you down, lad," old Fairford said. "All the decent men here know that you don't want to lie up: and all the wise ones know that you aren't sick from choice. Keep you still, or you'll ram an end of bone into your lung and ruin yourself for life."

Cruiser curled himself into a sleeping posture, and heard again at his ear a noise that he had learned to loathe, the cluck or gurgle of water slipping under the bottom boards only two inches from his cheek. He was weary past telling, as all his men were, and yet rest was denied, for the boat so leaped and descended, and the spray so splashed as she ran, that none could sleep for more than a few minutes. By now, too, the sun was in his might, smiting down upon them: no one there could hide from him, nor walk away from the cramped position, nor screen the pelting of the spray. The only comfort was the thought that the boat was on her course, moving past towards the end of this: what end, and when?

Cruiser woke suddenly from an instant's sleep as something big and rough scraped under the boat's bottom just below him. He felt the boat scrape over it, much as though she had driven over a sandbank. Sitting up on the instant, he heard Tarlton cry out:

"For the love of God, will you look at them things."

Sidling along by the boat on the weather side were three big sharks, which kept pace with her without any clearly apparent motion. From time to time the biggest of the three, which seemed the hungriest, would drive gently along the boat's side, running all along her length, perhaps having some pleasure from the friction. Just astern, keeping distance as easily as birds, were the fins of other sharks.

"They heard you send for the Doctor, Scotty," Tarlton said. "It's always a race between these boys and the undertaker. And I wish we'd a hook and a chain: we'd have one of these jokers with our kidneys and bacon. Give me hold of an oar, and I'll give the swine some play meat."

He swung up an oar, and brought the flat of it down with a smack on the surface of the sea. Instantly, and again without any clearly apparent motion, the shapes of dread were gone.

"That's the stuff to feed them," Tarlton said. "I was pearling one time out in the Pacific. Those boys are dead scared of a smack on the sea: it reminds them of threshers, what eat them."

The shapes were gone; not the memory of them. All there had heard too much of sharks following where Death was coming: a horror was upon all hands. Cruiser took a look at the compass, and remained at the con for a while, watching how the boat held her course. He chatted with the helmsman, then groped forward, clambered on to the mast-thwart, and stood there, holding to the mast, examining the nip of the halliards in the sheave lest it should be chafing. After he had looked at the nip, he looked carefully round the horizon, beginning dead aft, and searching each point from the tops of the now rousing seas. He had searched carefully perhaps ninety degrees of the horizon, when something made his heart stand still. He drew deep breath, shut his eyes, prayed, looked again, and said to Mr. Fairford, "Just step up alongside me, Mister, and take a look here."

Mr. Fairford did as he was bidden, and stared as Cruiser pointed in the direction of the weather bow. "That's what we're looking for, isn't it?" Cruiser asked.

"Yes, sir," Fairford answered, "that's what we're looking for, if we can fetch her up."

"Step up here, Kemble," Cruiser said, stepping down. "You've got the best eyes in the boat. Take a look-see and tell us what you make of her. Carry on, the rest of you. I spoke to Kemble, not to you."

Kemble clambered up on to the thwart and stared towards the port bow for about a minute. "She's a big clipper ship, sir," he said at last. "And heading this way, by what I make of her."

"Rig out the weft again," Cruiser said. He went to the helm and edged the boat nearer to the wind till she was heading for the stranger. Then he joined Kemble on the thwart and stared at her.

After a couple of minutes, Kemble ejaculated "Ah". Cruiser could see no reason for the cry, but he had the utmost respect for this old man of the sea so long-sighted and so used to staring into a glare to windward detecting and deciphering the least speck and smudge on distant skylines. "What makes you say that?" he asked.

"I'd like to watch her a minute longer, sir," old Kemble said. "She's not going from us."

"Knock off from your jobs," Cruiser said to the

men. "Get three oars out on each side and see if we can't help her along a little. There's a ship in sight: she seems to be heading towards us. You, Stratton, and Efans, take the bow-oars. Edgeworth and Tarlton, the midship oars. Coates, you pull stroke with Clutterbucke."

The men had lost much strength in the two days in the boat: they took to the oars and pulled. Even if they did not help the boat much, they still helped her. Kemble still stared, and at last said, "Well, sir, I don't quite know what to say."

"What do you think?"

"I don't know what to think, sir. She's a big clipper ship. She seems to me to be staying put. I don't believe she's under way."

"She might be a whaler, then," Cruiser said, "with her boats down. Do you see any boats? Any of you see any boats?"

"No, sir. She's no whaler," Kemble said. "She's a lofty big clipper ship. A whaler would have these stumps, and then a crow's nest. I've gone whaling. I'd pick out a whaler hull down."

The ship had been sighted at a distance of about three miles: the boat was making about five miles in the hour: she seemed to be crawling over a distance that did not diminish.

"Ah, there," Kemble said. "She's got her main-yards aback."

"What in the wide earth for? She's lost a man

overboard perhaps and has her boats down," Cruiser said. "Look out, there, Chedglow, can you see any boat at all?"

"No, sir."

"Lucky for us, sir," Mr. Fairford said. "Even if it's rough luck on the man that's overboard. They'll have the boats down for an hour and we may have time to fetch her up."

The slow minutes dragged as the boat crawled nearer and nearer. Presently Kemble said, "I'm inclined to think she's on fire, sir."

"Do you see smoke?"

"No, sir, no smoke: only there she is lying-by, with her courses in the gear. Whatever's wrong with her, it's an all-hand job."

"Very likely she's got this soft coal," Fairford said. "It gets red hot if you so much as look at it, and burns if you start a song. She's laying-by while all hands pump her full of water."

"Sometimes they blow the deck off with the steam," Edgeworth said, as they pulled. "You get a hundred tons of red hot coal down in the lower hold, and pour water on to it, you'll sometimes get a pocket of steam that'll lift a mast out of her."

"I'd rather be blown up in a barge than blasted in a Yarmouth skiff like this," Stratton growled.

The minutes passed slowly till they were within a mile and a half of her, and could see her fairly well as they came to the crests of seas.

"She's the *Cock*, sir," Rodmarton said.

"You mean the *Bird of Dawning?*"

"Yes, sir. She's the *Cock*. I've been in her. That's the *Cock*."

"I believe he's right, sir," Kemble said. "She is the *Cock*. She won't be likely to be on fire then. She'll have a man overboard."

"She might have sprung a leak," old Fairford said. "Started a butt, or hit a bit of wreck, and put all hands to getting a pad on the place."

"I'm sure I don't know what to think," old Kemble said again. "I think her boat's gone from these port davits. Now and again she takes a sheer, and it looks as if her boat were down."

"I believe she's sprung a leak," Cruiser said. "Isn't that water from her freeing-ports? They've all hands on deck pumping."

"It looks like it, sir," Kemble said. "It might be the run of the sea, though, plowtering up white."

Cruiser took Coates's oar for a mile and then climbed to the thwart again. All hearts and hopes were high now, that they would be seen and taken aboard. Even if the *Bird of Dawning* were on fire and about to blow up, or leaking and at point to sink, they would be able to stretch their legs, and eat and drink and perhaps sleep out of the boat that all so loathed now. By this time, the ship was plain to see, with her mainyard all aback, lifting and falling, plunging till her hull was hidden, then emerging, streaming.

"My God, sir," Kemble said, "there's something pretty wrong with that hooker. Her main royal's tattered itself, and they haven't sent a boy up."

Sure enough the port clue of the royal flung itself out and blew like a flag half-mast there. No one aboard her took any notice.

"Her boat *is* down," Cruiser said. "It's odd that we don't see her."

"My belief is, sir," old Fairford said, "that she's low in the water. She's abandoned, sinking, that's my belief."

"I believe you're right, Mister," Cruiser said. "She's lower in the water than she should be. I can't see anybody about her."

"Nor I, sir," Kemble said. "She's been abandoned, I do truly believe."

"Can anybody see steam or smoke about the water-line?" Cruiser asked. Nobody could, but all who watched her agreed that she was lower in the water than she should be.

"Sure she's leaking," Kemble said, "she's got a drag on her roll: look at that. The weight of the water in her checks her every time."

They were still far from her. Usually, she was almost stern-on to them, so that they could not see her well. From time to time, as the boat yawed a little or the ship took a sheer she would show her low broadside bowing to the sea and all the delicate details of her. Beyond all doubt, she was the *Bird of Dawning*. They had lain near her at Pagoda Anchorage for two months, and three of the men in the boat had sailed in her: she was certainly the *Cock*.

"Lay in your oars," Cruiser said. "Take the helm, Coates."

She was a clipper ship of thirteen hundred tons, with a short topgallant forecastle, a somewhat longer poop and a bold sheer. She was painted white above the water-line. About half the port broadside had been repainted within the last few days to fit the ship for her arrival in London, the rest was partly chipped, partly rusty from the passage. Her masts, spars, yards and blocks were all white. What little showed of her decks and deckhouses were also white. Both her boats seemed to be gone from her skids.

Her bows were of exceeding beauty; her stern elliptical.

She was weltering about, with a good deal of strain upon her gear. When she had been checked in her way by the backing of the mainyards, her main skysail had been furled, and men had hauled up the feet of the mainsail and crossjack, brailed in the spanker, and let the main and mizen staysails down with a run. All these sails now swung in their gear and tugged their sheet-blocks. The ship herself rolled in the plowter, scooped up the sea, and spouted it bright from all her freeing-ports. High aloft, the loosed main royal swung and lifted, till they could see the yard brickle.

"Sing out for your brother Joe, Roddy," Tarlton said.

"I'm not feeling like singing," Roddy answered. "I'm thinking where my brother Joe may be."

"Dere. Dere," Bauer cried. "I seen der hands at der braces. Dey go for to fill der mainyards."

"Fill your old back teeth," Tarlton said.

"Nein," Bauer said, "dey not see us, and fill der yards and go."

All had had a terror lest that should be the case. It was quite possible that all hands had been working in the hold, getting at a leak, or (less probably) some shift in the cargo, and that having finished they might come on deck, fill the mainyards and go. It was well possible that they might not see the boat, if they went thus, all hands busy on deck with their eyes aloft, and the Captain thinking only of a passage. They watched the mainyards in an agony, lest suddenly they should swing and fill. They did not. Instead, the lovely ship took a sheer, lifted her bows high, dipped them, rolled, at the dip so as to show a deck quite bare of crew, scooped up a long white roller along her sheer, taking many tons of it on board, and then seemed to shake her head as though agreeing that that kind of thing would not do.

"There's nobody on deck," Cruiser said. "You can see with half an eye that she's abandoned: both boats gone, and the falls dragging in the sea."

"It looks queer to me, sir," Kemble said. "Whatever has happened has happened to her suddenly. She was going along under all plain sail . . ."

"No, she wasn't," Edgeworth put in. "She had her stunsails out, and they ran them down on deck, or into the top, and never made them up. You can see them there."

"You're right," Kemble said. "She was making a passage with everything set. Then suddenly something happened: and they abandoned ship. What was it happened then? Why did they leave her?"

"Yes and when?" old Fairford asked. "It isn't like a crew to leave a sinking ship before she sinks. Boats generally stay by her till she goes. Her boats ought to be still standing by her, but they aren't."

"Don't you think," Cruiser said, "don't you think that they abandoned her because they had a chance of going? I should think that a ship came by and offered to take them off: and that then they took a chance?"

"Maybe, sir," Fairford said. "But I don't see any ship. And it's odd that a man like Captain

Miserden should think his ship sinking when she wasn't sinking."

"She's got a good dollop of water in her," Cruiser said. "Suppose they had a leak, and the pumps jammed or broke so that they couldn't free her: and everybody dead beat with pumping and eager to be out of her. Then if a ship came along and gave them a chance, they would take it, perhaps. And yet it's odd, too."

"It's very odd, if you ask me," old Fairford said.

"I've known leaks, plenty," Kemble said. "Odd things they are, too, some of them; and I've known bad ones very difficult to find and to get at. And I've known bad ones that would sometimes sew, no, so as you wouldn't get an inch in a day, and then next day would weep again a full foot. We used to say a fish had got into the hole: and maybe perhaps it had. It may have been a plank loose on a timber and sometimes working tight again. And we never knew quite where it was. That ship has got one of the sort, where they couldn't find it or get at it. Sometimes them sort will flood like a day of judgment coming in, enough to scare any man. Suppose theirs did. Then suppose, after they'd gone, it took up again. But whatever's wrong with her you may bet that that ship has got it bad."

"She's quite likely to go down on us," Cruiser said.

"There's another thing," Edgeworth said. "I was ashore, drunk, the day before we left Min River. I was damned drunk, and hit a big Chink, him come topsides. There was the port doctor fellow brought me off in his launch. I heard him say to Captain Duntisbourne, 'They've plague in all this province already, and what it will be in July here, God knows.' Suppose they've the plague on board there, and so many dead they couldn't work her, and had to abandon ship?"

"It's not likely," Fairford said. "Plague would have killed them before they were past Anjer."

"There's other things beside plague," Kemble said, "that breed slower. There's green-coffee-fever, what they get in the Java trade. Why shouldn't there be a green-tea-fever?"

"Because there isn't," Cruiser said. "You've all been in the China trade for years and never heard of any such thing. There isn't such a thing."

"There's other fevers that will kill," old Kemble said. "You don't have to be long at sea to find them. I've seen a brig come in to Swansea with copper-ore from the Havana: one hot summer it was: and only two men alive in her. All the rest were dead of yellow fever. And some who tried to discharge her died of it, too. You want to be careful how you tempt death going aboard a ship like that. She's got water in her, as you can see, but that may not be the real trouble. She may have all hands dead in their bunks, except those who got away from her."

"Yess, py Cot," Efans said, "she wass unter a curse, look you."

"We're not exactly under a blessing," Cruiser said. "I'm going aboard her, to have a look-see, curse or no curse."

By this time they were drawing close to the ship. As they drew nearer, her aspect became more ominous.

"There's another thing beside fevers," Clutterbucke said. "There's the wickedness of men. There's nothing worse than that. There are such things as pirates still. Some wicked men may have gone on board that ship and taken or killed her crew, and then taken her stores and what money she had on board."

"Or her crew may have done that: killed her officers and gone off in the boats," Tarlton said. "Gone on the grand account," he added, with a glance at Edgeworth, who was supposed to have been with Benito.

"There will pe scenes of plood in that ship, look you," Efans said.

"She had some Malays in her fo'c's'le," Rodmarton said, "Captain Miserden shipped them. They always hang together and sometimes go 'muck' together, like going mad; and when they go muck they kill everyone they meet and then they kill themselves."

"I don't want to seem depressing," Coates said, "but when she took that roll then, I'll swear I saw a body rolling."

"That will be it, then, sir," Fairford said. "Either pirates have come, or the crew has killed the officers and gone in the boats."

"There aren't pirates now," Cruiser said. But he knew as he said it, that pirates may at any time rise up in a ship's crew.

"Did you never hear of the *Flowery Land*, sir?" Stratton said.

"Depend upon it," old Kemble said, "this crew has been hazed or starved till they could stand it no more. They've killed the officers, and opened the ship's cocks to sink her, and cleared out."

"Dere's many homeward-bounders starves deir crews," Jacobson said. "Der poor mans is forced to eat der slush."

"I don't quite see why they haven't burned her," Tarlton said, "instead of leaving her to sink."

"Pirates don't burn," Stratton said. "A burning ship will bring down every ship within twenty miles."

Edgeworth was silent, but Cruiser looking at him, knew that at some time in his life Edgeworth had been with men who had given that very reason against burning a ship. He knew, too, that

Edgeworth did not repent, though perhaps would not have that past of his openly known.

"Lord, she's low in the water," Coates said. "She's just the twin of the *Blackgauntlet* the moment she went over. She'll go the same way, mark me."

Clutterbucke, who had been staring at the ship so intensely that his eyes had become visionary, now cried in a loud voice: "If she sinks on us, it will be the Lord's will, my brothers." He rocked to and fro, praying and weeping, and then began to sing, in his high clear tenor, from Gadsby's selection

> *"Let every drooping saint*
> *Keep waiting evermore;*
> *And though exceeding faint,*
> *Knock on at mercy's door;*
> *Still cry and shout till night is past,*
> *For daylight will spring up at last."*

He sang the last two lines over and over again as the boat drew up to the ship.

As they drew near her, she looked perhaps more to be pitied than feared. The little disorders against which the sailor is always contending, now triumphed unchecked and stamped her as deserted. They came quartering up to her, sometimes seeing her stern, sometimes her port broadside. Her boat's falls dragged in the sea on both sides. Sometimes in one of her rolls she hove them well out, as though she had hooked a fish, and swung them high and crashed them into her rail. Her staysails swung, jangling their sheets. She was groaning, cracking and jangling from blocks and ports and framework: her bells jangled sometimes; and buckets or paint pots which had rolled loose on her deck sometimes made a rattling roll from side to side, like the flourish of a little devil's drum delighting in the ruin. Now and again as the steady wind caught some fold of sail as she sheered, it would blow out with a roar, and flog and collapse, or lift high, trumpeting.

"She'll condemn some wealth in sails, sir," Mr. Fairford said. "If she goes on like this much longer."

"She will," Cruiser said. "Look, all of you, along her water-lines: the paint doesn't seem to have blistered."

"No, sir," they agreed, "the paint hasn't blistered. She hasn't been on fire below, sir."

"Not badly on fire, anyway; but she's got some water in her."

"If you'll excuse my saying it, sir," Kemble said, "I only say it to warn you. They've got deadly disease on board her, that's my theory, and opened the cocks to sink her before they cleared out."

"That's very likely," Cruiser said. "And it is just possible that they've left some dying men on board. It may be yellow fever: it may be small-pox. Now, I shall go aboard alone, or with you, Rodmarton, as you know her, and when I'm aboard, you'll drop astern on a line till I know what's the matter with her. You understand, Mister; let the two of us aboard, then shove off and keep clear, for I don't like the look of her."

"Nor I, sir," Fairford agreed. "I'll keep clear of her all right, if you'll pitch me a line off a pin."

"George! I've been wrong about her all the time. She's got a lovely stern," Cruiser said as they drew up to it, under oars, having now dropped the sail. The ellipse of it rose up high above them, and showed to all in a gilt grummet her name and port.

> *Bird of Dawning.*
> *London.*
> *The Light comes after me.*

Above and below the gilt grummet was her device, of a white cock with scarlet hackles, gripping a perch with gilt spurs.

"The Light comes after me," Edgeworth spelled. "Well, we're coming after you, you she-cow, and don't you forget it."

"Half a moment, before we come alongside," Cruiser said. "We must hail before we board. Sing out, all hands."

All hands lifted up their voices in a hail:

"*Cock*, ahoy. *Bird of Dawning*, ahoy."

They had not expected an answer to their hail: but an answer came. From the hen-coop abaft the mainmast, a cock faintly crowed at them.

"My word, a cock," Cruiser said.

"She can't be deserted, sir," Rodmarton said. "They'd never have left the poultry . . . They must be all dead of the plague."

"Who took the boats, then?" Cruiser asked. "They left in a hurry, thinking she was going down, and she hasn't gone." He knitted his brows, puzzled at the case. Standing up, he hailed again, *"Bird of Dawning,* ahoy." Again the cock crowed back at him, as though the ship herself were answering. Most of the men said that they were damned.

"The sooner we examine into her the better," Cruiser said. "She'll scare us all white, until we know." He was scared himself at the thought of the scenes of horror that might be in the houses there, only a few fathoms away. With the terror, there was hope of finding more stores, before the ship went down.

"Edge her in to the falls, Coates," he said. "Stand by to catch the forward life-line, Rodmarton, while I catch the one aft. Look out, port oars, that you don't smash any oars against her. Tend her with a ricker, Edgeworth: you, too, Kemble."

They pulled up alongside gingerly, Coates steering, Rodmarton forward, Cruiser in the stern-sheets ready to leap, the two old men ready to fend. The ship loomed up immense, as she rolled away from them, heaving out her grassy copper, and shewing bare, bright patches where the fall-blocks had stricken her. She paused in her roll for an instant, then with a rapidly increasing rattling jangle, she rolled down towards them, till her yard-arms looked like spears descending. "In your port oars," Cruiser said. "Half a stroke, starboard, lively now. Watch your tip, Rodmarton."

Nimbly as a cat in spite of his fatigue he leaped at the life-line that swung from the after-davit, caught it, went up it, swung to the rail and leaped down on to the deck. Rodmarton followed him rather less nimbly. Cruiser took a coil of running gear from the pin and leaned over the fife-rail. "Stand from under," he called. "Catch this line. Catch a turn with it round the forward thwart and drop astern on it till I tell you."

He paid out the line to them, and watched them drop astern, till they lay off the quarter, with all hands clustered forward in her, staring. Rodmarton stood by the starboard main fife-rail, looking thoroughly scared. The words of Kemble and the others had gone well home to him: he was thinking that his brother Joe might lie dead in his bunk in one of the deckhouses within a few yards of him.

Cruiser went to the well and hove up the rod:

there were three feet three inches of water in her.

"See that, Rodmarton?" he called. "She's got just over three feet in her. Try it, you: and check it."

Rodmarton tried it and made it the same.

"Yes, sir, three feet three, sir."

"And why should they desert her with only that?"

"I don't know, sir."

"It must have been much less than that. This ship was deserted yesterday, and she must have been leaking gaily ever since."

"It may have been like what Kemble said, sir; a fish got into it."

"A fish," Cruiser said. "An obliging fish, I should say."

"Yes, sir."

Cruiser stepped to the hen-coop and flung back its slide. A cock chuckled, hopped down to the deck and flapped and crowed: five hens followed him. Cruiser reached to the bin on the coop-top and flung them some grain, and filled their pan at the scuttle-butt.

"Won't you drink, sir?" Rodmarton said.

"You drink," Cruiser said. "I'll speak to the boat's crew." Going to the rail, he hailed the boat. "Give all hands a biscuit each and a pannikin of water, Mister," he cried. Going back to the scuttle-butt, he took a small drink himself. "This butt is full," he said. "It must have been filled in the dog-watch yesterday or the day before. I should think the day before, since the hens were shut up for the night. We'll go forward, first, Rodmarton, to see about your brother Joe."

"Joe was a good brother to me, sir," Rodmarton said, snivelling. "And if I'd not been so proud, I could have been with him now."

"I don't believe for a moment that this is a pest-ship," Cruiser said. "She's had men enough to get both boats over and haul up the courses and get the mainyards aback. You wouldn't have thought, would you, that being able to stand up straight and walk forward would be such pleasure? It is like having a new life."

"It is indeed, sir."

They were now near the after-end of the long, forward deckhouse which stretched from the fore-mast to the main hatch. A green door swung open, and crashed and clattered at the roll, in the after end of this deckhouse. "That's the round-house-door, sir," Rodmarton said, "where my brother Joe used to berth. I went to tea there with him, only two days before we sailed, and he give me those little London pantiles, all square, not like we got.

"And I don't think I dare look in, please sir, for fear of seeing them all dead."

Cruiser's habits of order were strong upon him.

"Lay aft, Rodmarton," he said, "and get a pull on that main royal clue-line before the sail splits." He went to the round-house-door, hooked it back open, and looked in.

It had been the round-house or cabin for the ship's idlers, the two chief boatswains, the two sail-makers, the cook and the carpenter. The two junior boatswains no doubt berthed in the fo'c's'le. The house was a neat cabin, with no trace of pestilence about it. The six bunks were deserted, with their curtains of green Min cloth swaying to the roll: the blankets neatly spread, ready for the night. The six chests were still lashed to the ringbolts, some to serve as seats at the tiny table, the others under the bunks. In the two spare bunks their canvas bags were piled. In the locker were their allowances, a tin of cold sea-pie with a spoon in it, a corked bottle half full of lime juice, and a bread-barge full of broken biscuit. Cruiser pocketed some of the bread, and looked about for some clue that would tell him what had happened. No clue was there.

The pipes were in the pipe-racks. Tacked to the match-board on the bulkheads in the bunks were odds and ends which shewed something of the tastes of the men who had slept there. The cook had two texts printed in colours, "God is Love" and "God bless our Home", the one with a decoration of partridges, the other with a Shetland pony.

They had probably been sent to him by his children: they seemed unbearably pathetic there. In a shelf at the foot of the carpenter's bunk was a model of the *Bird of Dawning*, rigged with spars of beef-bone, and very nearly finished, save for the running rigging of the mizen mast. In what Cruiser took to be brother Joe's bunk there were a couple of chest-shackles, not yet finished, with the pointing still in progress on them.

Cruiser went out to Rodmarton, gave him a hand at bunting up the main-royal, and handed him some biscuit.

"There's nobody dead there," he said. "You'd better eat this bread slowly. I'm going to the fo'c's'les. If I were you, I'd go into the round-house and take over your brother Joe's gear."

"Thank you, sir; I will, sir." Rodmarton, like most Englishmen, was a man of very deep affections not usually shewn. Cruiser left him in the round-house, and went into the starboard fo'c's'le, which was in the same superstructure just forward from it.

It was a big, roomy place; dry, clean and well-lighted, with bunks for fifteen seamen, whose chests and bags were still there. From what he could see, this starboard watch had been below, turned-in, when the alarm of all hands had been given. There was no trace of sickness or death there. From what he could see, the alarm had been in the day-time or the dog-watch, because the men had been lying on their blankets, not beneath them. The prints of their bodies lay stamped there; he could tell their sizes, and something of their characters.

At the forward end of the fo'c's'le was a hanging place for oilskins, which swung there on pegs, rather like a row of desiccated pirates upon a gibbet. The chests had not been emptied, even of their tobacco. The men had apparently sprung up, snatched a few things and had then left the ship. Their whack-pots were in the lockers still, and hook-pots half full of lime juice still hung on the edges of the bunks. As in all homeward-bound ships, the bunks contained things that the men were making, such as models of the *Bird of Dawning*, with the little blocks made of guji seeds, sharks' back-bones carefully dried and about to become walking-sticks, narwhals' horns on which the scrimshaw-worker was cutting crude designs of rope, sennits, ladies' hearts, arrows and clipper-ships; albatrosses' feet being made into tobacco-pouches; chest-shackles for going ashore; sail-makers' rubbers in beef-bone, representing shroud and stopper knots; and ships with their masts prone which were soon to be thrust down the necks of bottles half full of putty, coloured to represent the sea, and then by an adroit twitch of a thread rigged, with the masts erect, to rouse wonder in all beholders how the ships ever got there. All these little treasures had been left behind, unfinished, at the feet of bunks: some of them were good of their kind; and all had been made by blunt fingers, with the aid of a knife and a few pins, at the sacrifice of sleep in many watches below.

Cruiser crossed the deck to the port fo'c's'le on the other side of the bulkhead. It resembled its fellow, except that a meal had not been cleared away from the table when the crew left the fo'c's'le. The wreck of the meal had now been rolled off the table and flung hither and yon under bunks and behind chests. What meal it was, Cruiser found it hard to say: probably breakfast or supper, for the skilly-can, which may have contained a hot drink of some sort, was rolling with the whack-pots. Cruiser picked it up and scooped from it something of the molasses which had once sweetened its brew.

Forward of the fo'c's'le in the same superstructure was the ship's galley, shut up, either before or after the day's work, at the time of the desertion of the ship: the range was in good order, and the fire laid for kindling. Immediately forward of this was the donkey house, containing the engine, which had once been in charge of Rodmarton. Here Cruiser was startled indeed.

Both doors of the engine-rom were open. The

deck was strewn with coal-bags, spanners, and lumps of coal. Plainly, the vanished crew had been set to work to get the engine to work the pumps. He knew a little about engines; from what he could see this one was in good order: he did not doubt for a moment that it was in excellent order, like all the things under Captain Miserden's command. It was all greased, and oiled, and its bright parts kept polished. Its canvas cover lay folded beside it. The fires had been lit, but steam had not been raised, and the drive to the pumps had never been rigged. Rodmarton joined him here. Rodmarton was white and scared at the thought of his brother gone into a mystery: the deserted ship terrified him: he came to Cruiser for company.

"Look here, Rodmarton," Cruiser said, "this engine's in order, yet they haven't got steam and cleared her. Why not? Why on earth not?"

"It beats me, sir," Rodmarton said. "But I'll tell you what I'm afraid of, sir. I'm afraid one of them giant squid has come up and picked all hands off and ate them."

"What, and the boats, too?"

"Yes, sir, pulled the boats down."

"You can tell that to the marines, not to the deck department. Man, can't you see that she's sprung a leak somehow, some sudden, appalling leak, that leaped on them suddenly, and scared them all stiff and drove them out of her when they had the chance to be taken off? But why haven't they rigged the drive to the pump and got the engine on to it? They've the power here to free her. Why haven't they tried it?"

"Sir," Rodmarton said, "they have the hand-pumps rigged by the main bitts there, and I took a heave round on them, and could get nothing. It's my belief, sir, that the tea's got into the pump-box and jammed the suck. The pump's jammed sir, that's why they never rigged the drive."

"Jammed," Cruiser said, "I never thought of that. The tea leaves have jammed the intake of the pumps?"

"Yes, sir."

"Of course, if the pumps are jammed," he said slowly, "it would explain a good deal." But he thought to himself "How would the intake jam her? The ship has been swept and garnished, and all her timbers almost polished before any tea went into her: and her tea is all in tiers of boxes chinsed tight with grass-mat; how would loose tea leaves get down to the well?"

He found no answer to that question, so thrust it aside till he had settled something more pressing. He took a pannikin from the fo'c's'le, passed under the fo'c's'le head, and there pushed back the scuttle that led below.

He looked down into a darkness that was all close, hot and heavy, yet fragrant with the smell of the tea leaf. It was very dark below, he could see nothing but the gleam of a coaming below, and hear nothing but the crying of a ship's fabric that can never be wholly silent.

"I'm going down here," he said to Rodmarton, "I want to find this leak."

Rodmarton plainly shewed that he believed that the giant squid was down below; and something of his fear touched Cruiser as he swung over the coaming, and clambered down the nine iron rungs into the 'tween-decks. He went down slowly, feeling his way below him with his feet. He knew that somewhere down in the darkness was something evil which had driven nearly forty men in a hurry out of the ship. What that was, he had now to find and face. He did not believe in giant squids, but the light that he had left, shining at the scuttle-entrance, seemed dearer to him than any light that he had seen.

Soon, his feet touched the coaming of the fore-peak hatch; he swung round on to the laid 'tween-decks and looked about him. By the light from the scuttle above he saw close to him some casks lashed to the coaming bolts. Putting an arm into them, he found that they were half filled with sand for the scrubbing of decks, and with small pieces of holystone, wads of canvas, and suji-muji brushes, all designed for the smartening of the ship for London River. As his eyes became used to the gloom he saw the slope of the cables on each side, and the frame of strong scantlings which held in the coal for the cook and engine. Further aft, he could see the barrier of the shifting-boards, which fenced the tea in the waist. All the close heavy air was fragant with the tea. The noise of the ship labouring and plowtering, the clang of her freeing-ports, and the gurgling ominous running suck of the sea along her, making her whine, and whicker, were all more intense down below there. The gear was still tugging and jangling. Every now and then all the dark 'tween-decks seemed to shudder with patterings and goings: he knew that the noises were strains passing in the beams, but they sounded like feet. As he stood listening, and somewhat daunted, something heavy and swift ran across his feet. He leaped and kicked out, but the thing was already gone: it was only a big ship's rat, perhaps driven from the lower hold by the leak. His heart beat the quicker for it for some moments.

Remembering an old method of the sea, he groped to the ship's port side, pressed the pannikin against it and laid his ear to the pannikin. The sea-stethoscope brought to his ear a noise of gurgling and lapping, which he knew to be the noise of the water already in the ship. It was not the rushing noise of a dangerous leak. He took his pannikin from place to place, going to the breast-hooks, then to the starboard side, then moving aft to the cargo, then crossing again to the port side, and listening like a doctor for some irregular murmur, some dangerous sign or sound. There was no such sound in the forward part of the ship. "There's nothing dangerous at the moment, forward," he told himself. "Yet the water in her gives her a horrid feel at the end of each roll."

He felt at each roll that the ship had her death upon her, and might at any moment go suddenly down, and shut that little bright scuttle above him with the green weight of the sea.

He climbed back on deck, to the great relief of Rodmarton. "Rodmarton," he said, "get up on to the top of the deckhouse here with me. Clamber up to that ventilator and listen."

He, himself, clambered to the other forward ventilator, and listened at its frowsy mouth to what it had to say. It told just the same story that the pannikin had told, that there was a dead weight of water in the lower hold, but no shattering inrush.

"And yet," he said to himself, after he had tried both ventilators, "there must have been a shattering inrush. What has stopped it, and for how long is it stopped?" He shook his head at Rodmarton and said: "We'll move along aft and try there." In his head the thought ran, "She has probably started some butt amidships and in some odd way the cargo has caulked and chinsed it. If we could find the place we might get a mat over it and save her."

As he walked aft, he asked Rodmarton, if he had ever known the *Cock* to leak. "No, sir," Rodmarton said, "not when I was in her: she's as tight as a nut. She's still a new ship and she goes into graving dock every time. We never had to pump her. The last time I saw Joe I asked him if she'd opened at all, and he said the same."

They came to the booby hatch under the standard compass between the boat-skids. Cruiser pushed back the scuttle and let a waft of hot air blow by him. "If it isn't forward, it must be somewhere here," he said. He clambered slowly down, and stood in the 'tween-decks to accustom his eyes to the gloom.

As he stood there, holding to the iron ladder, and looking aft, he saw two green eyes looking at him from the bulkhead. They did not blink, they watched him intently, and for an instant they made him think of the squid. "Who's there?" he called. "Come out of it."

There was a rustling in the studding-sail locker and a faint mew: the thing came to his feet and rubbed his ankles: it was a little black cat. "Poor pussy," he said. "And couldn't they find you when they left her?" He stooped, stroked the little head, caught the purring creature to him and carried her up on deck. "Here's a pet for you," he said. "Give

her a drink of water, and see that she doesn't eat
the hens."

He walked to the port side and applied his pannikin as before. There was no sound of any in-pour
on that side. When he tried the starboard side, it
seemed to him that there was a new noise at his
ear. He tried forward, with no result, then, trying
aft, was convinced that somewhere on that side
water was struggling and lapsing into the ship. He
tried as far aft as the bulkhead which went right
across the 'tween-decks to screen off the sail-locker
and lazarette. The noise seemed to come from
rather far aft, now as a tinkle, now a splash, according to the roll of the ship: undoubtedly a leak
was there, of sorts.

He could not keep from wondering whether it
were not at the stern-post, or some other difficult
place, where a mat could not be put. He climbed
up to the deck and hailed Rodmarton. "She seems
to be weeping somewhere aft on the starboard side.
Come aft with me, will you?"

The break of the *Bird of Dawning's* poop was
recessed, in a curve, amidships. Within this curve,
a green door led to an alleyway, with the saloon at
the end. As was usual with those ships, the cabins
of the first and second mates lay on each side of the
alleyway; then came the steward's pantry and
cabin, then the companion leading up to the chart-
house, then the saloon itself stretching right across

the ship. Cruiser, who had been on board the ship at Pagoda Anchorage, remembered his way: Rodmarton had been aft as a seaman coming for tobacco and slops.

Stopping at the pantry, Cruiser groped in the half-darkness for candle and matches on the shelf, and finding them struck light, and then saw, in a bucket of water (for coolness) a bundle of tallow dips, which he took.

Just beyond him was the ship's big saloon, lit by a skylight and full of the sun. Only a few weeks before Cruiser had entered it as a suppliant, seeking for work; now here he was again: what was he now, and what was the ship now?

There was the table where Captain Miserden had sat to receive him, a big, white-faced, black-bearded man, with strange eyes. The saloon was finer than most ships' saloons. It had been designed for passengers making the Australian passage: its panels were of polished bird's-eye maplewood; there was much brass about the skylight: still bright, Cruiser noticed, as though it had been polished only the day before.

An open locker against the after-bulkhead caught his eye: it was the likeliest place for the ship's chronometers; he stepped to look within it, and saw that it contained the chronometers (there were notes of the rates still in the nest) but that the instruments were gone.

He hove up the hatchway which led to the lazarette and after 'tween-decks. A warm compound smell wafted up at him, from the variety of things stored there. Tea from the cargo was the dominant smell, but other suggestions of a grocer's shop were there. When he had clambered down and surveyed the place with his candles, he was freed from his fear that the crew had been starved away. It was a "homeward-bound" lazarette, but what stores remained seemed enough for the passage still before her. He stuck the lights where they would not fall and then stood to listen.

As he had dreaded, the sound of water running into the ship could be heard there without the help of any pannikin. Water was coming in, somewhere close to him, in some abundance, or so it seemed, for the echoes in that hollow place made the noise greater.

"No doubt about this," he said to himself. "She's got it somewhere aft here, on the starboard side. Now perhaps I can find it."

He laid his ear to the pannikin on the ship's side: the noise at once sharpened and seemed to draw near: it was close to him, under his feet and rather further aft. By moving aft, he reached a place at which it seemed to be directly below him in the ship's side, rather far aft. A pipe leading up the ship's side there gave him a clue. He ran up into the saloon, and opened a door on the starboard side aft. As he had hoped, it led to the captain's lavatory and bathroom. He tried plugs and taps, but got no water from them; and at once a hope sprang up in him that he had found the cause of the trouble. Instantly however, he had to beat down the thought. "It cannot be only that," he told himself. "It must be more than that. This ship must have had a flood pouring into her, and something or other has stopped the flood."

"Have you found anything, sir?" Rodmarton asked.

"I'm just going down for another look-see," he said. "Come on down, I've got to get a man-hole-lid open, and get down into the after-hold."

Down in the lazarette, close to where he had stood, was a man-hole-lid, which had certainly been lifted not long before. Cruiser hove it out of its place and peered down onto what looked like a little waterfall. Water was spouting in a jet through the ship's side into the hold there. As he held the candle he saw the jet arched almost like a pipe of bright metal shooting in and curving and splashing down.

"See that, Rodmarton," he said. "That's a part of it anyhow. It's the intake of the Captain's lavatory gone at the joint. Light some more candles from the bunch, I'm going down to have a look at it."

Very carefully, he swung himself down, got

foothold, and crawled with a light to the place. He had not expected what he found. The intake pipe had been cut through close to the ship's side; it had then been wilfully prized and wrenched aside, and splayed open to let water into the ship. There was no doubt about it. Someone had worked to let water into the ship.

"Do you find the skin gone, sir?" Rodmarton asked.

"No. It's the pipe. Nip forward to the carpenter's shop and see if he's got any big spigots: there are sure to be some. And get a slush-can and a maul, and any old clout you can come across."

While he waited for these things, he marvelled still more at his discovery. "Who did this, and why, and when?" he asked. "It cannot be the only leak. And yet, no other seems to be running. And there must have been another, to scare the crew out of the ship. The jammed pump of course came as an extra scare."

He remembered very clearly his own time with a captain who had wished to put his ship ashore. What if Captain Miserden had wished to be rid of the *Bird of Dawning?* What if the man, whoever he might be, who had cut through the pipe, had also jammed or choked the suction of the pumps?

Rodmarton appeared with gear from the carpenter's shop. "I've got some spigots, sir," he said, "and a maul and slush and stuff."

"Well, nip on down here, with some lights, and we'll tomm this hole tight."

Rodmarton swung down and stared at the cut pipe.

"Why, sir: it's been cut through on purpose."

"No doubt of that, but we can stop this easily enough, with a spigot, till we can get down to it and make a neat job of it."

"But can this be the only leak, sir?"

"Why, no," Cruiser said, "I don't see how it can be. But it may be the only active leak. I believe, now, that this ship knocked a hole in herself somewhere, somehow, on a bit of wreck, or wrenched a butt apart, or sheared off a rivet or something. Then she began to leak like fun. But water exerts a great pressure, and it often happens that when some weight of water is in a ship the very weight of the water will keep more from coming in. Now I believe that this ship has checked her leak in the same way. But I also believe that someone wanted her cast away, and cut through this pipe, and in some way got down to the well and choked the intake of the pumps. Then all hands were scared, and when the chance came to desert ship they deserted her. However, we'll soon know more about this. We'll chinse up this pipe and get those poor chaps out of the boat."

It was one minute's work to slush the hard-wood spigot, wrap it in a clout of worn canvas, slush the end, thrust it into the pipe and beat it home. The spigot dripped for an instant after it was in, then the drippings ceased.

"We'll get some putty or cement along presently," Cruiser said, "and make a good job of it; this will hold for the time. Now we'll get the boat on board."

He clambered back into the lazarette, hoisted up the gear, with the candles, and helped Rodmarton to replace the man-hole-lid.

"By the way, Rodmarton," he said, "when you were in this ship what hoses had you?"

"The usual wash-deck hoses forward, sir; and two long fire-hose, with copper-nozzles, in racks just forward of the mizen mast. The ship carried passengers her first voyage or two and the hoses were in case of fire in the quarters."

"I saw those hoses," Cruiser said, "when I came aboard this ship in the Min River. They're not in the racks now. The racks are empty."

"I didn't notice, sir."

"I did," Cruiser said, thinking to himself that the man who had removed the hoses had helped to the desertion of the ship. "Now on deck here, Rodmarton, by this little companion ladder, and get the ship's crew aboard."

As Rodmarton went up the captain's companion, Cruiser went along the alleyway, locked the door which led to the deck and pocketed the key. "Just as well," he thought, "to have no second road open to the rum, with men like Stratton and Efans about." He then went up the ladder to the poop, and found the boat's crew hauling their boat forward to the falls that dangled from the starboard davits.

"Up on board with you," he said. "We can salve this hooker, I do believe. Coates and Chedglow, you both stay in the boat till she's on the skids. MacNab, you, too; you'll only crock your bones again if you go trying to climb."

They brought the boat to the falls, and hooked her on. Man by man they swarmed up the life-lines, with ejaculations of wonder and delight to be out of the boat, able to stand erect, and to walk and to feel the deck of a ship below them. The two and a half days had taken the strength out of them. They had to take the boat's falls to the deck-capstan, and to hoist her one fall at a time. They got her up, swung her in, secured her, and helped MacNab out of her.

"Hold on a minute, all hands," Cruiser said, as the crowd stood below him, ready to scatter forward to raid the fo'c's'les.

He went to the boat's locker and removed the brandy.

"You've all had a hard time in the boat," he said. "You must splice the main brace. Keep aft here, till I give the word." He served out to each man there a strong grog, which they drank with thankfulness. After the grog he gave each man a handful of raisins. They sat about the main bitts eating for a few minutes; they were all smiling foolishly, looking up at the spars, touching deck and bitts to make sure that they were real, and anon rising to their feet, to walk a few steps for the pleasure of being able to do it.

Cruiser and Mr. Fairford ate their raisins at the break of the poop.

"What do you think, Mister?" he asked. "Will the crowd sail this hooker to London?"

"They're mostly English, sir," old Fairford said, "and my experience is, that you can get the English to do anything, if you put it to them the right way. The trouble with the English is they try all the wrong ways first."

"I'm not much of a hand at speaking," Cruiser said.

"They're not much judges of oratory, sir. 'Do this, damn your eyes', is the oratory they're used to."

"I know," Cruiser said, "but we've been in an open boat together for over two days." He walked onto the little platform which led to the standard compass: Mr. Fairford followed him.

"D'ye hear there?" Cruiser said, as the men started up at his approach. "We've been in a tight place together. Thank God we're out of it. We've got out of our boat into one of the crack ships of the fleet. Don't think you're out of danger in her. You're not. She's got more than three feet of water in her hold, and her pumps are jammed. I don't know what leaks she may still have. I've only stopped one small one.

"You've had a hard time in the boat and I'm going to see that you are well fed and rested. If you go eating and drinking in great quantities you'll suffer. Eat a very little every hour for the rest of the day, then you won't suffer.

"This ship has been left in a hurry. She may have a bad leak in her. She may flood suddenly again and go down like a stone. The first thing we'll do, is to provision this boat against our having to take to her again. We'll see this time that she has abundant water and thoroughly mended topsides.

"The gear of this ship's crew is in the fo'c's'le there: you're not to loot it and fight for it. It's going to be whacked out to you: then each will have a share.

"Now this ship may sink. We may have to take to the boat again. On the other hand, we may be able to salve her. I believe that we can salve her.

"I believe that we can sail her home and dock her in London Docks, and perhaps even come home first and win the prize.

"Why not try for that? You know what sailorizing is, two pounds ten a month and hard going. If you salve this ship and bring her home each man's share may be a couple of hundred pounds. If you'll try for that, I'll promise you hard work, but such good treatment that you'll remember this ship for ever. What do you say? Shan't we sail her home?"

The men looked about sheepishly.

"Come boys," old Fairford said. "You're not going to hang back when Captain Trewsbury asks you. You've all seen him in the boat, a young officer up against it, and how he has thought for you. Why, I don't think any old sailor of you all would have thought more for you and brought you through better. I say, you may thank God for him. Shan't we sail this ship home with him and get our names up? Don't leave the race to the *Min and Win* and the *Natuna* and tripe of that sort."

"We'll sail her home, sir," Edgeworth said.

"We'll sail her home with you, sir," Rodmarton said.

"I wass say, sir," Efans said, "we wass not far from Fayal. I say we put into Fayal and claim to be sent home. We wass all shipwrecked men, look you. It wass our rights to be sent home, not to work our ways. Let a new crews ship, look you, in Fayal, yess, and we co home in the mail steamers, with a nurse at our pedsides."

"Fayal your Welsh grandmother," Kemble said.

"Shut your head about your rights. Are you going to do us all out of two hundred pounds?"

"I say the same as Efans," Stratton said, "I'm not going to be bullied out of my rights, because old walrus-whiskers believes he'll get salvage-money. We have a right to be taken to the nearest port and shipped for home."

"Come away from that," Tarlton said. "You and your right to be shipped for home! You may have a right to be shipped for home. Do you suppose you'll find a Consul who'll ship you home? Do you suppose the mail-ships haven't fixed it with the Consuls so that they shall not carry shipwrecked men? Lord, I've been shipwrecked. I thought, Lord save us, that I'd be sent home in a mail steamer, with a stewardess to ask if the sheets were aired. Did I get? Did I, hell? No, the Consul said to me, 'There's a fine ship in the bay short of hands. You can sign in her and get the advance; that's my last word to you, my man.' So I signed on board the 'fine ship': one of these down-easters put in with her topmasts gone. Hard? She worked her iron into me and out of me. And that's the kind of mail-steamer you'll get sent home in: a New Bedford whaler, put in with scurvy, who'll be at sea for the next three years as like as not."

"And that's God's truth," Kemble said. "We'll sail her home, Captain Trewsbury. If Stratton and Efans are set on going to Fayal, they can walk

there and count the milestones." He looked round
for support, and plainly had it from nearly all
there. Jacobson might have spoken up for Fayal,
but had had most of the devil knocked out of him
by the time in the boat. Bauer would have liked a
spree in Fayal, but the thought of a two-hundred-
pound spree in London was too much for him: the
others were for Cruiser. Young Coates spoke out
his mind, as was his way. "And I say we're damned
lucky, and the sooner we get her on her course, as
the Captain asks, I say the damned well better."

"Thank you," Cruiser said. "We'll try for the
London River. But bear in mind, that this ship
may go down on us. Stratton, Efans, and Jacobson,
you will put this ship's scuttle-butt into the boat,
and fill it with fresh water. Then you'll fill all the
buckets in the boat with fresh water. This time
we'll see that you do it. Mr. Fairford, will you
take Kemble forward, and whack out all the gear,
clothes and blankets and stuff, so that each man
has a fair kit? But before you go, Mister, I must
rearrange the watches a bit. Perrot, who is in my
watch, will be cook, and MacNab, who can't do
much except look-out and steward's jobs at present, will be steward, and look-out and lamp-man.
Nailsworth, I want you to be in my watch as
boatswain. Kemble, I want you to be boatswain in
Mr. Fairford's watch. You will both bunk in the

round-house. Chedglow, you will go to Mr. Fairford's watch.

"Nailsworth, and you Tarlton, you can get at the
boat in a short while, and give her a thorough overhaul; but the first thing is to fill the mainyards
and get this ship onto her course."

He was perhaps more thoroughly fagged than
anybody there, for he had had less rest, and all the
life in him had been given to put life into the
crowd. He felt dead-beaten, yet saw endless things
to be done. The fact that he was out of the boat,
even if it were to be only for a part of a day, was
such bliss that it was hard to keep from tears. He
felt that the first thing to do was to get the chronometers out of the boat to safety. "And I must
go through the Captain's things," he thought,
"and I must get the pumps rigged. And I must
take the sun, and give these fellows a course."

When he had stowed the chronometers safely,
he came on deck, where Mr. Fairford was serving
out the gear of the vanished crew, beginning with
the fine weather things. Mr. Fairford, helped by
Kemble and Edgeworth, was building up fourteen
little heaps of clothes. "Dungaree trowsers for
this fellow. A pair of dungaree trowsers here. Now
another pair here. That makes decency for all
hands; now the shirts and jumpers."

Cruiser called to the men who were hanging
about, to clap onto some of the gear and snug it

up: while they did this, singing out at the ropes, he went to the pump at the main-bitts. It was a strong winch pump, rigged with a traveller to the donkey-engine, and with hand brakes for six hands when steam was not being used. Rodmarton had said that it was jammed in the intake, which seemed to Cruiser to be likely. He took the winch-brake and hove upon it, and called to two hands to come to heave upon it. "Handsomely, now," he said. "Don't break anything."

They did not break anything, something was so jamming the action that the winch-brakes would not go round.

"Der tea was jam up der suck," Bauer said. Cruiser did not answer, because to him it felt as though something had jammed or broken in the mechanism close to the winch-brakes. He knew that the ship had had foul play, and that someone had wanted her to be sunk. Someone had cut through that pipe. Someone had removed the fire hoses from their handy racks on deck. Why should not somebody have wrecked the pump so as to finish his dirty job?

"Rodmarton," he said. "You're the best mechanic we've got. Go forward to the carpenter's shop and get what wrenches and spanners you can find. And Perrot, get forward, too, and get the galley fire lit. Chedglow, lay aft into the steward's pantry; you, too, MacNab and Coates, and get out some bully-beef tins, or soup-and-bully: make us a strong soup, Doctor, as soon as you can."

While Rodmarton brought the spanners, Cruiser brought some lanterns from the steward's pantry and called Rodmarton down into the 'tween-decks. The tea rose in a cone to the main hatch, but a space had been built clear round the main mast with strong shifting boards. Cruiser came to the shaft of the pump and held his lantern to it. "Look here," he said. "And look here, sir," Rodmarton said, stooping to the deck. "Here's all a kit of tools."

Just below the deck, at a height convenient for a man to get at the nuts and bolts, there was a strong iron clamping joint, which had been opened and still was open. Its nuts and bolts lay on the deck, methodically screwed together and so stowed in a kit-bag that they could not roll away. Having cast loose the joint, someone evidently a sailor, and a man of considerable strength had put a chain stopper on the plungers and bowsed the stopper well home to the main mast by means of a handy billy. Anyone trying to force the pump-brakes round from the deck above would be almost certain to smash the plungers across.

"Well, of all the wicked sights," Rodmarton said. "It looks as though someone might have done it a purpose."

"That was done on purpose," Cruiser said. "Surely you can see that. Now let's get to it."

He cast loose the hitch on the handy-billy fall, unhooked the tackle, and slowly and carefully removed the chain, which might have been a length of old topgallant sheet. The plungers did not seem to have been bent. The putter on of the stopper, whoever he was, had used so much chain that he had if anything overdone it and made a cushion of it.

"Whatever would he go for to do a thing like that for?" Rodmarton asked.

"He was up to no good," Cruiser said, as he began to re-fix the clamping-joint.

"Whoever could it have been?" Rodmarton asked.

"Strange things happen at sea," Cruiser said. As Rodmarton took the spanner to the nuts, Cruiser examined the tool-kit-bag that had been lying on the deck. He saw that they were new tools, in a new kit-bag: they looked to him like a set indented for by the Captain for the ship's use and only just out of store. As it occurred to him that the point would be important in any enquiry, he called Rodmarton's attention to them before he removed them.

When they were again on deck, he sounded the well. The leak still stood at three feet three inches. He had been on board for rather more than seventy minutes, during which the leak had not increased.

"Turn to here, half a dozen of you," Cruiser said. "Man this pump a moment. Heave round as handsomely as if you were walking on eggs. Handsomely does it."

They manned the brakes and very gently began to turn them round. After half a dozen turns the water spouted onto the deck and away into the scuppers. Cruiser took a place at the brakes, and felt for himself that the pump was working easily. "There it is," he said, "the pump is all clear. You can shift a ton of water in a minute and a half with her. You could free this ship in a couple of hours. But I'm not going to break your backs with pumping. Rodmarton, you go forward with Clutterbucke and see if you can get steam and rig the drive along."

He went to Fairford and told him the news. "Someone had jammed the pump," he said, "but had not wrecked it, luckily; perhaps he was afraid of making a noise. I'm getting steam, or hope to get it, and then we'll free her by the donkey. What I'm afraid of is, that there's some other leak that is being kept under by the pressure of the water, and that when we start freeing her, she'll fill again."

"As to that, sir, we might find the place and get a mat over it, or a sail into it, if it should be anything big. I would not worry, Captain Trewsbury: if we have to go back into the boat, we'll still be a lot better off than we were this morning. I suppose you haven't found anything to show, why they left her, sir?"

"Nothing at all. It's a mystery to me."

"If I might make a suggestion, sir, I would not lose time getting her to a course. No doubt this ship and the *Blackgauntlet* were leading the fleet, but others will be near, sir, if you'll forgive my saying so."

"Yes, I shall get her to her course, as soon as I've got a fix." He went aft into Captain Miserden's chart-room, just abaft the mizen mast; the door had been hooked open, and some of the drawers in the lockers were wide open and untidy. The Captain's sextant and barometer had gone: the tell-tale compass had gone from the ceiling. Cruiser noted these things with the mental comment, that both barometer and compass had been unscrewed, as though the desertion of the ship had been expected and prepared for at leisure. The log-book, meteorological log, abstract, and the ship's clearance papers had gone: also all the charts. Thrusting back the slide of the window, he reached for the log-slate hooked to the outer bulkhead. On the slate, someone had written with a bold sea hand:—

"D.R.2. Winds variable light NE
Sq with R."

There was no date to the entry, which might have
referred to a voyage made with Noah.

All the jottings and rough-books, all the tables
and logarithms that had been used in that room
until the day before in finding the ship's position,
had been removed. Cruiser took those that he had
used in the boat, worked up a hasty fix, that would
serve till he could check it by observation, then
having shaped a course, he prepared to go on deck.
As he was about to leave the chart-room, he noticed a little drawer underneath the mahogany
stand in which the water-carafe stood; he pulled
it open, thinking that it might contain some jottings of the ship's position. It did not: it contained
a pistol, with five chambers loaded. He put it into
his pocket and walked out on deck. "Man the
wheel here," he said. "Stand by, all hands."

At his orders, the great mainyards swung and
filled, the ship which had been kicking and buck-
ing for so long, steadied for a few instants, then
leaned in her roll, then leaned further, rolled
back a little, and then slid forward, so that a wave
splashed high at her bow and rolled over abaft
her waist and crumbled away into pale green
bubbles astern. The ship was on her course and
under way again.

There was a good deal to be done on deck, getting pulls on the braces and freshening the nips on nearly all the gear: it was fully half an hour before anyone had any leisure; but when the yards were trim, a little party of malcontents came aft together and hung about the booby-hatch waiting for Cruiser to notice them. He had seen them, indeed he had expected them, but for a little while he took no notice of them. They were Efans, in command, Stratton, second in command, Jacobson of the party because he was half-witted, and Bauer of the party because it offered some little variety to the life. They were coming aft "to see the Captain" in the time-honoured way. The rest of the crew were giving them no sympathy and in no way supporting them, yet it was plain that all hands knew what was toward. They were not hanging back in the jobs they were doing, indeed, all seemed to be suspiciously eager at them, yet all, without exception, had an eye on the group and on the Captain.

"Here are these four come-day-go-days wants to see you, sir," Fairford explained.

"I'll deal with them later, Mister," Cruiser said, going aft to look at the compass. He stood there an instant, looking now at the card, now at the mizen topgallant sail, full of wind and sharp-edged with it. "How is she, Edgeworth?" he asked the helmsman.

"Steering as easy as an old shoe, sir."

"The water in her is holding her down."

"Yes, sir, she's not herself."

"This is better than that ship's boat."

"Yes, sir," Edgeworth said. "You may just bet it is, sir." He watched the trim of the sails, and glancing aft at the stream of the wake judged that she was going about seven knots, and could be made to do more. There was exhilaration in feeling her striding away thus: the bliss of it after the boat was untellable. Yet he dared not give way to exultation, just behind the joy was still that spectre: "This ship has been abandoned in a hurry. She has her death about her and may even now go down like a stone."

He strolled quietly to the rail at the break of the poop and looked down at the party of growlers. "What's the matter?" he asked.

"This ship, sir, look you," Efans said. "It wass not right, sir, to take poor men to their teaths. This ship has peen apandoned, look you, full of water, yess. We will not work her, sir, no, unless you go for Fayal. We will not go to watery teath in her, it wass not right."

"No, sir," Stratton said. "We're not going to work her, unless you take her to Fayal and have her into dry dock." He nudged Bauer and Jacobson. Jacobson said nothing. Bauer said, "It was a tam shame to risk men's lives, so."

"If this ship leaks," Cruiser said, "so that she

is a danger, I shall sail her to her nearest port. If
not, she'll keep the course I set. And if you refuse
to obey my commands I'll shoot the whites out
of your eyes." He took the pistol from his pocket,
so that they could see it.

"Let me hear no more from any of you about
not working her. Get to the jobs I set you, putting
water into the boat. Get to it." They got to it:
Cruiser had the pleasure of hearing Efans say,
"Cot's sake, man Stratton, I nefer knew that he
had a pig pistol, nefer."

Stratton muttered something under his breath,
probably about some people being funny dogs, and
that was the end of the breeze; it had been what
old Fairford called "a bit of kite-flying to see
which way the wind set." Cruiser watched the
rebels till they had watered the boat, he then sent
the three of them to the royal yards to loose the
sails. By the time the royals were set and trimmed
it was time to take the sun. He got a good observation, worked out his position exactly, pricked
it off upon the chart, had the log hove and saw
that she was making eight knots. The Cook had
dinner, of sorts, for all hands at about noon, when
Cruiser's watch on deck began.

"Mr. Fairford," he said, as he took the deck,
"you can choose any cabin you like down below.
I shall keep the chart-room here for when I'm not

on deck, but as I have still some hope of a passage, I may not be much below."

"Perhaps I shan't be much either, sir," old Fairford said. "When one comes to be my age, one doesn't need as much sleep as one did, but I'll be glad of a watch below now, sir, I'll confess, after that boat."

After he had turned-in, Rodmarton reported the rigging of the drive, and the getting of steam. Cruiser came down to the main deck to watch the setting going of the pumps. The leak had not increased since the morning, it was still a steady three feet three.

"Had you much of a bother with the engine?" Cruiser asked.

"No, sir, none," Rodmarton said, "I know this engine like an old friend: and they've got all the spare parts put away in oil in the bosun's locker. I knew where to put my hand on everything. Captain Miserden always was very particular about the engine; he said it saved him an anchor once. She started up just like a bird."

"Still; go handsomely," Cruiser said.

The steam was applied, the drive throbbed along to the barrels, and in a moment the pump was flinging two jets of water onto the deck. The water came up brown with tea, for the lowest tiers of cargo were ruined. They watched it carefully, Cruiser anxiously, for he expected to hear a ripping crack from somewhere in the pump-box putting the pump out of action.

"I can't understand," he said, "why the man who tried to wreck the pump didn't drop a few spanners down the shaft, instead of securing the plungers."

"Perhaps he did, sir," Rodmarton said. "We shall very soon see."

However, there came no jolting, stripping final crash from inside the pump-box, the pump worked and the water gushed. Cruiser watched the well anxiously now, lest his fear should be justified, that the leak was controlled and held under by the weight of water in the ship. He expected a sudden inrush as the weight was lessened. He watched the leak dropping, to three feet, to two feet nine, then down to two feet, yet still no more came in; the water dropped regularly, so much pumping, so much decrease in the well, so many minutes of pump, so many inches less leak.

"I can't understand it," he said to himself. "They could have freed her. If they had made the least little search, they could have found the leak and the stopper on the pump. Who was it that wanted her put away, and contrived all this?"

He was desperately short-handed. With a man at the wheel there were six men to a watch and of those six one or two were weakly youths, and all were much the worse for being in the boat.

"What coal have you, Rodmarton?" he asked.

"I should think about three and a half ton in the forepeak, sir."

"Could you keep steam in her with that till we dock?"

"Yes, sir, enough to work the deck-capstan. You could swing the braces with the engine if you'd a mind to it."

Even so, that afternoon watch was hard work for the men on deck. The wind was fresh and fair, the ship going well before it under most of her plain sail, and going the livelier as the water came out of her. The gear aloft was good, yet with the ship moving as she was, the men were at it all the time, getting a small pull of this and that, or a better set on the other thing. Cruiser would gladly have set a foretopmast studding-sail, but thought it wiser to wait till the crew had had some more food and rest. By four bells in the watch the pumps sucked dry, the well was empty: by six bells he had satisfied himself that there was no more water coming into the ship. He sent Nailsworth with Rodmarton down to the cut pipe in the lazarette. There with some cement from the carpenter's shop they made a good job of the repair, so that it was as tight as a nut.

All through the rest of the watch, whenever the work of the ship gave him a moment's pause, he wondered at the change in his fortunes and at the reasons for it. He could see no reason why the ship should have been deserted: no amount of thought made the matter clearer to him.

"I must have some sleep, sometime," he said to himself; "then, when I have slept perhaps I may have some light on it, or find something that may explain it."

He had a word with Nailsworth towards the end of the watch. "What do you think of it, Nailsworth?" he asked. "Why was this ship deserted?"

"I cannot think, sir. It seems to me to lie between somebody's madness and somebody's wickedness. It has been very fortunate for us, sir."

"It has indeed."

"What would you recommend, Nailsworth, for men who have been through what we have been through?"

"Food and rest, sir. They won't expect much rest in a ship, for the work has to be done; but you could feed them up a bit, if there are the stores for it."

"Yes, I can do that. There are the stores."

He gave orders for a good supper for all hands. After his watch he turned-in in the chart-room for a blessed dog-watch of sleep which gave him a new lease of life. When he came on deck at four bells, just before sunset, he was told that a ship was in sight. Mr. Fairford was examining her through a telescope which he had found in the cabin of the mate.

"She's hull down, sir. I can't see what she is. A lofty ship; one of the China fleet, I should say. Will you take a look-see, sir?"

Cruiser took the telescope for a look. It was a good old glass, much the worse for wear and difficult to adjust. When he had focussed it, he saw the little smudge take a shape which he knew to be that of a ship with a skysail, and with studding sails set. He watched her for a minute or two, till he was satisfied that she was on the same course as the *Bird of Dawning*. He handed the glass back to Mr. Fairford.

"She's one of the fleet," he said. "She looks to me like the *Streaming Star*."

"I thought that, at first, sir," Fairford said, "Kemble thought she's the *Natuna*."

"We seem to be holding her."

"Yes, sir, she's not gaining. If they'd only stayed by her this ship would have been just about leading by twenty-four hours clear."

"She's in the first flight still," Cruiser said.

"Yes, sir, but short-handed as we are we can't drive her."

"Can't we?" Cruiser said, "we will though. Forward there, rig out your gear and get the fore-topmast stunsail set."

He drove her all through that night, with a

fair wind blowing fresh. When he came on deck
for the forenoon watch next morning, the water
was still blowing strong and true, heaping the sea
astern them, and wetting the foresail to the yard.
The ship was not in sight; it was a dirtier day
with a smudged horizon. She might have been
close to them and they none the wiser. They were
now tearing through it at ten knots an hour, under
conditions which shewed the *Bird of Dawning* at
her best. She liked a lot of wind on her quarter;
with that she would run at ease without strain,
"steady as the Scripture," old Fairford called it,
hardly filling a scupper as she ran.

Cruiser left the deck in charge of Fairford for
an hour, while he took a survey of the ship.

The well had no water in it, the only leak must
therefore have been the cut pipe. Perhaps some
thing or paper in the ship might shew why she
had been abandoned.

Coates had given him an account of the ship's
stores. As he had judged for himself in passing
through the lazarette, these were ample for the
passage home: some seven cwt. of bread, three
casks of salt pork, one cwt. of peas, 2 cwt. of rice,
150 lbs. of soup-and-bouilli, much Australian
tinned mutton, plenty of small stores, much mar-
malade, 200 lbs. of raisins, 1 cwt. of currants, some
gallons of lime juice, a cask of molasses, half a
cask of sugar and a cask of flour. In the captain's

private stores were jam, pickles, sardines, and a
tin of butter, which had gone across the equator
twice and may have lost some of its dairy fresh-
ness. There were also some tinned plum-puddings
and tongues. Altogether, there was ample food to
feed the survivors of the *Blackgauntlet* on double
rations to London River. The water in the tanks
was abundant. The boatswain's stores were also
abundant as the stores of a China clipper had to be.
She had rope, sails, canvas, small stuff, spare spars
and tar enough to take her round the world and
back.

Cruiser took the cabin-keys from the labelled
keyboard in the chart-room and went down into
the cabin, asking himself what manner of man the
Captain of the *Bird of Dawning* had been. He had
seen him and remembered him from the meeting
as a big, black-haired man with a white face and
a kindly manner. He had heard no ill spoken of
him except that he was "a religious man, fond of
his glass." All the captains in the China fleet were
religious men, and fond of a glass on occasion. Men
under Cruiser had sailed with Captain Miserden:
they had never seen him drunk nor the worse for
drink: but Cruiser had to answer the question why
the ship had been abandoned: drunkenness in the
Captain was one possible explanation. Cruiser felt
that he would begin with that.

At a first glance, it looked as though the Captain had been fond of a cocktail. There were two big glass carafes in the saloon, one containing rum, the other gin; by them were bottles of liquid sugar and orange bitters and two glasses containing swizzle sticks. Yet on examining the steward's stores account-book, which hung from a hook in the pantry, he found that the rum and gin in the ship at Foochow amounted to only twelve quart bottles of each, or barely enough to allow Captain and Mates one modest cocktail a day apiece. Certainly the Captain could not have been a drinker. Even the medical comforts contained only three dozen bottles of brandy, not more than two of which had been opened. It was among the medical comforts that Cruiser first found some suggestion of what Captain Miserden was.

All the stores were in excellent order, arranged in lockers on each side of the rudder shaft. The locker to port was the usual ship's medicine-chest with bandages, splints, dressings, and diagrams of men, clamped to cabin tables, undergoing simple operations; some thirty jars of drugs, and scales for weighing the same. The starboard locker at a first glance seemed to contain similar things, there were tins of arrowroot and of beef-jelly, a few tins of preserved milk, and a little ginger and camphor. The main bulk of the goods in this locker proved to be patent medicines for the Captain's private consumption. There were so many of these that Cruiser turned them out onto the cabin deck.

The first to come to hand was a box almost full of "Dr. Jenkinson's Cholera Powders, the only known specific for this Fatal Complaint". Next came a discreet bottle for Female Ailments, not otherwise described, and a large assortment of cheap medicines:—

Doctor Hoborow's Mixture for the Blood.

Old Doctor Gubbins's Liver Remedy, with a picture of old Doctor Gubbins being told by an Eminent Scientist that the Remedy was essential to Health.

Rhubarb Pills, for use in the Spring.

Dr. Mainspring's Mariner's Joy, for the most obstinate cases.

Bile Pills.

Liver Pills.

Dr. Primrose's Kidney Pellets, as prescribed by the famous Dr. Primrose to the unfortunate Queen of the French.

Dr. Gubbins's Spring Mixture, for the Blood.
"   "   Autumn   "   "   "   "
"These Sovereign specifics correct Nature in those difficult seasons when the Body politic is adjusting itself to changed conditions."

Nature's Remedy, "Vegetable Pills prepared from plants known to the Red Indians, who by their daily use attain to the ages of 100: even 120 being not uncommon."

Senna Tea, "two tablets dissolved in the cup that cheers ensures a happy household."

"The Salt of Life, being the active principle of Epsom and Glauber Salts extracted by a new process."

In addition to these, there were wrappers and empty boxes which marked where others had lain. "Dr. Gubbins's Nutrient Corrective, being a Medical Food derived from Active Vegetable Principles by the World Famous Lemuel Gubbins." There was a picture of Dr. Gubbins, who seemed to be a mixture of Euripides and the Duke of Wellington.

"Use Olopant and smile at Disease." A Mother of seven wrote to say that she had and did.

There were many, many others, most of which had been opened and tried: plainly Captain Miserden must have dosed himself with some of these remedies every day and night since his ship left England. "That is something to go upon, perhaps," he thought. "He had a bee in his bonnet about patent medicines." He turned his mind back to his one memory of Captain Miserden, that strange-looking, white-faced bright-eyed man who had spoken to him there in that cabin. "He looked a bit odd," Cruiser thought. "But then ship's captains often do look odd: it's a very lonely life."

There was nothing else in the lockers that shewed anything of the Captain's mind. There were some jars of ginger, and of lichees, some China ham and a few cases of nutmegs, which were no doubt his own private venture: there were also about two piculs of tea, carefully stowed at the ship's side, either a private venture, or brought as gifts to friends. There was nothing in all this to shew why the ship had been deserted. Why, in the name of wonder, had she been deserted?

The slop-chest was the next thing examined. It was in one of the little cabins off the alleyway. It had been neatly kept. All the stores were in pigeon-holes, marked with tickets that shewed the contents and the quantity remaining. Though the ship was homeward-bound, the slop-chest contained a fair number of articles, pipes, tobacco, matches, foul-weather clothing, south-westers, knives, shoes, etc., not yet taken up. Cruiser helped himself to several things of which he stood in need. There was a neatly-kept account book of the slops. Cruiser, looking through it, saw that Rodmarton's brother had drawn a pound of tobacco from them only three days before.

"There'll be nothing down here," Cruiser thought to himself. "I'd better search the chart-room."

He went up again to the little hard, bare, chart-room which still seemed haunted by Captain

Miserden. He had looked through the upper drawers in the lockers there, when hoping to find instruments, charts or the ship's log. These had all been removed; but there were other lockers in the cabin, under the settee, and these he had not yet looked at. He pulled open one. It contained a few blue linen handkerchiefs, some writing pads and pencils, a box of dividers, a pair of protractors, a little French guide to Navigation, and a cardboard box containing spare sextant mirrors done up in tissue paper. He shut this drawer and opened another, wondering where the Captain had kept his clothes. "I suppose," he thought, "I suppose his steward has them in some locker down below."

The second drawer contained a row of books, placed backs upward along the drawer so as to chock each other. These books had seen a good deal of service, they were much used, and had been more than once in salt water. Cruiser took out the first volume which came to hand: it had not been thrust well home into the row and seemed indeed to be offering itself to his hand. It was a mean sort of book in a bad binding and ill print. He opened it at the title page and read:—

Habakkuk Unveiled.
Mudde.

On the flyleaf was the Captain's signature, in a

bold flowing well-formed sea-hand, R. Miserden, Capt. 1857, with a note below, in fainter ink:

"I bought this Book for my Eternal Salvation at the house of the Prophet, 27 Seacole Lane, Millwall, on my 35th Birthday—R.M."

On the title page, the purpose of the book was declared.

Habakkuk Unveiled.
being an Interpretation of the Prophecies
Concerning the Destruction of the World
Now shortly to happen
The whole being a Revelation of the Prophet's Mission
granted in Vision to the Prophet's Follower
Ebenezer Mudde
of the First church of Habakkuk. The year of
Wrath, 1853.

He glanced at the book, which contained a fiery doctrine about the coming end of the world. Miserden had read it very carefully, with ejaculations pencilled in the margin, such as "Lord grant it". "O that I may see it". "Hark to truth" etc. Under one fiery passage at a chapter ending he had written "This light is too blinding." Cruiser looked at the light according to Ebenezer Mudde. He read, "Already the brimstone is prepared, the tow teased and the powder of blasting mealed. The first trumpet has blown, the second is about to blow. At the third, the flame shall be put to the heap, and then too late the wretches of this world will hold their hands to Habakkuk, who will answer them with fearful justice, 'Too late.' "

The next book was The Form of Prayer to be used at the Visitations of the Fire in the gatherings of the First Church of Habakkuk, as Revealed to the Prophet's Follower, Ebenezer Mudde. Towards the end of this book were printed metrical versions of the Book of Habakkuk arranged to be sung to well-known tunes, and at the end some blank pages, into which Captain Miserden had entered jottings of Ebenezer Mudde's sermons:—
"E. M. spoke with much Fire on H. III. 7. searching words, wh convinced F of being in the Prophet's Wrath."

"F fasted till she was conscious of Fire."

"Very conscious of Fire."

"Comfortable sermon from E. M. on the second Trumpet."

"E. M. on the supping up of the East Wind. O that such words should not be in every sinful heart."

"F and I fasted and put on white raiment expecting the Second Trumpet this day."

The next book was called

Habakkuk Takes Horse

For a Ride of Denunciation through the Land of Dagon, being England.

A Word of the Preparation for
The Second Trumpet
Now about to blow.
by
Ebenezer Mudde, F.P. (follower of the Prophet).
The 7th year of the wrath of Habakkuk.

The next was a printed account of the Revelation of Habakkuk to his handmaid Fraterna Miserden, who after long being the devoted wife of Roger Miserden, sea captain, and a faulty follower of the Prophet, received by Visitation the Revelation of the Prophet, and put aside carnal life that she might persuade others to the eternal truth of the fire. It was a slim little book with a ghastly engraving of Fraterna woodenly persuading others.

The next books were note-books containing jottings by Captain Miserden over a term of years.

"Called on the Prophet, who at last vouchsafed the South East trades."

"Habakkuk bade me stand in with the land, against my carnal judgment; on standing in, lo, I had the landwind, which brought us clear of the Swatows."

"All hands scraping paintwork, this being the Prophet's Direct Command to me R.M."

"Spoke the *Thermopylæ* and *Forward Ho*. Spoke to Mr. Todd about the church. He seemed impressed."

"N.B. to labour with Todd."

"Lent Mr. Todd the word according to the Follower. Shall labour with him till he perceive the Fire."

"Laboured with Mr. Todd at supper. The Prophet visited me this even, carrying away the mainstunsail boom and splitting the sail."

"Mr. Todd again. A stony soil. But fire shall consume even stones. All hands at paintwork."

"Finished the main deck. Fasted for a fair wind."

"Scourged myself with the lesser scourge for a fair wind as well as for Mr. Todd's soul."

"Hopes of Mr. Todd's soul before we sight the Bishops."

"The Prophet directed me to tack ship against my carnal judgment. Lo, within three hours, Mr. Todd desired more doctrine and spoke of promptings of the Fire. Finished the poop with a second coat of oil."

"The Prophet vouchsafed such wind as makes me hope we may win yet. Scourged against carnal man. Drank one half pint of Dr. Gubbins' Mixture against the same. The *Thermopylæ* (?) hull down astern."

"Mr. Todd desires to meet the Follower. O joyful day. Directed the Sailmaker to play the Accordion in the dogwatch."

There were several of these books. Cruiser

glanced through them hurriedly. They convinced him that Captain Miserden had for years been a follower of a strange ecstatic: and that his religion was a very real thing to him, and that it had led to a voluntary separation from his wife. Apparently he did not often try to convert his officers, only now and again, when there was some chance of success! It seemed however that the sailmaker and the carpenter were both followers of Mr. Mudde. Cruiser wondered whether this odd religious belief, with its scourgings, its ecstasies, its use of violent medicines, added to the loneliness of a sea captain's life, had not turned Captain Miserden's brain.

The last book in the drawer was a photograph album with a thickly embossed cover, clasped with a brass clip. Cruiser opened it. There were a few photographs in it of Fraterna Miserden, and of her parents, all looking stiff and grim in their best clothes. Later in the book were photographs of a strange-looking man, with long gray hair and beard. From his look, Cruiser judged that he had some narrow intensity but small intelligence, he had the look of sect and of authority. Somehow Cruiser seemed to have seen the face leaning over some small counter, selling grocery. The figure was dressed to the waist in the black of Sunday coat and waistcoat. Over his trousers he wore something between a Masonic apron and a kilt. There was a figure painted or embroidered upon this robe: it represented Habakkuk brandishing three arrows with his right hand, while with his left he offered a scroll to a little kneeling man. Underneath this portrait was written "Ebenezer Mudde, F.P. to his Brother in the Fire, Roger Miserden." Two pages later in the book there was a photograph of a tiny brick conventicle somewhere not far from docks, for the masts of ships shewed in it, with this same figure, topped by a tall hat and without the apron, standing with Roger and Fraterna Miserden, and with a third somewhat aloof figure, who might perhaps have been Mr. Todd.

"That is as much as I'm likely to know," Cruiser thought, "but there may be more somewhere. If the Prophet directed him to cut through the intake pipe and choke the pump and persuade all hands to abandon ship, he would certainly have done it. That seems the likeliest explanation yet."

He found nothing else to explain the abandonment. The ship had abundant food, water and stores: she was in good order aloft: her crew, as far as they could tell, was complete and in health till the day they left her; her hull was sound; her cargo in trim. Suddenly someone had determined to sink her and had contrived to scare all hands out of her. It seemed to Cruiser that nobody but the Captain could have had the power to do this.

A memory of a line in Shakespeare came to him: "It is too hard a knot for me to untie". He had to leave it at that.

He found the Captain's wardrobe at last in one of the disused cabins in the alleyway: all his go-ashore things were there, laid up with camphor in tissue paper, including his tall hat. With them, were some withered yellowed flowers tied up in a faded satin bow. Cruiser thought that perhaps they had been carried by Fraterna on her wedding day.

Going on deck, he called Rodmarton. "Tell me," he said, "when you were with Captain Miserden, was he a religious Captain? Did he preach on Sundays and hold a service?"

"No, sir. He always gave us Sundays. He held a little prayer-meeting on Sundays, but only the Carpenter and the Sailmaker used to go. People said it wasn't true religion."

"Did you know a Mr. Todd?"

"Yes, sir: he was mate in her."

"What sort of a man was he?"

"A fine seaman at sea, sir: but he always got drunk ashore, and then he would tell Captain Miserden off."

"In what way?"

"He used to shout out: 'That's Captain Miserden, that is. Gubbins' got his body, and Mudde's got his soul. Hey, Captain Miserden, have you got the Fire yet?' We never knew what he meant. The Captain stood it very well, sir; he never answered a word, but he would talk to Mr. Todd when he was sober, and then Mr. Todd used to weep."

Cruiser thought over this for a while, then he walked across to Nailsworth.

"Nailsworth," he said, "did you ever hear of a ship's captain going mad?"

"Yes, sir," Nailsworth said, "and in a trade like the China trade it is even common. It is a solitary life, sir, without any relaxations or companionships, and on the passage home, when the rule is 'never to undress between pilots' and never to leave the deck for more than half an hour, the mental strain is very great, especially if the winds fail or are foul. My impression is, sir, that half the clipper captains are a little mad."

"Thank you, Nailsworth," Cruiser said. He looked Nailsworth in the eye and knew that he was talking to a doctor. Why was he not still a doctor? He could not ask him. Cruiser was now a clipper captain, leading a solitary life, and driving a big ship for the prize.

Within two days, the ship's company had recovered their strength and had settled down to the ship's routine. They were short-handed, according to the ideas of that time, for the rule of one foremast hand to every hundred tons, though customary throughout the next generation, was not then dreamed of. Cruiser nursed his scanty crew. He fed them liberally, spared them when he could, and contrived new leads to much of the gear, so that all heavy work could be done by the capstan or the engine. Still, even with no painting to do, and the tarring-down put off until another voyage, the work of the ship was very severe to watches of only six men each. On the second day, the wester, which had been blowing steadily, increased in strength and blew a full true gale, with abundant rain keeping down the sea. They ran before this, day after day, in exultation, striding over an expanse of two thousand miles across. Presently, it became blind going, so that they went by log and a guess; yet still the wind increased, till Mr. Fairford looked grave and old Kemble shook his head. Mr. Fairford coming up to Cruiser as the night closed in suggested that if anything were coming in, it would be handled more easily in daylight. Cruiser had not been below for more than twenty minutes at a time for a week. He had slept, if at all, in a hammock slung under the weather mizen pin-rail; the exultation of the wind and the going had entered into him; he shook the rain from his face and grinned back at Fairford.

"Take anything in," he said. "I was just thinking if we couldn't set a royal."

Fairford was too old a sailor to say anything: he looked at the royal mast, and looked to windward, and looked at Cruiser.

Fairford said nothing more about shortening sail. He made one more suggestion: "I suppose you wouldn't care for a cast of the lead, sir, about midnight to-night? We should be about on Soundings, wouldn't we?"

"We're all right," Cruiser said. "Why, Mister, you couldn't have the heart to stop her, could you?"

"It's a good slant, sir," Fairford said. "But blind going's bad going, if you ask me."

"She's all right, Mister."

"Very good, Captain Trewsbury." Fairford walked to the break of the poop. Efans, the sea-lawyer, was talking to Stratton. "These poys, look you, they wass not prudent men: they take the sticks clean out of her, as sure as Cot's my uncle."

All night long she drove before the thrust of the wester, in a succession of staggering and surging leaps that sent the crests of the waves flying white before her. At midnight she was running twelve, at two, thirteen, and at the changing of the watch fourteen knots. Though she had ever steered easily, she was now more than one man's task: the lee wheel was manned, and kept busy.

At five in the morning Cruiser turned out after an hour of uneasy sleep in his hammock to find the ship roaring on up Channel in the breaking darkness, a high gray Channel sea running under a wild heaven, and the teeth of the waves gleaming out from the gray. He lurched to the mate, who was forward, putting an extra tackle on the fore-tack. When the tack was home, he asked:

"Have you picked up any light, Mister?"

"No, sir, all blind as you see."

"Well, we must be there or thereabouts."

"Yes, sir. It's been a good slant."

"Get a hand aloft when it lightens a bit; he may be able to see the land."

"Very good, Captain Trewsbury." The mate hesitated for a moment, then said:

"If you please, sir, we're doing more than fourteen, and we haven't had a sight for four days. We're well into the Channel: and thick as it is we may be on top of anything before we see it."

"No: keep her going," Cruiser said. "Our luck's in. We'll not throw it away."

"Very good, Captain Trewsbury."

The ship was running on, with the same desperate haste, an hour later when Trewsbury returned. It was now in the wildness of an angry morning, with a low, hurrying heaven and leaping sea, that shewed green under the gray, and rose and slipped away with a roar. The ship was careering with an aching straining crying from every inch of her, aloft and below. Her shrouds strained and whined and sang, the wind boomed in her sail, the sheet blocks beat, the chain of their pendants whacked the masts. All the mighty weight of ship and cargo heaved itself aloft, and surged and descended and swayed, smashing the seas white, boring into and up and out of the hills and the hollows of the water, and singing as she did it, and making all hands, as they toiled, to sing.

"Run, you bright bird," Trewsbury said, "that's what you were born to."

There was no chance of a sight with that low heaven: the man aloft could see nothing: all hands were on deck getting the anchors over. There came a sudden cry from them of "Steamer, dead ahead."

She must have seen them on the instant, and ported on the instant, enough to clear. Cruiser saw her as it were climbing slowly and perilously to port for twenty seconds: then as he leaped for the signal flags to ask "Where are we?" she was surging past close alongside, a little gray coastal tramp, with a high bridge over her central structure, butting hard into it with a stay foresail dark with wet to steady her, and her muzzle white to the eyes. As she had just fired, a stream of black smoke blew away and down from her, with sudden sparks in it, as Cruiser thought. Cruiser saw two figures in yellow oilskins staring at them from behind the dodger. He knew well with what admiration and delight those sailors stared. Then the little coaster's stern hove up in a smother, as her head dipped to it, and she was past and away, with one man behind the dodger waving a hand. The reek of her smoke struck Cruiser's nostrils; then she was gone from them, her name unknown.

The mate was at Cruiser's side.

"That shows you how we're in the fairway, sir," he said, "we may be on top of something at any minute. We've only a minute to clear anything, in this."

"I know it."

"Yes, sir."

"Did you ever know of a China clipper throwing away a fair wind in soundings?"

"No, sir."

"Did you ever hear of a China clipper being sunk in the Channel when running?"

"No, Captain Trewsbury, and I don't want to be the first."

"Well, I do want to be the first, Mister, and I mean to be it, the first to London Docks, if you understand. And to get there, I have to use whatever chance throws in my way. It's going to break, presently."

There came a hail from the main cross-trees, where the look-out had a speaking trumpet. "Ship on starboard bow." They turned to look at her,

and Cruiser who was ready now ran up the signal
flags of "What is my position?"

As the flags blew out clear the ship hove up
alongside. She was a big full-rigged ship, painted
black, and very loftily rigged with skysail yards
on all three masts. She was now under her fore
and main lower topsails and fore topmast staysail,
beating her way down Channel. She was streaming
with glittering water. At each 'scend the sea ran
white along her rail, which bowed to it and lipped
it in. Then, out of the pause, the bowed fabric
seemed to dive forward, though with difficulty.
Cruiser saw the watch gathered on the poop, all
staring: even the man at the wheel was staring.
The ship beat past them on a lurching leap, her
maindeck full and spouting, no one answering the
signal, not even acknowledging it.

"There's discourtesy," the mate said. "She
wouldn't even dip her colours."

"She never saw our signal," Cruiser said. "She's
an outward-bounder, with everything on top and
nothing to hand. Besides she was watching us."

"We must be well worth the watching, sir," the
mate said, moving away. To himself, as he moved,
he added "and I hope all who meet us will watch
out for us."

It grew lighter in the sky, but no lighter to
landward, they were running in a blind and moving seascape not a thousand yards across, all cloud

and water, both mad. The ship strode into it, and streaked her way across it, smashing onto the grayness a track of a paleness and a greenness of many million bubbles, over which the petrels scuttered.

Where they were Cruiser did not know and did not much care. The exultation that was so movingly in the ship was in himself. They were getting up Channel with a marvellous slant, and who could tell that they were not leading the fleet? It would clear up presently, and they would see where they were, or pass something that would tell them.

"Forward there," he called. "Up there two of you, and get a good burton on the foreyard. Lively now, I'm going to give her a stunsail."

"Burton on the foreyard: ay, ay, sir."

He turned to the helmsmen. Coates, who had the weather spokes, was enjoying it; he loved to see a ship driven; but Bauer at the lee wheel was scared.

"How is she, Coates?" he asked.

"She's begun to be a bit kittenish," Coates said, "but nothing to hurt, sir."

"You're keeping a good course. You can steer, Coates."

"Yes, sir. And she can kick, I tell you."

"Keep your eyes forward, Bauer," Cruiser said. "There's nothing for you to look at behind you."

There was, though. There was a toppling, toppling running array of heaping water ever slipping over at the top.

"If you let her broach-to, Bauer," he said, "you'll be the first man drowned and the last man God will forgive and that's what you'll get by it."

Bauer smiled a sickly smile and licked his dry lips and said "Yes, sir."

"All ready the burton, forward?"

"All ready, sir."

"Bowse it well taut." He went forward to see to the setting of the sail.

As the courses of the *Bird of Dawning* were very deep as well as square, the lower studding sail was a great sail, needing much care in the setting, in such a wind as was blowing. The boom was run forward and guyed. All hands mustered to the job. They well knew that if it were not done smartly, the sail would go. A wild sea spread from under their feet into the hurrying cloud; but those there felt, from the push of the rain that came down upon them, that the grayness was about to go. The rain that had streamed from all things relented suddenly and died into a pattering.

"Let her go," Cruiser called. The tackles skirled as the men went away with them; he paid out the tripping line as they ran. The boom dipped under as it went and the great sail darkened with the wet half up it. As the stops came adrift, the sail lifted and strove to flog itself clear, but the checks of the gear came onto it and stayed it. One instant before it had been a bulge of canvas, flapping at folds where the wind could catch it, now it was a straining curve of sail, held by check and counter-check, leaning like a wing to the ship over all that hurry of leaping sea. She put down her foot, and the foot of the sail stooped into it, as a gull stoops upon the wing. She rose, with the water dripping from the scoop, and again plunged and arose shaking.

"That's got her where she lives," Clutterbucke said. "That's made her lift her feet."

"Just as well she's got that burton on her yard-arm."

The effect on the ship was instantaneous. She had been leaping, now she seemed to lift from sea to sea, and to tread down their crests into sub-jection.

"I think she'll stand a topmast stunsail," Cruiser said to himself.

He went aft to watch the steering, which was grown the livelier for the sail. From the poop, he had a new impression of the power of her drive: she was swooping and swerving, like a thing alive; in fact, she was a thing alive: she had ceased to be wood and iron, laden with cases: she was some-thing of the spirit of the wind, and of the kindled wit of man, that laughed as she flew.

Suddenly, as he stood by the wheel, watching

her head, and letting his eyes run aloft to the curves of the leeches under strain, the grayness in the heaven parted as though the sheets had given, with the effect of a sail suddenly let go and clued up. The cloud tattered itself loose to windward and rived itself apart, and blue sky shewed and spread. Instantly, a blueness and a brightness came upon the water. To leeward before them the storm passed away like a scroll. There, to port, far away, was the Chesil Beach, with the Needles beyond it, and the far and faint line of England, stretching astern to the Start. The sun appeared, and beauty came with him, so that all the tumbling and heaping brightness rejoiced.

One of the first things revealed, was a fine clipper ship two miles ahead, lying almost the same course. On the starboard quarter, perhaps two miles away, another lofty ship came racing up Channel, and far astern, a third shewed. This third was perhaps not one of the China fleet.

"We've turned into the straight," Cruiser said. "There seem to be three left in it."

"Yes, sir," Fairford said, "unless the race is already won."

"We'll learn soon enough if it's already won," Cruiser said. "Get a tackle on the yard-arm there," he called. "All hands set studding sails." The mate and the men marvelled, but they leaped to the order. They were now as keen as Cruiser to bring their ship home. Not a man thought that perhaps the race had been already won by someone; to them the race was now beginning.

Cruiser was on the fo'c's'le head with the telescope trying to make out the ship ahead. Under the tapering clouds of sail he could see a dark green hull, with an old-fashioned transom look about her stern. She could be no other than the *Caer Ocvran*. She had been running with prudence, not knowing where she was; now that the sky had cleared she was making sail.

"All ready, the foretopmast stunsail, sir," Mr. Fairford reported, adding under his breath, "If you think she'll stand them, sir."

"No time for prudence now," Cruiser said, "hoist away there—lively now."

One at a time, the mighty wings of studding sail swayed aloft and shook themselves out of their bundles with a roaring into service. Cruiser saw the topsail yard lift and the booms buckle as the strain came upon them; but the gear held. A whiteness boiled along the *Bird's* side and flew in a sheet over the waist as she felt the new power given to her. Cruiser watched for a minute, standing well forward, eyeing the straining booms. "They'll hold," he thought, "as long as the wind keeps steady and the helmsmen behave." He crossed the fo'c's'le and eyed the ship ahead. She had set her lower studding sail, and no doubt was setting more, as fast as the men could move, but the *Bird of Dawning* seemed sailing two feet to her one.

He watched for half a moment; Fairford and others were at his side, staring.

"Ah, she's holding us," Fairford said suddenly. "Yes, she's holding us. There go her topmast studding sails: beautifully done, too. She's got forty hands at stations. It's something to have a full crew."

"We've got twelve," Cruiser said. "Twelve good men upset the Roman Empire. Get the topgallant stunsails on her."

The men ran to it: he slipped aft with the telescope, partly to con the ship, partly to see what the ship astern might be. He steadied the glass against a mizen shroud and stared at the ship astern. She was on the starboard quarter, and plainly much nearer than she had been. She was not more than a mile and a half away. Not much of her shewed except a tower of leaning sail, winged out with studding sails, a jib-boom poising and bowing, and a roll of white water under her bows. He broke off from his staring to rate Bauer at the lee wheel. "Never mind what's astern of you," he called. "Watch your steering or you'll have the masts out of her and we'll skin you alive."

He looked again at the ship astern. Someone forward had said that she was the *Min and Win*.

He was satisfied that she was not the *Min and Win*, but a much bigger and newer ship, the *Fu-Kien*, commanded by a reckless dare-devil known as Bloody Bill China. "Well, what Bill can carry, we can drag," he said, so he leaped down into the waist, to the job of getting more sail onto a ship that already had plenty.

"Doctor, there," he called to Perrot, "and you, Chedglow, get breakfast along on deck. Chedglow get tongues and sardines and what you like out of the stores: the best there is. Hands must breakfast as they can, on deck, three at a time." He watched the setting of the new sail and its effect upon the ship. She was holding her own now, perhaps gaining a very little on the *Caer Ocvran*, and hardly losing to the *Fu-Kien*.

"She's gaining on us, though," Cruiser muttered. He could see now, plainly, her anchors over the bows dripping brightness whenever she rose from the sea. "Well, I'll try what the skysail will do. Up there, one of you, and loose the skysail."

They loosed and hoisted it, and had the sight of the pole bending like a whip of whalebone to the strain. Bill replied by loosing his main skysail, which blew away in the setting. They raced on now hardly changing position. All hands in all three ships had all that they could do: getting a pull here, a pull there, a better set on this and a better trim to the other. Even Stratton, sullen as he was, seemed interested in the race, even Efans forgot his rights, in the thought of how much better Captain Duntisbourne would have handled her. They raced in the laughing morning, while the coast slipped by them, all the landmarks long looked for.

With blown-down streamers of smoke, a squadron of iron-clads moved across the sea in front of them, going in line ahead from Spithead under steam with no canvas set. They were in a beam sea, making heavy weather of it, they laboured exceedingly, streaming like the half tide rock, yet keeping station. The sailors commented on their order aloft, the yards squared to a T, the bunts triced up with jiggers into perfect cones and secured with black gaskets a foot across. Two of them were barque-rigged, with double topsail yards. Cruiser dipped his colours to them, and then with rapid hoists of flags asked if the China Race had already been won. There were no code hoists for this question: he had to spell it and was not sure of being understood. One of the ships hoisted the negative pennant, or so he thought, but he could not be sure, as the flag was blowing away from him, and even if it were the pennant he thought that it might be some private naval signal, or even a refusal to answer.

Cruiser had had prepared for two days on the poop a contrivance for sending letters and tele-

grams ashore in case of luck or need. He had
lashed to a ship's life-buoy in upright positions
two blue and white boat-flags, which the *Bird of
Dawning's* boats had borne in the Foochow Re-
gatta. He had then bent to the buoy a long line of
small stuff ready to lower it over the side. To this
buoy, he now lashed with great care two bottles of
brandy, frapped with bagwrinkle, and a canvas
packet, sewn up in oilskin, which contained a sovereign, presumably the only coin on board, that
had been found in Captain Miserden's trowser
pocket, and an urgent appeal to the finder to send
two telegrams there plainly written out, ready to
be sent.

Soon after the iron-clads had passed, a big
smack, under a reefed mainsail and jib, hove up,
all gleaming, ahead. She was crossing their bows,
making for some point on the Hampshire coast.
It was what Cruiser had most longed for, during
that morning. He signalled to her with a red
weft that he wished to speak, and luckily the fish-
erman understood, and hove up into the wind with
a shaking sail to let the *Bird of Dawning* pass.

As the great ship surged by, Cruiser in the
mizen rigging shouted to the smack through his
speaking trumpet asking them to send off the telegrams. He pointed to the buoy, which the mate
smartly lowered to the sea and paid out upon.
They saw the buoy lift high on the sea, with its

flags blowing clear, and in an instant it was tossed away upon the following surge to the smack's bows. A man leaned over with a boat-hook, fished for it, caught it and hove it inboard, then bent over it as the sail filled. Cruiser saw the bottle pass from hand to hand while the skipper looked at the writing. The skipper presently waved vigorously to shew that he understood.

"I only hope that he does understand," Cruiser thought, "and that nobody else has worked the same traverse." One telegram was to the London and Dover Tug Company to have two tugs for the *Bird of Dawning* off the South Foreland, the other was to his brother, now a young lawyer in London, to meet the ship in the Downs and advise about the claims for salvage.

"Mike is the only lawyer I know," Cruiser thought, "and I've been abroad for a year: if he should have died, I shall be up a gum-tree."

As he had expected, the change of the lifting of the gale brought with it a lessening of the wind, and a shifting of it to two points to the northward. All three ships now had set every sail that they could carry, to the royal studding sails and trust-to-gods. Cruiser had guyed out a boom below the jib-boom and had set a spritsail: Bloody Bill China had bonnets on his courses and contrivances that he called puffballs in the roaches of his topsails. What the *Caer Ocvran* was doing they could not clearly see, she was almost dead ahead of them. The three ships were drawing nearer to each other, the *Caer Ocvran* coming back, the *Fu-Kien* coming on. If the race had not been already won by some ship in ahead of them it was the finest finish seen since the China prize was raced for.

An outward-bound ship came ratching past with the sprays like clouds of smoke at her bows. Her mate and various boys were on her fo'c's'le at work: they all knocked off to see those racers, no such sight had been seen in the Channel, as those three driven clippers making the utmost of the day. Cruiser signalled to her an urgent signal, and asked, spelling the hoists, "Has any China ship arrived yet?" He could see the ship's captain with a couple of boys busy at the signal halliards, acknowledging each hoist. The answer, when they made it, was the affirmative pennant without any ship's number, to show the winning ship.

"So we're beaten to it then, sir," Fairford said. "I wonder if the *Natuna* got it."

Cruiser stared after the now receding ship, now being spoken by Bloody Bill, to whom she gave nothing but her own number, the *Inkerman* of London, and a dipped ensign.

"I don't believe she understood," Cruiser said, "and I'm not going to take that as gospel. We'll race these two ships at least."

Still, something of the zest was gone from the

contest when he thought that after all another ship might have docked even a couple of days before, and now lay discharging, with a gilt cock at her masthead. Then as the day drew on, the tide slackened and the wind dropped and shifted still more to the north: it gave them a beam sea and much anxiety for their gear, which held, but only just held.

At one that afternoon, as they passed Beachy all three ships began to feel the turn of the tide, the flying kites had to come in lest they should pitch the spars away. Then in little short spells of twenty minutes the wind would lull and the kites would be set again; and in this kind of sailing Bloody Bill China had an advantage: as Cruiser could see, he had the boys aloft in the tops all the time ready to race up to loose the light sails or take them in. He was creeping up a little and a little, and was now only about a mile astern, having gained certainly a mile and a half in five hours. In another five hours the *Fu-Kien* would be half a mile ahead having the pick of the tugs at the South Foreland. The *Caer Ocvran* was at a slight disadvantage, being not quite so happy in fresh or clearing weather as in light airs. However, her Captain was fighting for every inch she lost. Cruiser with his small crew had only the miracle of the ship in his favour. He felt more and more keenly every instant that the ship was the best ship in the race. In other voyages she may not have been so: in this race all had conspired together, her builder and some happy combination in her trim, to make her supreme, but now she was short of hands, unable to do her best.

A darkness gathered into the heaven astern of them as the secondary moved up. The hours of the afternoon dragged by as the ships strained up Channel, all drawing nearer, all watched by thousands ashore who now guessed that those three moving beauties were the clippers of the China fleet.

Just off the Fairlight a little steamer, going with coals for Fowey, edged close in to the *Bird of Dawning*, so as to have a good look at her. Cruiser hailed her through the trumpet.

"Ahoy, there, the *Chaffinch*, what China ship won the Race?"

"No ship," the *Chaffinch's* skipper shouted back. "You are the Race. Go in and win."

"Thank you," Cruiser shouted, "is that straight?"

"Yes. Get to it. Knock the bastards silly."

This was greeted with a cheer from all hands: they had a chance still.

There came a sudden hurrying, grayness astern: it sent before it a hissing noise which put Cruiser's heart into his boots. He shouted out "Let go your royal halliards. Stand by topgallant braces," and

had let fly the main royal halliards as a rain squall
swept over them and blotted out ships, sea and land
in a deluge that filled the scuppers. Out of the
deluge there came wind in a gust that tore the
flying royals into tatters. Something more than
the royals went, the topgallant stunsails went at
tack and halliards, blew out in the rain like dirty
flags, flogged once, twice and away, with whips of
their gear lashing round anything they touched.
The masts bent, the yards curved at the arms under
the pull of the sheets, and the ship leaped forward
as though suddenly lashed.

The men ran to the gear: nothing more was lost:
the split sails were cleared and new ones bent but
not set. The rain made a darkness about them for
twenty minutes, during which Cruiser had two
men on the fo'c's'le looking out.

As the squall cleared off, the sun drawing to the
west, shone out and made a rainbow upon its darkness. Under the arch of colours, they saw the *Caer
Ocvran* not two hundred yards from them on the
starboard bow. She seemed to be stuck there in
tossing waters that whitened about her in a great
bubble.

Through the glass, Cruiser could plainly see her
Captain, pacing his weather poop, glancing quickly
aloft and at the *Bird of Dawning*. "Ah, yes, sir,"
Fairford said, as he watched, "you can glance, and

you can curse the helmsman, but the *Bird of Dawning's* got you beat to the wide."

"That's Captain Winstone," Cruiser said. "He was mate of the *Bidassoa* when I was in her. Look at that, now: did you ever see a ship so wet?"

"She's famous for it, sir; the *Caer*; a fine ship, too."

Presently they were abreast of her, and forging ahead upon her, so that they could see her in her glory. She had a straight sheer and a transom stern, having been built upon the lines of the famous French frigate, *L'Aigle*. In a light air, no ship of her time could touch her, and she could run with the swiftest. She had a name through the seven seas for being wet: her decks now were running bright: for she was a caution in a head sea. They were watching and tending her now, getting some of her after-sail off her to keep her from burying her bow. Cruiser dipped his colours to her as he passed, but would not hail his old captain. As he drew clear, he saw her famous figurehead of Queen Gwenivere bowing down into the smother, then rising and pausing, then plunging down till the fo'c's'le-rail was lipping green.

"Look at that," Cruiser said. "Did you ever see a ship pitch like that?"

As he spoke, she took a deeper 'scend than usual, and rose with a snapped stunsail boom lifting on a loose wing.

The *Fu-Kien* drew clear of the *Caer Ocvran* on her lee-side: she was now a quarter of a mile away and gaining perhaps twenty yards a minute. Dungeness lay ahead, distant perhaps eight miles, and somewhere about Dungeness there would be pilots and perhaps tugs. There or thereabouts the race would be decided, another hour would see it out. Cruiser's men had been hard at it all day, and were shewing signs of wear. They drank strong tea, syrupy with sugar and laced with brandy, as they got their hawsers ready forward and eyed the distant winning post.

All the issue from the gate of the Channel were about them: all the ships of a tide or two before from London and Antwerp, all the fishermen of Kent and Sussex. Every seaman who came past had no eyes for anything but those two superb clippers disputing for pride of place.

When the squall had passed by, both had set every rag that could be brought to draw: they were now straining under clouds of canvas with a strong beam wind, and a head tide. Tarlton, who had been in the *Fu-Kien*, was not encouraging. "Just the wind she likes most," he said. "She's a glutton for it. And she laps up a head sea like a rum milk-punch." All the marvellous evening shone out mile after mile as they raced: the French coast plain as far as Calais, England white to windward, with occasional windows flashing like jewels, and a darkness of passing storm beyond. Occasional violent gusts kept men in both ships at the upper halliards; and still the *Fu-Kien* gained.

Cruiser was watching her now; she was not more than a hundred yards astern and to leeward, her decks full of men, and spare sails, all made up for bending, on each hatch, and the ship herself a picture of perfection, all bright for port, the paint-work and tarring finished; the hull black, with a white sheer-straik to set off her sheer, the yards black, man-of-war fashion, but with white yard-arms, and her masts all scraped clean with glass, of shining yellow pine. All her brass was bright, and the scroll below her bowsprit had been freshly gilt. She was driving on easily with great laughing leaps. Cruiser could see, in the bearing of the men in her, their certainty that they were winning. Both ships were hauling their wind now to turn the bend. Both could see now, coming out from Dungeness, the pilot cutter, standing towards them, not two miles away, and beyond, making for them what seemed to be tugs, but might be small coasters.

"Too bad, sir," old Fairford said, "we'd have done it if we'd had a bit more luck."

Cruiser was feeling broken-hearted at being passed on the post, but he could not take this view of it. "No, no," he said, "we've had such luck as no sailors ever had before. Think of what has come to us." All the same, he had to move away. When he was on the lee-poop staring at the *Fu-Kien*, old Fairford could not see how bitterly he felt.

As they hauled their wind, the *Fu-Kien* forged ahead upon them, standing close in upon them, intending to weather upon them and drive across their bows. Bloody Bill China was there on his poop, an unmistakable big figure with a hard tall gray hat jammed sideways on his head and a long pistol in his right hand. "That's Bloody Bill, sir," Tarlton said to Mr. Fairford, "Bloody Bill China, sir, the Captain. You'll see him send a bottle of brandy out to the yard-arm in a moment."

Sure enough, a lad with a line went up the mizen-rigging and out to the crojick yard with it, rove it through a jewel block at the yard-arm, and brought it down on deck. A bottle of brandy was hauled out to the yard-arm upon it and dangled there. "That's Bloody Bill's way, sir," Tarlton said. "If ever he weathers on a ship he shoots a bottle of brandy at the yard-arm and then splits another on all hands."

Twenty faces stared at the *Bird of Dawning* from the *Fu-Kien's* side. Those men of the sea, negroes, Malays and Europeans, grinned and cheered as their ship slid past.

Bloody Bill China, who was certainly half drunk, shouted something to his steward who was standing near the break of the poop beside a grog-kid. The steward put a corkscrew into the cork of a bottle which he held. Bloody Bill strode to the ship's rail, and yelled at Cruiser, whom he took to be Captain Miserden, "Give my love to the Prophet Habakkuk."

Voices from the *Fu-Kien's* waist, eager for the promised grog, and full of joy in their victory, shouted *Habakkuk, Yah Yah, Habakkuk*, and instantly the *Fu-Kien's* main mast was ahead of the *Bird of Dawning's* mizen, and at once the *Fu-Kien's* crew manned the rail and cheered, and beat the fire signal on both her bells. Bloody Bill China brandished his pistol above his head, brought it down, and fired it as he fell: the bottle at the yard-arm was shattered—the brandy spilled. Instantly the steward drew his cork and Bloody Bill China shouted "Grog-oh. The *Fu-Kien* wins the China race."

She tore past the *Bird of Dawning*. She cleared her by a cable, then by three hundred yards. "Look out, sir," Tarlton cried to Cruiser. "He'll cross your bows as sure as God made Sunday."

And instantly, Bloody Bill China did; he luffed up out of bravado, so as to get to windward of the *Bird of Dawning*.

He was going to cross her bows, just to shew her. As he luffed, one of the violent gusts beat down upon both ships. Cruiser saw it coming and let go in time, but it caught the *Fu-Kien* fairly, and whipped her topgallant masts clean off in succession as one might count one, two, three. The great weight of gear swung to and fro on each mast, the fore-upper topsail went at the weather clue, the main upper topsail halliards parted and the yard coming down brought the lower topsail with it bending the truss and cockbilling the yard. The helmsman let her go off, she fell off, thumping and thrashing while gear came flying down from the ruin. With a crash, the wreck of the fore-topgallant mast, with its three yards, and stunsail booms and weight of sail and half a mile of rigging collapsed about the forehatch.

It all had happened in a moment. Cruiser had been warned and had just time to heave the helm up. The *Bird of Dawning* always steered like a bird: she answered to a touch; she answered to it now, but the *Fu-Kien* was right athwart her hawse not three hundred yards away, falling off and coming down on her, with all the wreck on her main mast visibly shaking the whole mast. One active daredevil soul was already racing with an axe to the splintered mast head, to hack through the shrouds.

Cruiser saw her come round almost on her heel, straight at the *Bird of Dawning*. For about half a minute it seemed certain that the two would go into each other and sink each other. The mizen royal yard slid out of its bands and smote the *Fu-Kien's* deck end-on like a harpoon. The terrified helmsman hove the helm hard down; the ship, having still way on her, swung back into the wind. With a running, ripping, walloping crash, her main topgallant wreck came down into her waist, going through the bunt of the mainsail as it went.

The *Bird of Dawning* went past her and missed her by thirty yards. As they passed, Bloody Bill China leaped onto the top of the wheel-box, hurled his hard hat at Cruiser, and while it was still in the air, settling to the sea, put three bullets through it with his pistol: he then hurled his pistol after it and leaped down cursing onto the main-deck to clear the wreck.

Cruiser left him to clear it; there, ranging down upon him was the pilot cutter. In another minute, that graceful boat rounded to with her pilot, who caught the tackle flung, and in an instant was swung high, and brought upon the *Bird of Dawning's* deck.

The Pilot was a short man of enormous breadth, with a gentle manner. He seemed puzzled at the smallness of the crew and at the unusual untidiness of the deck, the planks not scrubbed nor oiled, the paint not freshened. He came up the weather ladder to Cruiser and shook him by the hand.

"I'm proud to welcome you, Captain," he said.

"You're the first China clipper to take a pilot this year."

About five minutes later, two tugs bore down upon them. Cruiser hoped as they drew near, that they would be those telegraphed for by him. They were, however, two pirates, anxious to make the most of the situation. "Take you in, and dock you, for £100 a tug, Captain," their spokesman said.

"Are you the London and Dover Tug Company?"

"No, Captain; the South Foreland Tug Company. What about it?"

"Nothing doing."

"Now, Captain," the tugman cried. "You give us your line. £100 a tug is nothing to you if you win the prize. And with us you can't fail to win the prize. What's £100 a tug to honour and glory?"

"I'll give you £50 a tug," Cruiser said.

"Is that your last word?"

"Yes."

"Adew, my bucko," the tugman cried. Both tugs sheered off, in what Cruiser took to be the familiar gesture of a tugman driving a bargain. In this he was wrong, both tugs bore down on the *Fu-Kien* in such obvious distress astern. They had no doubt hoped that they might get a little salvage there. He saw them hang round the stern of the *Fu-Kien* while they drove their bargain and though Bill China was an ill man to bargain with, they drove it, for he saw them take position ahead to take the *Fu-Kien's* lines. But there was some little delay in their getting the lines, because the *Fu-Kien's* forward deck was a jumble of wreck not yet cleared. Old Fairford shook his head. "Ah, Captain Trewsbury," he said, "if you'll excuse my saying it, sir, 'Agree with thy adversary quickly' is wisdom when you're dealing with tugs. Now we're past the bend of the land this wind will fall and be tricky: we'll be as like as not becalmed before we're in the Downs: and there aren't too many tugs, sir. It'd be hard to see the *Fu-Kien* go past with those two fellows. Besides, sir, if the wind should fall light, as it will, we shall have the *Caer Ocvran* on us again. They say her Captain can get way on her by blowing a flute on the poop."

"I daresay I was an ass," Cruiser said, "but we'll soon know."

There came a shout from forward on the starboard side. Efans came running aft.

"What's the matter?" Cruiser asked.

"The *Serica*, sir. She's been on the French side look you, and is standing over ahead of us."

"What of it?" Cruiser asked. "She can't sail against the wind."

He had watched that ship to leeward for some time, wondering if she could be one of the fleet. He had not thought her to be the *Serica*. If she were the *Serica*, then she, too, would be in the running, and might get a tug before him, and beat them all. He looked at her through the telescope, and thought that she was liker the *Min and Win;* but a ship ahead of them by any name would be ugly. "Well, I suppose I was an ass," he concluded, to himself, as the evening closed in, and the sun dipped into the clouds above England.

As old Fairford had foretold from the depth of his knowledge, the wind fell light and was tricky. Sheltered there in the Channel under the lee of the land, with the tide still ebbing, there was little lop on the water, which was of a dark gray now, under the cliffs, and stretching green, with pinkish mottlings from the clouds, to distant France. Dover Pier and Castle and cliffs rose up: and there, bearing down upon him, were two tugs with tall scarlet smoke-stacks banded at the top with black. "There are the London and Dover tugs," he said.

"Them's them," old Fairford said. "The *Morning and Evening Star*." He sheered away to utter his real comment unheard:— "And them two the *Fu-Kien's* got will eat the pair of them for breakfast."

As the *Evening Star* swung round, and came almost alongside, Cruiser saw his brother, the lawyer, standing on the bridge with the tug-captain.

"Hallo, Mike," he hailed, "how goes it?"

"Hallo, Cyril."

"You got my telegram?"

"Yes. I've settled with these tugs. I've settled everything."

"Give us your line, Captain," the tugman cried. The lines were tossed down: in a few minutes the hawsers were passed and the tow to London River had begun.

Soon after they had started towing, and before it had become too dark to see, the ship that men had thought to be the *Serica* showed clearly that she could not be the China clipper, but some unknown lofty ship bound for Dunkirk. Cruiser was able to judge the speed of the *Fu-Kien* under tow as less than his. He had a start of at least a couple of miles of her, and hoped to be able to maintain it.

In the last of the light, he saw the *Caer Ocvran* come gliding up on a breath, and signalling for steam. There was no tug for her. Presently the wind ceased, so that even the *Caer Ocvran* lay still in the calm.

The September night closed-in upon them as they drew into the Downs. Deal lights twinkled to port; on ahead, on the starboard bow, the full stream light gleamed out and vanished and again gleamed. Presently, as they finished with the sails and came from aloft in the dark, a big moon rose

on the one hand, while on the other came the
Kentish lights, Ramsgate Harbour and the North
Foreland. A mile or two more brought them round
the Elbow, into the great expanse starred with
beacons, the Prince's Channel and the Girdler,
with Shoebury far beyond. The night came cold
and quiet, with a clear sky, into which the moon
rose triumphing.

All through the night they towed, from the
Channels to the Deeps and from the Deeps into
the Reaches. The hard work of the voyage was
over, but all hands stayed on deck ready for a
call. Perrot made them suppers at odd times;
some of them slept and others sang. Edgeworth
stretched canvas over the ends of a cask and made
a drum.

Before morning came, as Cruiser walked with
the Pilot watching sleeping England and the un-
sleeping life of the river, a Kentish cock crowed
for morning in some unseen roost. The faint magi-
cal noise reached the *Bird of Dawning,* and instantly her cock flapped on his perch in the coop
and crowed in answer. Far away ashore on both
sides of the river the cry passed from roost to
roost. Cockcrow surely will rouse the dead at the
dawn of judgment.

Soon light came into the sky: factory whistles
blew to work, chimneys smoked; bells rang and
the life of the port became busy about them. At

eight o'clock, as they drew near to dock, a big
steamer, coming down, beat her bells to them;
her crowd of passengers, stewards and deckhands
clustered at the rail and cheered them: she blew
her siren, and passed them, dipping colours. Now
down the river towards them came a flotilla of
tugs, river-craft, skiffs, wherries and launches, all
crowded, all gay with flags. The Pierhead loomed
up, black with people. The dockside railway men
began to let off detonators. All those multitudes
cheered and cheered, waved flags and streamers,
flung their hats aloft and cried for the *Bird of
Dawning*.

"You're for it, Captain," the Pilot said, "and
if you'll cast an eye down the Reach you'll see
your rival."

Far down the river, too far down perhaps to be
a serious rival, a big ship without topgallant masts
was towing up in a cloud of black smoke.

"She's the *Fu-Kien*," Cruiser said.

"She's got three tugs to her," the Pilot said.
"She'll run you close still. The worst of these
races is that they're never decided till the ship's
docked. And we're far from docked yet."

"Yes, there's many a slip," Cruiser said. "And
she's coming up fast."

"If we can get the gates closed behind us, before she's ready to enter, we'll beat her," the
Pilot said, "but in this river anything may delay

us, a barge or one of your admirers in a skiff here."

The crew of the *Bird of Dawning* had done their best to fit her for her coming in. Ever since dawn they had been at her, getting harbour stows on her sails, squaring her yards, washing down, coiling-up, and brightening her brass. All her flags were aloft between trucks, and her colours and number at the peak. Now, as she loitered down and checked and took position to enter dock, the boats closed-in upon her and the world of the shore came crowding on board, press-men first, to get the story, ship-owners and their friends, men who had betted on the race, ship-designers, ships' builders and ship's captains, with the runners and the sharks who live on sailors. They were pressing everywhere, bearing a hand at the gear, questioning, cheering and cutting bits of rope as souvenirs.

Now, slowly, the ship moved up to the dock-gate, with both tugs ahead. Kemble steered her; old Fairford stood on her fo'c's'le; Cruiser eyed her aft. As the figurehead drew past the gate, the tense crowd on the wharves seemed to grow white. A man, stepping forward, put fire to the breech of a signal cannon. At the crash of the gun, the Father of the Port, an old white-headed sea-captain, took off his white tophat and cried, "Three cheers for the *Bird of Dawning*, winner of the

China Tea Race." Then all the crowds broke into a roaring of cheering: all ships in the port beat bells, fired guns, hooted with sirens and cheered with throats.

Old Fairford lifted his hat and cried "Three cheers for Old Pierhead." That little crowd of neversinks cheered and cheered as they passed into the dock.

Then old Fairford cried "Three cheers, boys, for Captain Trewsbury." As they finished the cheers Edgeworth leaped to his drum and beat upon it, others beat marline-spikes together, and all sang the words and tune of *See, the Conquering Hero Comes*.

More yet remained to be done. As the ship took sheer to sidle in, Coates and Chedglow went aloft to the main truck and secured to the spindle of the wind-vane the gilt cock made by Clutterbucke some days before. He steadied to the wind there and swung proudly as a *Bird of Dawning* should. The two lads came slithering down the backstays to the deck.

As they slid down, they saw the dock-gates slowly draw together and lock themselves close. They were shut. Three hundred yards downstream, the *Fu-Kien* checked her way: she was beaten. Now the Bird of Dawning's bow-and-stern-fasts were pitched over the bollards ashore.

All hands, crew and visitors, took them to the capstan, and old Edgeworth began his song:

> *"I thought I heard the Captain say,*
> *Leave her, Johnny, leave her.*
> *I thought I heard the Captain say,*
> *It's time for us to leave her."*

They walked her up "for a full due" to the
dockside, till her fenders touched the coping.
"That'll do, men," old Fairford said.

They had been told to keep in touch with
Cruiser till the claims were settled: he felt certain
that he would see them again: but as he stood amid
the strangers at the break of the poop, seeing those
men, with whom he had gone into the presence of
death, now leaping down to leave her, he felt
that a marvellous time had ended. They all came
to shake hands with him before going, according
to their natures, some of them deeply moved,
hoping that they would sail together again, some
of them loud in praise, some silent in sympathy.
Efans said, "When you get command of a fine
ship, sir, you take me as poatswain, look you."
Stratton hung back for a while, but at last drew
truculently near and said, "I suppose we might
shake hands." "Yes," Cruiser said; so they shook
hands together; and then the *Bird of Dawning*

was docked and the crowd gone, save for old Fairford, who was going to stay by her.

In time, the claims were settled. Cruiser and
his crew received, in all between them, £41,000,
for the salvage of ship and freight and cargo.
Cruiser's own share was half of this; but in addition to his share, he received £100 for the winning
of the race and £600 bonus for having brought
the first tea of the season to the market. One of
the *Bird of Dawning's* builders, who had betted
largely upon his ship's success, sent him £500.
The underwriters gave him a gold repeater watch
worth a hundred guineas. The M.M.S.A. sent him
an illuminated scroll and a silver coffee service.
The Captain's Room at Lloyds sent him a telescope, a painting of the *Bird of Dawning* and a
cheque for £100. The *Conway* gave him a pair of
binoculars suitably inscribed; the *Worcester* gave
him another pair. The Brothers of Trinity House
gave him a luncheon, Liverpool gave him a dinner
and the freedom of the city. The sailors of Great
Britain gave him a walking stick made of a shark's
backbone bound with chased silver. The school-
boys of Great Britain gave him a magnificent
paintbox with fifty tubes of colour and twenty
brushes. The schoolgirls of Great Britain gave him
a travelling bag with silver fittings. Bloody Bill
China gave him a new hat.

The greatest lady in Great Britain (and in the world at that time) sent for him that he might tell her his adventures. What she gave to him, he would never tell, but long afterwards it was buried with him. It was a little pocket Bible inscribed by the Royal hand.

The very beautiful girl whom he had long loved, and who had long loved him, gave him her hand; and all the crew of the *Bird of Dawning*, except Efans, who was in gaol, and Stratton, who had meant to come but was not sufficiently sober to risk it, came to the wedding.

And so we will take leave of Cruiser Trewsbury.

The ship which sank the *Blackgauntlet* was, in time, proved to have been the *Mareotis*, of Alexandria, belonging to a Levantine firm, who after some years of litigation had to pay damages and compensations, a share of which came to Cruiser.

As for Captain Miserden and his crew, they were all landed at Bahia from the steamer *Alvaredo*, which had gone past the *Blackgauntlet's* boat the night before they sighted the derelict. They were returned to England by mail steamer and landed at Plymouth a few days after the *Bird of Dawning* had docked. Captain Miserden was very frank about it, that he had been told by the Prophet Habakkuk to cut through a pipe, wreck the pumps and tell the crew to abandon ship. He had obeyed the Fire, he said, and the Fire could neither lie nor err. Helped by his Carpenter and Sailmaker, he had persuaded his crew to leave the ship and go off in the *Alvaredo*.

He was put under restraint for some two years and then released, with the medical advice not to go to sea again. He joined the Ministry of Ebenezer Mudde, and lived humbly and righteously for many years with him, as a ship's chandler, who on one counter of his chandlery sold comments on the Prophet Habakkuk with interpretations of the Burning Coals and the Wind.

GLOSSARY

A.B.	An "Able-bodied" seaman; formerly one who had served five or seven years at sea.
Amberline	A light line or cord.
Backstays	After-supports to masts.
Bagwrinkle	A padding of rope yarn.
Beam sea	A sea breaking at right angles to a ship's course.
Binnacle	The case in which the compass is held.
Bonnets	Extra sails laced to the feet of courses.
Booms	The space filled with the ship's spare spars. The spare spars themselves.
Braces	Running rigging by which the yards are trimmed to one side or the other.
Break of the poop	The forward end of a ship's after-superstructure.
Breaker	A wooden cask or small barrel.
Broaching-to	Suddenly shifting course so that the ship's head points into the direction from which the wind is coming.

Brought aback	In such a position that the sails are pressed by the wind against the masts.
Bulkhead	A ship's partition or wall.
Bulwarks	The ship's sides, especially those parts of them which fence the upper deck.
Bunts	The central portions of square sails.
Caught by the lee	Taken unawares by a dangerous sudden shift of wind, as in a revolving storm.
Chocked	Secured against rolling about.
Clinker-built	Having overlapping planks.
Clipper	A name given to a ship of speed and beauty.
Clove hitch	A simple fastening.
Clue	The lower corner of a square sail.
Coach-work-mat	A plaited cover.
Coaming	A raised rim round an opening in a deck.
Cockbilled	Pulled askew.
Coir	Cocoanut fibre.
Companion	A hatchway, or opening to a cabin.
Cringle	A round, flanged ring of metal sewn into sails at particular points.
Crojick or Cross-jack	The lowest yard upon the mizen mast of a full-rigged ship; also the sail set upon this yard.

Crutch	A movable rowlock.
Davits	Curved iron appliances to which ships' boats may be hoisted.
Day's work or Dead reckoning	A means of computing a ship's position from her course and the distance traversed.
Dead reckoning	See Day's work.
Dodger	A screen.
Dog-watch	A short evening watch, from 4 to 6 or from 6 to 8.
Drogue	A floating sea-anchor, to which a ship or boat may ride in foul weather.
Dungaree	A thin stuff like coarse cotton.
Fall	A stretch of running rigging, especially that part handled in hauling.
Fetch-bag	A canvas bag, with a wooden bottom, used for sailmakers' tools.
Fid	A wooden marline-spike.
Fife rail	A teak ledge stuck about with belaying pins for the securing of rigging.
First watch	From 8 P.M. to midnight.
Fo'c's'le or Forecastle	A deckhouse or other living space allotted to seamen. The men living in such space.
Forenoon watch	From 8 A.M. to 12 noon.
Frapped	Wrapped and tied round.
Gear	Things proper to the work in hand; such as running rigging.

Grummet	A ring or garland of rope.
Gudgeon	A metal socket.
Gunwale	The upper edge of a boat's planking.
Halliards	Ropes by which sails are hoisted.
Handy-billy	A portable tackle or pulley for obtaining greater power.
Hank	A twist or roll of light line or twine.
Harness cask	A tub containing salt meat.
Jibboom	A spar secured to the extremity of the bowsprit.
Jiggers	Small arrangements or pulleys.
Jury rudder	A makeshift rudder improvised in case of accident.
Killick	Small grapnel anchors for boats, usually with four prongs.
Kites	Light topmost sails.
Lazarette	A strong-room in which provisions are stored.
Leeches	The edges of sails.
Liverpool pennants	Rope yarns used instead of buttons.
Log ship	A quadrant of hard wood used in estimating a ship's speed.
Luff	To turn the ship towards the direction of the wind.
Main bitts	A strong wooden frame, surrounding the main mast, to which much gear is secured.

Mainyards aback	An arrangement by which the wind presses the sails of the main mast against the mast and stops the ship.
Marler or Marline-spike	A steel spike, about 15 inches long, used in splicing ropes, etc.
Middle watch	From midnight till 4 A.M.
Midshipman's nuts	The hard central portions of ship's biscuits.
Mizen mast	The aftermost of a ship's three masts.
Morning watch	From 4 to 8 A.M.
Nettles or Knittles	Light cords such as are used to spread and support hammocks.
O.S.	An Ordinary Seaman, not yet able to qualify as A.B.
Paddy's Milestone	Ailsa Craig.
Painter	A line by which a boat may be secured to anything.
Pannikin	A tin cup containing nearly half a pint.
Pantile	A ship's biscuit, usually a round hard object weighing 4 ounces.
Picul	The load a man can carry at one time: about 120 lb.
Pin or Belaying pin	An iron or wooden bar to which ropes may be secured.
Poop	A ship's after-superstructure.
Puff-balls or Save-alls	Extra sails laced to the feet of square sails.

Quarter	A little to one side of the after-end of a ship.
Ratching or Reaching	Beating against the wind.
Rickers	Short lengths of wood, poles or light spars.
Roaches	The curved feet of "square" sails.
Round-house	A part of a deckhouse set aside for the berthing place of a ship's warrant officers.
Royals	Light sails set above the topgallant sails in square-rigged ships.
Scupper	A channel at the ship's side for the carrying off of water.
Scuttle-butt	A tub containing drinking water.
Sheer	The line, curved or straight, of a ship's rail.
Shrouds	Lateral supports to masts.
Sight	Observation of sun, moon or star for determining the ship's position.
Skids	Supports on which a ship's boats stand.
Skysail	A little sail set above the royals in lofty square-rigged ships.
Slops	Clothes, kit, tobacco, knives, etc., etc., issued to sailors during a voyage and charged against their wages.
Slush	Melted fat.
Spanker gaff	A spar by which the head of the spanker, a fore and aft sail set upon

	the aftermost mast of a ship, may be extended.
Splice the main brace	Drink and be merry.
Spunyarn	A light tarry line spun from rope yarns.
Stays	Powerful forward supports to masts.
Steerage way	Motion sufficient to enable the ship to be steered.
Stern sheets	A clear space at the after-end of a boat.
Straik	A streak or line of planking.
Studding sail	A sail set at the extremity of a yard to increase the area of a ship's canvas.
Tack block	A purchase pulley used at the corners of certain sails.
Thimbles	Small metal rounds or eyes spliced into ropes, or sewn into sails, for various purposes.
Thole-pin	A wooden pin fitted into a boat's gunwale as a fulcrum for an oar.
Topgallant masts	Upper spars.
Transom stern	Shaped like the straight back-board of a boat.
Triced	Hoisted.
Truss	An iron crutch or hinge supporting a yard upon a mast.
Trust-to-gods or Hope-in-heavens	Little light topmost sails.

Watch	A division (usually one-half of a ship's company). The space of duty kept by such division at one time.
Weft	A flag knotted in the middle as a signal of distress.
Whack	An allowance.